Borough
of
Churches

Borough
of
Churches

Robert Dumont

To order additional copies of this book, contact:
Xlibris Corporation
1-888-795-4274
www.Xlibris.com
Orders@Xlibris.com
16569

Contents

THESE STORIES ARE DEDICATED TO
THE MEMORY OF URSULE MOLINARO.
SPECIAL THANKS TO MY DAUGHTER ALEXANDRA
FOR THE COVER PHOTO.

CHRISTMAS LIGHTS

"It's not supposed to snow here in the city, but up there you never know."

After searching the gray barren sky, Charles Gardner closed the living room window which overlooked the park and the river. The traffic on Riverside Drive was virtually nonexistent. "We should still give ourselves an extra ten or fifteen minutes to find a cab." But he knew it was useless to try and hurry things along. His wife's preparations followed their own course, independent of him, and could not be hastened. He sat down heavily on the sofa and leafed through the *New York Times* once again. He tried, without success, to concentrate on an article in Section 1 concerning the current political and economic situation in the African nation of Gabon. He skimmed a piece on Christmas customs in various non-Christian societies throughout the world but couldn't get interested in that either. Finally, he gave up and turned to the sports section to see what holiday football games would be on television today.

"Don't worry—almost ready," his wife called out from the bedroom.

"Take your time," he answered.

"Don't be sarcastic Charles."

"I mean it, take your time."

"Oh come on Charles, you know how you get when we have to be somewhere."

"No really. Look Virginia, it's Christmas and I'm enjoying the hell out of this holiday. I'm merry. I'm bright. I've had enough sleep. I'm fine, not worried a bit."

"Well since you've got time to read the paper then you've got time to put the rest of the cookies I baked into the plastic sandwich bags, otherwise we'll end up eating them ourselves."

He jumped up all at once and went into the bedroom. "As a matter of fact I'm not ready after all." He went to his sweater drawer and began going through it.

"Oh please Charles. Don't change sweaters again. What's wrong with the one you have on?"

"It doesn't feel right. It doesn't fit right."

"Then wear the one that my mother sent."

"It doesn't match what I have on."

"Oh please. It matches fine. Don't be so particular."

"All right, all right," he grumbled. Picking up a brush, he stood in front of the mirror hanging above his wife's chest of drawers and gave his already neatly parted hair a couple of swipes. He then went into the kitchen and started putting the chocolate chip cookies six at a time into the small zip lock bags. He glanced at the clock in the living room and saw that there actually was plenty of time before they had to catch their train. Charles decided he would wait and call his parents from Connecticut. He had always called on Christmas Eve in past years, but he and Virginia were at their friends Miriam and Josh's the night before and their small one bedroom apartment was too noisy with people and music for a phone conversation. Even though they were Jewish they were not at all observant, so Miriam and Josh had thrown a Christmas party that lasted until 11:00 when everyone put on their coats and left for the Midnight Mass at the Cathedral of St. John the Divine. As the group crossed 110th Street and then Amsterdam Avenue in the cold, frosted darkness, the two hosts eagerly described the procession, the liturgy, the choir, and the Cathedral itself as if these things were all elements of some Broadway production.

Charles and Virginia sat with their friends towards the rear of the enormous church that was awash with a brilliant white light. All along the side aisles people were hurrying and milling about. The air was filled with the smell of incense and pine. To Charles, the contrasts between this spectacle and the spare, simple Christmas services he remembered attending while growing up in the Midwest could not have been more striking. After the procession got underway and the music rose he had a difficult time following what was happening, even with the aid of the printed program. Josh and Miriam and the rest of their friends didn't even bother with the program or the hymnal. They chattered and smirked and looked around and stood up and sat down along with everyone else. For a while Virginia seemed quite interested in everything, but just when Charles was beginning to find his place with the liturgy and letting himself be carried away by the sheer magnificence of it all, she reminded him that they had to leave since they were getting up early in the morning to catch the train to Connecticut.

After he finished putting the cookies in the plastic bags he poured some extra food into the cats' dish and replenished the water bowl. One of the cats showed up when he shook the food box. It sniffed the dish and turned away uninterested. "Merry Christmas you ungrateful little wretch." Charles followed the cat and tugged her tail. She turned around with feigned irritation but then rubbed her head on his ankle. He kneeled down and was stroking her, and then as if she were a child he began telling the cat the Christmas story—about everything from the birth in the stable and the arrival of the three wise men, to the custom of gift-giving and the visit of Santa Claus.

Virginia came out of the bedroom. She was ready. They put on their coats and grabbed two large department store bags full of wrapped presents, bottles of wine, candies, and the cookies.

"Is this everything?"

"Yes."

"Are you sure?"

"Yes."

"Are you sure you're sure?"

"Yes."

"Good-by *mein Katz und* Merry Christmas," Charles called out to the empty apartment as he closed the door.

"Think we'll have trouble getting a cab?" Virginia asked as they rode the elevator.

"Probably. Who in the hell's going to be out on Christmas driving a cab? We should head over to Broadway and then go up to 125th Street to get the train."

In the lobby they saw Hector the night doorman who had been pressed into service to work an extra shift for the holiday. Virginia gave him a bag of cookies and Charles was ready with an envelope. On the street the numbing wind swept off the river and pushed at their backs as they walked towards Broadway. There was an empty cab waiting at a red light at the corner which they climbed into immediately.

*

"Did Mohammed like his cookies?" Charles asked as they crossed 125th Street and entered the railway station.

"He gave me such a nice smile—poor guy, driving a cab on Christmas day. He said he'd take them to his kids. He acted like it was his only Christmas present. I hope you gave him a big tip."

Virginia waited by a magazine stand while Charles bought their tickets. The waiting room was cold and dingy. There were an equal number of sleeping street people and waiting passengers seated or slumped on the scarred wooden benches. A draft moved through the room each time the door opened from the outside. Charles rejoined his wife. The newsstand also sold coffee so he bought a cup for each of them. "Looks like we've got lots of time. That driver really got us here fast."

"Which track will our train be on? It's not posted?"

"The ticket seller said that there would be an announcement."

"Man if you knew me—if you was truly my friend or my kin, you would know what my name is—you'd know that everybody calls me Mary." A black woman, a prostitute no doubt, Charles thought, wearing a fake fur coat, high heel boots, and a silver-haired wig shouted at a man who was lurking behind a metal column and leering at her. Neither was concerned about the attention they were attracting. The man came out from behind the column, passed by a few feet away from her, said something to her in a low voice, and started to grin. She gave him a cold look then turned away indignantly.

He made a second pass by her and this time was making audible smacking noises with his pursed lips. She refused to look at him but shouted for the whole place to hear—"None of that shit mister. No sir! You take that shit someplace else. Uh-huh. You hear me now? No sir! Huh-uh!"

The man retreated to the other side of the column but kept peeking out from behind it every few seconds.

A Christmas morning, sleepy-eyed cop came through a door in the rear and strolled through the waiting room. He had caught most of the show up to this point, but unless something further developed, he gave every indication that he was just going to finish his cigarette and his coffee and not say anything.

"You'd think they'd have a black cop up here," Virginia said. "Remember what happened when those two white cops beat up that black kid who went to, where was it? Yale?"

"Attention. Attention. Ladies and Gentlemen. Boys and Girls. The 10:09 train to New Haven will be arriving in five minutes on track number 4. That's track number 4 for the 10:09 train to New Haven which has just left Grand Central Station. Thank you very much Ladies and Gentlemen. Boys and Girls. And Merry Christmas to all."

Charles shrugged. "Let's go up by the platforms and wait."

*

The train rolled slowly through Bronx neighborhoods of drab, brown walkups and housing projects, past whole sections of burned out and abandoned buildings with broken windows and crumbling facades, and past entire blocks of massive piles of rubble and assorted debris. Here and there weed-choked vacant lots appeared where buildings had been cleared and nature was allowed to take its course. The train seemed to pick up speed with the first signs of suburbia—initially some low-rise factories and commercial strips, then tree-lined streets and single-family detached houses, a golf course, more houses somewhat larger than the ones before, and then shopping centers and churches surrounded by expansive parking lots, and now wooded areas through which Charles could glimpse still larger houses.

Virginia read a magazine before succumbing to the drowsy bounce and sway of the quiet train and closed her eyes. Charles divided his attention between his newspaper and the ongoing suburban vistas of Westchester and Fairfield counties. Because he was from a medium-sized town originally, in a different part of the country, the allure of the big city was still palpable for him, even while living and working there. At times the tensions and frustrations of coping with New York wore him down, but these periods would usually pass with the changing of a season. A spontaneous surge of enthusiasm would inevitably follow a bout of mild dispiritedness. He always told himself he could have the best of both worlds by keeping in touch with things in his hometown, while at the same time responding to the challenge of a broader world and wider perspective that the city offered.

Lately he realized how tenuous the connections with his hometown were becoming. Only his parents were still living there and they were thinking of moving to Arizona to be closer to his sister who was married and living outside of Phoenix. His older brother Rex, after finishing college, had spent much of his life just wandering around the country, turning up in

California or in New York for brief periods; or being heard from while stopping over for longer stays in Florida, then Colorado, then Minnesota. The last report Charles had was that Rex was sharing a house with a group of people in Seattle. Charles wondered if his brother would be home for Christmas. Probably not. It suddenly occurred to Charles that it had been eight or nine months since he had gone to Times Square to buy a copy of his hometown paper.

In their three years of marriage he and Virginia had not visited his parents at all, and Charles had not been home for Christmas in several years. Growing up in the east, Virginia had only a vague idea of what lay beyond Pennsylvania. She had met his parents only once—when they came back for the wedding. They had spent a few days in New York afterwards, gone to a couple of shows, walked around, taken the Circle Line cruise, all the while claiming they were having a wonderful time. But they had left a day ahead of schedule simply because they were exhausted.

"Tickets, tickets, tickets please." A young conductor with blonde hair flowing out from beneath his cap and liquid blue eyes which gave him the air of an undiscovered movie star, stood in the aisle. Charles fumbled in his pockets and then produced the tickets. The conductor perfunctorily punched them and told Charles to remain on the train all the way to the last stop. Charles nodded and resumed looking at his paper. A few moments later two women became agitated and started shouting in Spanish when the conductor approached them. Apparently they were on the wrong train.

"Poughkeepsie, Poughkeepsie!" they repeated to each other and to the conductor.

"No Poughkeepsie," he answered, "New Haven. This train . . . New Haven."

"Poughkeepsie—Poughkeepsie!" was their only response. They were insisting, and then pleading, and then nearly in a panic when they realized they were not on the train to Poughkeepsie.

Charles stood up and tried to assist with his self-taught, rather limited Spanish. Both the conductor and the two women began speaking to him simultaneously. He had no idea what the women were saying. Their excited Spanish was streaming out, while the conductor was telling Charles that all they had to do was get off at the next stop, cross the platform, and head back to New York in order to change at the 125th Street station for the Hudson Line. He laid out all the exact times for this sequence of maneuvers until even Charles was confused. Finally, a well-dressed, middle-aged man wearing a silk ascot around his neck came down the aisle and intervened. He spoke to the women in calm, fluent Spanish. The conductor and the women now turned their total attention towards him. He was explaining to the conductor in unaccented English that the women had confused the track numbers in Grand Central. The conductor again went through the necessary itinerary for getting the women on the train to Poughkeepsie.

"What was that all about?" Virginia yawned when Charles sat back down.

"Two women on the wrong train. They're trying to calm them down."

Finally the conductor and the well-dressed man got it all sorted out and made them understand how they could get back to New York from the next station. But after the conductor resumed punching tickets and after the well-dressed man took his seat, the two women began talking back and forth to each other and were on the verge of working themselves into a state of hysteria all over again. Just then the train de-accelerated for the unscheduled stop. The conductor hurried back to the women to get them moving and help them with their bags of Christmas presents.

Charles watched the women and the platform recede as the train left the station. The wind was whipping out of the north now and the sun was attempting to burst through a thick membrane of clouds but seemed helpless to warm anything.

As they moved through the Connecticut suburbs Charles noticed the random patches of snow that had fallen the night before, of which there had been no sign in New York City. All the way to Bridgeport he stared out at the silent wintry day while Virginia once more slept with a magazine on her lap. He reminded himself again to call his parents as soon as he arrived at his sister and brother-in-law's house. He wondered how late the Mass had lasted the night before. He wished he could have stayed longer, even without the company of their friends, sitting in the brilliant light, smelling the incense and pine, listening to the music and the prayers, and thinking of how far he'd traveled, and from where, to find himself in such a splendid and sumptuous setting on Christmas Eve.

When the train arrived in Bridgeport a black family of four got on—a husband, the wife, and two little girls. The woman was lugging a shopping bag full of presents and the father carried an enormous wrapped package under his arm. The woman and the children sat down in facing seats and she made room for him. She looked up and spoke to him sharply as he flopped down with a sullen expression. Suddenly, right after the warning buzzer sounded, the man bounded from his seat, leaving the package behind, and made it outside just as the chimes sounded and the doors closed. He stood on the platform brooding as the train left the station. An expression of utter bewilderment and then enormous sadness appeared on the woman's face as she sat there with her shopping bags full of presents. After a long while she turned her attention to the two girls who had been looking fixedly at their mother the whole time, but who now were staring at nothing at all as the train gathered speed.

"Tickets, tickets, tickets please." The conductor moved down the aisle.

*

"How was the trip?" asked Mary, Virginia's older sister.

"I slept all the way," Virginia laughed. "Trains just knock me right out."

Mary maneuvered the car onto the turnpike and into the stream of light traffic. It was definitely colder here in New Haven and Charles had caught a chill while waiting in front of the station. Though the temperature in the car was quite warm, he was still shivering and kept rubbing his hands together.

"How are you Charles? How is work?" Mary was her usual solicitous self. He was never sure if she were not subtly patronizing him sometimes. "Virginia tells me you recently got some kind of promotion."

"Sort of. More work, more responsibility. But not more money for now. How's Bill? And the kids?"

"Everyone is doing great. Richard got a pair of walkie-talkies, a sled, and a baseball glove. Patricia got the collector's doll she's been wanting. It's a little old for her but she's so good with her other things, and she wanted it so much. And both of them got a new saddle for their pony."

"What did you get for Bill?" Virginia asked.

"I got him some skis which were the right ones and for a change he won't have to return a gift I bought for him. When we were in New York he took me to a ski shop and showed me exactly what he wanted and practically made me buy them while we were there. I had to phone the shop the next day to keep it secret and be sure they could deliver them."

"What did Mom send?"

"Oh she just sent the same thing she has for the last few years. Money for the kids and a smoked ham for all of us. I thought we'd try and call her later tonight after dinner. Too bad she can't be up here but ever since she met Ed she doesn't want to leave Florida. Remember how she used to hate it down there?"

"Let her have her fun," Virginia said. "She's earned it."

Sure she has, Charles thought, even though he and Virginia were still waiting for an invitation to visit. "Any snow up here Mary?" He didn't want to change the subject, just to interrupt the silence that had momentarily enveloped the three of them.

"No not really. A little last night and maybe some more tonight. The roads are a little slick. We had hoped for snow so they boys could use their sleds."

The boys? Charles wondered. He couldn't stop shivering.

"How are Michael and Susan doing?" asked Virginia. She always seemed to find her sister's neighbors to be most congenial, although Charles never felt all that comfortable with them. He assumed there was something about the suburbs that accounted for the fact that the two families could be so much a part of each other's lives. The kids and the adults were always in and out of each other's houses nearly every day. Certainly the link was initially through the kids but it was beyond that now. It was a circle so tightly drawn that certainly not Charles, and probably not Virginia, could really penetrate it. But, he thought, today is Christmas. And if he would not be with the family he remembered as his family—his parents, his brother and sister—then these people would be his family. Perhaps another circle could be drawn, one that would somehow encompass this other one.

Mary exited the turnpike and drove through the center of the small village. There were more cars here than on the turnpike, most of them headed for one of the three churches on the town green. She drove a few more miles past the village proper to where the houses were further apart and set back from the road on one and two-acre lots, constructed in the typical New England rustic style. The wooded hills seemed barren and harsh with the winter brown landscape unrelieved by the dusting of snow. Under metallic skies and with a chill wind blowing off Long Island Sound, Christmas day in Connecticut now had a look of desolation about it. And Charles was still shivering.

They came over a slight incline, rounded a curve, and immediately Mary and Bill's house came into view on the left. At the end of the driveway and near the garage there were two cars parked. Michael and Susan's blue Volvo station wagon Charles recognized, but the other car was a Jeep with a vibrant red exterior and California plates.

"Who does the Jeep belong to?" he asked his sister-in-law.

"Oh that belongs to Susan's mother. She's been up here for the last several days. Tomorrow she and Gert are going up to Vermont to go skiing."

Who's Gert? Charles wondered. Am I supposed to know him or what? Somehow on Christmas he didn't feel like having to make all these new acquaintances.

"Is Gert her husband?" asked Virginia.

"No, they're just friends. They've been traveling together for a while. He's very interesting. He's an engineer and has his own consulting business in San Francisco. They travel a lot. I think they met on a ski trip."

"Well I hope you've got enough food for everybody." Charles attempted to sound agreeable.

"Oh yes, of course we do. But that's not all," said Mary. "Michael's mother is here from Ireland. She's been staying with them since Thanksgiving. This is only the second time she's ever been to the United States. She's pretty quiet. I guess it's all too much for her—the holidays, the kids, being here."

Mary helped Charles and Virginia gather their presents out of the car and the three of them went into the house through the back door. As they were taking off their coats they heard the sound of a piano being played. Then it broke off and there was children's laughter. Next there was a random banging of dissonant chords, as if someone were using his elbows to press the keys.

"That must have been Gert playing before, but I guess the kids decided to help him out," Mary laughed.

Bill greeted Virginia and Charles when they walked into the warm kitchen. He was wearing an apron with a calendar with each month of the New Year—1980—printed on it. As usual he was in charge of preparing the Christmas dinner.

"Well Bill, how's the turkey doing this year?" Virginia put down on a counter the bag of gifts she was carrying and peeked into the oven. Mary called for the children to come and see their aunt and uncle and to exchange presents.

"Oh Bill this smells wonderful," Virginia enthused. "It's going to be so delicious."

"It better be or I'm in trouble with a whole lot of people. Would either of you two like some eggnog? Michael and Susan brought it."

"I think I'll have a beer," said Charles as he opened the refrigerator door and helped himself to the supply that Bill always kept there.

Richard who was ten, and then Patricia, who was seven, came running into the kitchen followed by their friends Martin and Katie, Michael's and Susan's children. They all four were keyed up with excitement—red in the face, short of breath, and unable to stop laughing.

"Calm down a minute kids," said Mary. "Let's see what Charles and Virginia brought."

"Okay Richie, okay Patty, here you are. And here's something for Martin and Katie too." Virginia dug to the bottom of the shopping bag. "This is for you and Bill," she said as she handed a package to her sister. "I've got something for Michael and Susan too. And cookies for everybody."

Charles was surprised that his wife had brought presents for her sister's friends and their children. But he was even more surprised when Susan came into the kitchen with two wrapped packages, one for him and one for Virginia.

Susan's mother whose name was Rose next appeared in the kitchen, along with Gert. She had a healthy, ruddy complexion and an easy, unforced smile. She wore her long dark hair in a braid that gave her the air of someone possessed of a perennially youthful spirit. Gert was of medium height, stocky build, and had a neatly trimmed salt and pepper beard. He took the lead in introducing both himself and Rose to Charles and Virginia. He had a self-assured manner and immediately stationed himself between Mary and Virginia and began looking back and forth at the two of them. "*Jah*, two real beauties these sisters are. That's for sure." He spoke with a thick but not unpleasant German accent.

The kids were shouting as they tore into their presents—baseball posters for the boys and *Little House on the Prairie* books for the girls.

"Mom look! Reggie Jackson."

"Grandma look! Ron Guidry."

"That's great boys," said Bill. "Did you pick those out Charles? You really know who they like."

"How about someone from the Red Sox for me?" Michael said, now entering the crowded kitchen and leading his mother. "How come all of the kids in this town like the New York teams and all of the adults follow Boston?"

"These American sports I don't understand," said Gert. "These are baseball players? Baseball is the worst. I never know what's going on. And your football! So much confusion and crashing into each other, and then they spend so much time just standing around." He put his palms in the air and shook his head with an exaggerated expression of bewilderment.

Everyone smiled and stood in a circle surrounding the children and Gert. To Charles it seemed a kind of intimacy had been perhaps too quickly presumed if not actually attained; as if everyone actually shared in or ought to sympathize with Gert's bewilderment. Michael introduced his mother, Mrs. Riley, to Charles and Virginia. In contrast to Susan's mother, Mrs. Riley gave the appearance of a much older, less-hardy woman. She had wispy white hair, was rather frail, and quite reserved. Other than a curt nod she scarcely acknowledged Charles and Virginia, while the children's unlimited energy was apparently having an unsettling effect upon her.

The children followed each other out of the room in great haste. The women all wanted to busy themselves with some kind of a task or to inspect the turkey but Bill made it clear he was in charge. He told them he'd take them up on their offer to help in another hour. "In the meantime, just relax." Michael greeted Virginia with a hug and winked at Charles. He poured some eggnog for his mother. Charles stood for a moment next to Virginia who was listening to Susan saying that she was going to have an exhibition of her paintings at a gallery in Soho in the Spring, and then in the summer she and the kids were going to be in France through July before meeting Michael in Ireland in August.

Charles went to the refrigerator and got himself another beer. "How's your work going?" he asked Bill who was busy peeling potatoes. Bill had recently started his own business in computer consulting. That's what Virginia said anyway. Charles had not the slightest idea what that meant.

"Work is all right. I've got several projects going. I have to fly to Texas right after the holidays and set up a payroll system for an electronics company. How about you Charles? Didn't I hear that you just got some kind of a promotion? You're still at the bookstore for now, right? Do you have a chance to get much writing done?"

"Oh sure I keep after it. I work at it when I can. Evenings mostly, when I'm not too tired."

While Bill was dealing with the steaming pots on the stove, Charles left the kitchen. He heard the sound of the television coming from the den. It sounded like a kids show or maybe coverage of a parade. He wandered through the empty living room strewn with ribbon and wrapping paper and piles of gifts in half-open boxes. The enormous Christmas tree in the corner, its lights blazing, cast a varicolored glow against the gray dreary day visible through the windows. He went into the den. He had no idea who'd turned on the TV. He flipped through the channels and there was a football game, the Fiesta Bowl from Arizona, about to begin. It was a sparkling clear day in Tucson and the cameras pulled back to show the low ridge of humpback mountains that surrounded the stadium. The University of Nebraska was playing Brigham Young—he knew that from the *Times*—and the winner was sure to be ranked in the Top 5 after the game. He immediately conjured up in his mind the image of broad-shouldered, thick-necked farm boys competing against a group of religious zealots with white shirts and crew cuts. Actually, he was struck during the introductions by the fact that so many of the players on both teams were from California or Florida or even New York.

He had just settled down into a chair after the kickoff and the first few plays from scrimmage when Virginia came into the room.

"So there you are."

"This is a great game Virginia, the Fiesta Bowl. Nebraska vs. BYU."

"Why are you in here? Why don't you come out with the rest of us?"

"Is dinner ready?"

"Did you ask Bill if you could help?"

"Oh I'll help afterwards. Bill's got everything under control. I'll watch the game for a few minutes."

"No you won't. You'll come out with the rest of us and not be rude."

"I am not being rude. I'm watching the game. Why don't you ask Gert if he wants to watch? Tell him I'll explain all the rules to him."

"Oh Charles—!"

Virginia turned and left the room. Charles sank deeper into his chair and sipped his beer. The room felt cold and drafty. Bill and Mary's house had abundant New England charm and quaintness all right, but it was not particularly well insulated. Just sitting there, after awhile, he developed the shivers again.

The game proved to be totally uninteresting. Nebraska dominated on defense and scored nearly every time they touched the ball. It was 20 to 0 at the end of the first quarter and Nebraska had the ball once more. Charles stood up and decided he'd better make an appearance in the living room where he now heard the voices of the adults coming from. He didn't bother to turn off the TV set.

As he entered the room Gert was speaking animatedly on the subject of American politics. He understood even less than he did baseball and football, the intricacies of the series of primaries and caucuses held for the purpose of choosing presidential candidates from the two major parties. "I cannot understand how members of the same party can speak so harshly of each other—the things Kennedy is saying about Carter, what Bush says about Reagan. In Europe you would be kicked out of the party for speaking like that. And New Hampshire, such a small and insignificant state, but more important apparently than California when it comes to deciding . . . . "

Susan's mother said that she wished that the United States had a party similar to the Greens in Germany.

Charles remained silent as a general consensus was reached, or at least no one bothered to contradict Gert's assertion that the U.S. had a particularly poor system of choosing its leaders. Somehow the next topic of conversation concerned California drivers vs. East Coast drivers vs. European drivers. Of course Gert was very outspoken on this topic as well.

"In California they drive so skillfully." Rose was again nodding in agreement as Gert held forth. "I don't like to drive here at all in the East if I can help it—and New York City is the worst."

"What about the *Autobahn*? I hear they it can be pretty dangerous," Charles offered mildly.

"Not like New York!" Gert was quite vehement as he spoke, rolling his eyes and making theatrical gestures. "Everyone always turning left or right from the middle lane and cutting you off, running red lights like crazy, and never giving you room when you are getting onto an expressway."

"And the potholes there are just awful," Rose added, screwing up her face in disgust. "But what can you expect. It's New York. They're so broke they can't do anything about it."

"Well California might get there too." Charles had heard enough. He had not lived in New York long enough to either shrug off the opinions of outsiders or go them one better with their complaints. He felt compelled to defend New York, or at least try to explain it. But Virginia gave him a look that said maybe he should go watch that football game after all.

Bill shouted from the kitchen. He said that those who had

been so anxious to help a while ago should now report for duty. Everyone crowded into the kitchen but it was apparent that only the women were really ready to work. Charles got another beer out of the refrigerator and Gert busied himself with sniffing the pots on the stove. Michael offered a few wisecracks, then spied the kids outside and volunteered to go round them up for dinner. Mrs. Riley, who had little to say to this point, seemed even more disconcerted by the constant commotion. While the others were busy mashing potatoes, thickening the gravy, carving the turkey, opening bottles of wine, finishing with setting the table in the dining room— Charles made an offhand comment to her concerning American holiday customs. "Over here everyone sure likes to get in on the act," he said.

He stood there smiling blandly while she went from appearing to be slightly confused to surprised to deeply offended. It was as if he'd made some sort of rude or vulgar comment. He didn't know if she'd heard him incorrectly or was just unaccustomed to being spoken to so informally by a virtual stranger. He felt ill at ease himself and was relieved when Virginia collared him and gave him the job of slicing bread and putting it in the basket on the table.

Michael and the kids came in from outside—shouting, short of breath, red-cheeked. Those kids are always charging in or charging out the room Charles thought to himself. He noticed that Mrs. Riley now sat in the kitchen clutching tightly her glass of eggnog and looking as if the room were spinning.

At dinner each generation sat down together to eat. The boys joked about saying grace. "Good bread, good meat, good God, let's eat." When Gert acted puzzled Susan explained how grace was still said before meals if at no other time than Thanksgiving and Christmas.

"*Jah* I know that, but in Germany we would never confuse going to church with sitting down to a feast. I always wondered about that. I have read that President Jimmy Carter says a prayer before every meal in the White House. But this I never see in California."

"In Protestant homes in the South and Midwest it's still traditional," Charles said. A round of jokes ensued regarding just who were the "real" Americans and whether they said anything before, during, or after meals, busy as they were belching and wiping the grease off their mouths with their shirtsleeves. In the middle of this Bill held up a bottle of the California wine they were drinking and said, "Real Americans, here in the East anyway, only drink French wine at Christmas. How'd this get on the table? Must've been left over from Thanksgiving." Everyone laughed.

The conversation drifted and turned for a while in response to whatever remarks the children made, allowing them to determine the point at which a subject was exhausted or required further witty repartee. But after awhile things grew quiet. Everyone became preoccupied with the meal and the food on their plate. And then, rather quickly it seemed to Charles, in view of the lengthy preparations that were required, dinner was finished. While they were still pushing back in their chairs from the table and attention was diverted, Mary began bringing forth from the kitchen an array of cakes, pies, cheeses, and fruits which produced a litany of protests and mock cries of anguish.

"It's too much, oh it's all too much," the adults said while the children shrieked with delight. Desert was going to be painfully delicious.

Charles ate a piece of apple pie and then a piece of chocolate cake and had two cups of coffee. He asked Michael for a cigarette, lit it, then put it out when the children objected.

Everyone became more and more cheerful. Another bottle of wine was opened. The measured agreeableness of the afternoon and the jokey atmosphere at dinner were giving way to something now that was becoming an actual celebration. Even Mrs. Riley appeared to be slightly less uncomfortable, owing partly to the fact that she had gotten rather plastered.

The adults sat practically stupefied as the kids chattered away, succeeding at last in talking Gert into going into the living room with them to play the piano again.

Charles and Michael lit cigarettes after the children were gone. The two grandmothers and Susan took it upon themselves to clear the table while Virginia and Mary went upstairs to call their mother. Charles and Bill and Michael lingered over the table awhile, finishing off the last of the bottle of wine. It was only then that Charles realized he hadn't called home yet. He wondered if it was too late. But then he heard Bill speaking to him.

"Are you and Virginia staying over or going back to New York tonight?" his brother-in-law was asking him.

"We'd planned on going back. We really have to. We both work tomorrow."

"I'll drive you to the station whenever you want to go. The trains run every other hour on holidays."

"Thanks Bill. We're in no hurry." Actually, Charles was somewhat concerned about their departure time—that and the fact that the long ride back to New York would no doubt seem interminable. Bill and Michael were now discussing local matters. A broken stop light on the way into town, a new house being built up the road, the daily commute to New Haven on the turnpike. From the living room could be heard a tentative rendition of *The Twelve Days of Christmas* being played by Gert who was apparently unfamiliar with the song. The children shouted at him each time he broke down and had to start over again.

There was a crash in the kitchen. The piano playing and the conversation stopped. The girls scurried into the kitchen and then Patricia came out. "Katie's grandma dropped the turkey!" she announced. With everyone in the kitchen and the turkey carcass and the roasting pan on the floor, Mrs. Riley stood in the corner chuckling to herself. Susan and Rose were on hands and knees cleaning up.

"Anybody hurt?" asked Bill, and he laughed heartily. Gert

remarked that it was still such a heavy bird even after we'd eaten so much of it. Charles volunteered to help out in the kitchen. The kids talked Gert into going back to the piano. Michael poured his mother another glass of eggnog and led her out of the kitchen. She was smiling sheepishly as he told her to just come into the living room and listen to the music.

Virginia and Mary came downstairs and took charge of the kitchen. They told Rose to go into the living room too and enjoy the music. Charles was ordered to finish clearing the dining room table and then to take out the garbage later. As he made trips back and forth from the dining room to the kitchen he heard his wife and her sister telling Susan about their mother in Florida. "She says the weather's been perfect down there ever since Thanksgiving." Charles got himself another beer and went into the living room to listen to the music.

Everyone surrounded Gert who had begun to hit his stride at the piano. They were singing a spirited version of *God Rest Ye Merry Gentlemen*. Richard, who was taking lessons on the flute at school, was looking at some sheet music and trying to play along. He hit several sour notes which caused the girls to roll their eyes. Often, he would skip entire phrases altogether when he fell too far behind.

The singing grew more and more boisterous now that Bill and Michael were taking part. Susan and Mary and Virginia came in and joined in on *We Three Kings of Orient Are*. Michael's mother sat on the sofa between Martin and Katie who were holding sheets of paper with the words to the songs for her. She appeared very content, surrounded by her grandchildren, and was singing with much enthusiasm. Her voice rose at times above the music and Charles could hear her small but remarkably clear and sweet voice. It did not tremble or seem at all tired.

The next song was *Angels We Have Heard on High*. During the refrain, with Richard's flute rising, and everyone enthusiastically lifting their voices and drawing out the archaic

Latin words—"*Gloria in excelsis Deo*," Mrs. Riley closed her eyes and put her head back. Charles listened closely to her voice which actually sounded quite lovely here in this room, as if she were bringing forth something from her many Christmases past that was well beyond the ken of everyone else's intermingled memories. Something more remote yet perhaps far more vivid. Charles held the sheet with the words but he did not sing. He looked around at the faces of the others and listened as the music filled the room with what he could only reckon was some perceptible form of the Christmas spirit. It was a feeling of almost miraculous clarity, as if these moments had waited the entire year to be re-born only to disappear immediately for another year and reside in one's unconscious memory as a sense of longing that gives way to a sense of anticipation when Christmas was once again approaching.

Charles could see out the window that it was snowing. He left the living room, walked through the dining room, and went outside to stand on the back porch. The cold quickened his senses as he stared out over a line of trees that topped a hill at the base of the dark and inscrutable sky. A floodlight in the backyard was on and in the zone of light the wide snowflakes tumbled and blew. So quiet now. Here. The music so far away. The soft silence of snow falling at night. Another gift.

He went inside, into the kitchen, to get the garbage, and came back outside. As he was walking down the driveway towards the garage he noticed the effect of the moon behind a cloud that caused it to resemble a bowl of light hovering overhead. He studied the chiaroscuro patterns of the darkness and the churning illuminated cloud. Another nearly miraculous moment. After he arrived at the side of the garage where there were three metal garbage cans aligned he lifted the lid of the middle one, put the plastic garbage bag inside, and replaced the lid. He wondered again if his brother was home for Christmas. Probably not. He would have already heard something about it if he were. Charles wanted to get Rex's address and phone number in Seattle, or at least find out if that's where he was still living. Maybe he'd give his brother a call one of these days. Surprise him. Too bad they really didn't keep in touch.

Charles looked up at the sky once more. The bowl of light was still there.

Instead of going back into the house Charles walked across the yard towards the barn which was actually a small stable with a low hayloft on one side of the doorway and two narrow stalls on the other. Although it was pitch black inside, when Charles entered he could sense the presence of something in the darkness. He had no idea where the light switch was so he reached in his pockets and found a matchbook. He lit the match and suddenly he and the children's pony, Brownie, simultaneously startled one another. He knew the kids had a pony, but thought that it was kept somewhere else in the winter. As the match flame died he moved closer to the stalls and began talking to Brownie.

"Hey Brownie, hey little pony—don't you know it's Christmas? Are you out here all alone? Didn't anyone remember you?" He lit another match and the pony again was frightened. He heard it kick against the wall with its rear foot. He picked up a handful of hay and started feeding her. He did not light another match as his eyes were now adjusted to the darkness. As the pony ate, Charles stroked her mane and petted her neck. She was a gentle pony, with short legs and wide flanks. He'd seen the kids ride her often in the summer, or sit in the small cart to which Brownie had been hitched, and she would pull them behind her.

The barn sat at the bottom of the hill that was fenced off from the yard behind the house. There was a door on the other side of the pony's stall that opened onto the hillside where she was allowed to graze. Charles walked out of the barn, climbed the fence, and tried the door. It was secured only with a hook and eye, which he easily unfastened. He called inside to Brownie and she emerged slowly out of the darkness. It was still snowing very hard. Charles climbed onto Brownie's back and he felt her rear legs buckle. His legs dangled over her sides so that once he got his balance he could touch the ground with his toes and take much of the weight off her back.

The bowl of light was now visible above the top of the line of trees at the crest of the hill. Rather than the moon it was probably the lights from an airplane Charles decided. But why, he wondered, did it seem to remain stationery whenever he looked at it? He strained to hear the plane's motor. Everything was so silent here in the woods with the snow falling. If Brownie had been a stronger, stouter horse, instead of a children's pony, he would have liked to have ridden her to the top of the hill in pursuit of that bowl of light, to get a better view of it, to be closer to it. But they remained where they were. Brownie, with her nose to the ground, kept sniffing for shoots of grass, while Charles stared at the sky. The snow was falling all around.

At last he put the pony back in her stable and locked the door. When he went back into the house the cold air followed him inside. The piano playing and singing had stopped. In the den the TV was on—*A Christmas Carol* with Alistair Sims was just beginning—but no one was watching. He heard one of the boys shout "Snow!" and the scene in the living room broke up. Everyone rushed to a window in order to see, except for Mrs. Riley. She was sitting alone on the sofa. She appeared to be asleep.

"What is it?" she asked Charles, awakening suddenly when he passed by her. "Have you recently come from Ireland?"

"It's snowing," he told her.

"Ah yes, snowing it is. And would you know if it is snowing in Ireland? Was it snowing when you left?"

After a long silence. "I should imagine it was," Charles answered.

"I should imagine it was too. The snow in Ireland. At Christmas. So beautiful. Oh how I love to imagine." Mrs. Riley leaned back, slowly shook her head, and closed her eyes. Within a matter of seconds, it seemed to Charles, she had dropped off to sleep once again.

BOROUGH OF CHURCHES

His uncle announced that he was going out for coffee. "You want me to bring you back a cup of something Tommy?"

Thomas Barrett Anderson Jr. sat behind his old-fashioned, roll-top desk, staring out the dirty window toward the World Trade Center which glistened in the morning sunlight. The old man's words had interrupted a recurring reverie.

"No thanks Uncle Jack. Just a pack of cigarettes and a copy of the *Journal* if you don't mind."

Anderson watched impassively while his uncle searched first through a desk drawer and then fished in his pockets for change. He noticed once more what he had been trying all morning not to notice—that Uncle Jack had neglected to shave for the second day in a row. At last, reaching into his own pocket, he produced a few crumpled dollar bills and handed them over with an air of silent resignation.

Uncle Jack slipped a plaid summer-weight sport coat over his wrinkled white shirt. He went to the coat rack beside the door and from a hanger removed a rumpled trench coat that was missing the belt as well as several buttons and had dark stains on each frayed lapel. He started to put it on. Before thrusting his arm through the second sleeve he hesitated. "Hey

Tommy, what say if I borrow your overcoat? That's a stiff wind out there and my jacket is a little light?" Without waiting for an answer, he hung up the rumpled trench coat and pulled from another hanger a heavy wool overcoat and put it on. "Didn't realize how cold it was when I left home this morning . . . That's cigarettes and a *Journal*, right Tommy?"

Anderson had resumed his gaze out the dirty window. He did not answer. When he heard the door close he leaned back in his chair and sighed. Taking the last cigarette from an old pack he found in a drawer of the large roll-top desk, he lit it with a disposable lighter which he returned to the breast pocket of his suit jacket. His suit was of considerably less quality than the wool overcoat. Cut from an inexpensive synthetic cloth and not being particularly well sewn, the jacket bulged and puckered along the seams and if he stood up it hung too low in the back. The trousers were very tight around the waist and showed signs of wear where shiny patches had formed on the seat and at the knees. He wished he had not let his uncle take the overcoat. The rank odor of the trench coat was even more noticeable in his absence. But to object would no doubt have provoked the usual torrent of bitter remarks about the overcoat actually belonging to Tom's father who had been able to afford such a coat, while his brother-in-law walked around in rags. Besides, Uncle Jack always claimed he was drumming up business whenever he went out for coffee, although Tom knew he was right now on his way to the OTB parlor to place his daily wager. Afterwards, he would be checking in at a place called O'Brien's Authentic Irish Pub for a little morning "tasting."

Tom took a long drag on his cigarette and closed his eyes. The hiss of the radiator and dull distant rumble of street noise was pierced by the ringing telephone.

"Anderson Personnel . . . "

"Anderson? Rosenberg here—"

"Arthur my friend. It's so good to hear from you. What can I do for you today?" Tom spoke smoothly and affected a pleasant yet business-like tone. He leaned back in his chair. Cradling the phone to his ear, he folded his hands and placed them neatly on his lap. This was a pose he remembered seeing his father assume countless time when talking to clients. His cigarette burned itself out in the ashtray.

"Goddamnit Anderson, that last kid you sent over—that Spanish kid—what's his name? Martinez? Well this Martinez didn't show up for work for three days in a row until this morning. So I figured I'd give him a break. I don't ask no questions. Just put him right to work. I hand him an envelope at eight to deliver to Midtown by nine, and here it is, eleven-thirty, and I haven't heard a word from him. I don't know if he's lost or skipped out or what? And I got one screaming customer too!"

"Well Art, I'm so sorry to hear this. I suppose you're going to have to let him go."

"You're goddamned right Anderson! And I'm not paying you a dime in commissions on him either. He must be a drug head or something. I don't know and I don't care. And you told me he has a family and needs to work while he goes to school at night. What do you take me for anyway? Look Anderson, the last three people you've sent over I've had to fire. That old broken-down drunken sailor; that little street hustler from Jersey; and now this Martinez character. What in the hell is going on over there Anderson? Where are you getting these guys? You know your old man and me go back a long ways together and he'd never have sent these types over here for me to have to deal with. He'd have figured these guys' angles right there in the office and bounced their asses back out on the street before they had time to take theirs hats off."

"Art believe me, I had no idea." Anderson frowned. He no longer looked composed. He stuck his finger deep into the cigarette pack and wiggled it around before tearing off the stamp and foil and examining the pack to see if possibly one last cigarette still remained. "They lie on the application forms Art and there's nothing I can do." How many more times would he have to hear from Rosenberg about his father he wondered? "You know how it is Art—the kind of people who are coming to New York these days. Times have changed." He crushed the empty pack into a ball and leaned forward, putting his elbows on the desk. "Say, how's old Charley Callahan doing? He's still with you I'll bet."

Rosenberg was slightly calmer. "Yeah, yeah, he's still here . . . "

"He'll never leave you Art, not old spare-a-five Charley. What about Tiny Tim and Smitty and Sweet Pete the Poet?" Rosenberg never seemed to mention the good ones.

"Look Anderson—"

"Yes Art?"

"I need someone right now, tomorrow morning at the latest. Give me an old man if you can dig one up. I don't care if he's half-blind and half-dead, just so long as he's not a drunk. And no more illegal aliens. I'm still catching hell from the government over that Mexican your uncle sent over here last year. I don't want any hippies or crazies either. I'm warning you Anderson, if you don't start giving me better service—"

"Okay Art, let me check my files and make a few calls. I'll get back to you after lunch . . . " The receiver went dead in his ear while he was still talking. Rosenberg never bothered with good-by. Tom looked again toward the World Trade Center where Rosenberg and his Ace Messenger Service had its offices. His gaze followed the length of the narrow street, which terminated abruptly at the plaza surrounding the twin towers. The shadowed base of one of the towers appeared to have been driven like a wedge between the rows of low-rise buildings which lined the approaching street on either side, while its shining upper stories, reflecting the brilliant sunlight, soared into a lucent blue sky. Of course there were no files to check. And Rosenberg was right about the kind of people Tom had been sending him. But times really had changed, Rosenberg would have to understand that—like Tom did—and like his father, no doubt, would have if he were still alive.

∗

The Anderson Personnel Agency was located on the fourth floor of a six-story, nineteenth-century office building on Maiden Lane in lower Manhattan. According to a recent article in the *Times*, the building and the ones on either side of it were about to be acquired by a Japanese bank and were going to be demolished so that the bank could construct a New York City headquarters. But Rupert, the Jamaican elevator operator, and Lefty, who ran the newsstand downstairs, said now the latest word was that the building would not be demolished, but renovated and converted into residential apartments. Everything was still in the talking stage though, and might not get much further than that. Or at least so Tom hoped.

The office itself consisted of one very large room much more spacious than was necessary for only the two desks, few chairs, a single file cabinet, and the low, backless bench and coat rack which flanked the door. Three-quarters of the room was wasted space and received scarcely any light through the dirty windows or from the dim fluorescent desk lamps. An overhead light fixture had shorted out years before and no one from the building had ever come to fix it. But the rent was very low. Tom knew he could never find anything, no matter how small, in a building like the World Trade Center that would be affordable. And the way things were now, costs had to be kept to a minimum. That was the main consideration.

His father had not had to concern himself with such matters when he had founded the agency in the late 1920's and seen it become one of the most successful in all lower Manhattan. Despite the Depression, and then later during the war years, business had grown steadily. Even after his brother-in-law Jack, who had been laid off from a position with a brokerage house and then classified as 4F for military service, joined the firm, business still continued to increase. Following the war things were better than ever with the agency running classified ads in several of the daily newspapers and various trade publications.

A large chalkboard sign downstairs on the sidewalk had to be changed every day to show the new positions available, with listings for positions with law firms, accounting firms, banks, brokerage houses, insurance companies, and the stock and commodities exchanges. There was a also separate and still larger chalkboard sign with listings for a whole array of jobs with the steamship lines and in the shipping industries: bookings clerks, inward and outward clerks, bill of lading clerks, operations managers, traffic supervisors, and so many more that this sign had to be updated every two hours. It had taken more than a dozen people to run the agency then, and Anderson Personnel had occupied every office except one on the fourth floor of the Maiden Lane building.

Tom still retained vivid childhood memories of riding the subway in from Brooklyn with his father on Saturday mornings, walking the empty streets of lower Manhattan, and climbing the stairs to the fourth floor office. While his father worked at his enormous roll-top desk, Tom would sit at Uncle Jack's vacant desk and play with the dictating machine or rustle through the stacks of paper in imitation of his father.

Thomas Barrett Anderson Sr. had always assumed that his son would join him in the business after finishing college. Lacking an education himself, a college degree was the one thing he most wanted and expected from his son. But things were postponed when Tom dropped out of NYU after an indifferent freshman year and enlisted in the army. He spent two years in Germany and another year stationed in Georgia, the only times in his life he'd been away from New York. Following his discharge he returned to Brooklyn and married Sadie, a girl from the neighborhood, who was soon pregnant with their first and only child—Mickey. Tom tried college for a second time to please his father. He enrolled in a couple of evening courses at Brooklyn College and worked days for a while, first as a shoe salesman at the A & S department store, and then later he had a brief, unsuccessful career selling used cars in Bay Ridge.

His mother tried to convince his father, meanwhile, that Tom was only getting some valuable practical experience before resuming his studies full-time. But after Mickey was born and at the urging of Sadie, Tom decided to quit school again and ask his father for a job. Anderson Sr. finally relented because he had come to realize that Tom was never going to finish college, and because his brother-in-law Jack was of no help to him at the office with his fondness for drink, weakness for the horses, and all around unreliability.

It shortly after this that Tom's father developed a series of health problems. First it was ulcers, after that he was diagnosed with diabetes, and then he had a severe heart attack. Each of these in turn rendered him less and less able to oversee the agency and adapt it to the changes affecting it. Though Tom could recite all the reasons why business declined so precipitously—clients moving to Midtown, the stock markets becoming more automated, the departure of the maritime industry from Manhattan—there was nothing he could do about it, even if it had not become increasingly apparent that he was not the businessman his father was. And now, after so many years, Tom still resented the fact that he had been left with so many problems and no obvious solutions. He still resented that before he died, his father refused to give him credit for what he had accomplished. Because in spite of everything, Tom had somehow managed to keep the business afloat and the office open. What he resented most however was Sadie with her expectations—her demands!—that he provide her with something more than a merely comfortable, middle-class lifestyle, and her repeated threats to leave him. Perhaps everyone had expected too much of him all along, even if he had at one time shared in those expectations.

In his own mind, joining his father's business was only to have been a temporary solution until he really did go back to college, or until something better came along, or until he settled on what he was best suited for, whatever it was to be.

But events had long since overtaken him. He never went back to college. And nothing else ever came along; or if it did he was unable to recognize it. His life became a routine, which consisted of just showing up at the office every day, week after week, month after month, year after year; even as his father was dying, even after his wife finally did leave him, even as the Anderson Personnel Agency continued to languish.

*

The phone was ringing again.

He hesitated to answer it for a moment. Probably Rosenberg calling back to complain some more. But at last he picked it up.

"Anderson Personnel . . . "

"Just what do you think you're doing Tom! Just what in the hell do you think you're doing! I'm telling you, you can't do this to me, to us."

It was Sadie. He couldn't even remember the last time he'd spoken to his ex-wife.

"What are you talking about Sadie?"

"You know damned good and well what I'm talking about. I'm talking about Mickey. I finally heard from him. He's in California—but you already know that."

"How would I know that? What do you mean?"

"He finally wrote, only a post card mind you. He's staying at some kind of religious retreat in the mountains. It's a commune and there's a holy man or swami around who runs things."

"When did this happen? How long has he been there? I thought he was still living upstate."

"How should I know?"

"Why shouldn't you know?"

"Look Tom, he left home over a year ago. Since then you'd think I was dead as far as he was concerned. But that's not the point. The point is I know you gave him money so he wouldn't have to work. The point is you always tried to turn him against me and now you probably think you've succeeded."

"Sadie, you don't know what you're talking about."

"Oh is that right?"

"Yes—goddamn it!—that's right. I haven't given him any money since he was in school. What money do I have to give him anyway? He never calls me or writes to me. Where in the hell did you ever get such an idea? Probably from your husband the big-shot lawyer."

"You leave Leonard out of this. He's tried hard to be a father to Mickey, like the father you never were."

"Sadie you're nuts, you know that? Is this why you called? Just so you could start something—right Sadie?"

"I'm not starting anything, but I'm telling you that I want my son back. I've already taken measures."

"Taken measures? What do you mean?"

"I've hired a man, a man who will find him and take him somewhere so Leonard and I can talk to him, talk some sense into him."

"You're going to have him kidnapped in other words. That sounds like something your husband could arrange. But Mickey's an adult now Sadie, you can't get away with it."

"Don't tell me what I can get away with Tom. He's my son and I want him back and you'd better not stand in my way."

"I'm not standing in your way, only—"

"Only what?"

"Only—maybe the reason he's fallen in with these people is because of you, you and your big-shot husband with your limousines, your private clubs, your high society pals, with your—"

"Shut up Tom. And don't forget what I told you."

"I can't believe that he had it in him to stand up against you two. But don't think for a minute I had anything to do with it Sadie. I never see him. He doesn't give a shit about me, you two saw to that."

The phone went dead in Tom's ear. He slammed it down

when he realized she was no longer on the line. His face flushed with anger, he turned his chair around and his gaze once again sought the dirty window.

*

"Say Tommy boy—what's the good word?"

"Oh hello Louie. Where've you been lately?"

Louis Moscello, head of the Moscello Musical Talent Agency of Maiden Lane, New York City, walked into the office without knocking. The Moscello Musical Talent Agency was the only other tenant on the fourth floor of the building.

"Whattaya mean where've I been? I told you I was going to Puerto Rico with my daughter and her husband. Had a great time. Played golf all day and went to the casinos every night." Louie took a chair from beside Jack's desk and dragged it over to the window. "Didn't you get my card?" He took out a pipe and loaded it with his cheap drugstore tobacco. He left the door of Anderson Personnel ajar, as well as the door to his own office across the hall, so that he could hear the phone ring, footsteps falling on the stairs, or the clatter of the elevator.

As usual, Louie had brought with him copies of the *Daily News* and the *Post* and was ready to resume his interminable commentary on the sports and the rest of the news.

"How about those Mets? They're gonna be stuck in the same rut again this year. Take it from me. But the Yanks are looking good. This guy Steinbrenner says he will do whatever it takes to win. Did you see they fixed up Yankee Stadium? Maybe we can go to a game—me, you, and Jack. Your dad and I used to go to Dodger games, before he got sick."

Tom sighed and frowned and shrugged. He shuffled some papers then opened and closed a drawer of the roll-top desk. He fished a long cigarette stub out of the ashtray, blew off the ashes, and lit it.

"And this guy running for mayor—this Koch—he looks like

he's got his head on straight. Wants to put a cop on every corner. But what can he do? The city's broke. And these people who say we should trust the Russians now, can you believe it! I don't know where they're coming from. I tell you, Tommy boy, there's going to be a war. Korea, Viet Nam—they were just a warm-up for the big one. Take it from me. Hey! How's my pal Jack? Where is he?"

"Uncle Jack is fine Louie. He went out for coffee but should be back soon."

The syrupy smell of Louie's tobacco was all-too familiar to Tom. Louie had known Tom's father and had occupied the same office on the fourth floor of the Maiden Lane building for the last forty years. Why he was located downtown in the Financial District instead of up near Tin Pan Alley Tom never understood. Though he once in awhile took out an ad in a trade journal or musical magazine, offering to assist in selling the rights to songs written by unknown, undiscovered composers and otherwise promote their work, Louie was actually retired and had had no clients for some time. He lived with his daughter and her husband in Bensonhurst. Every day he had breakfast with his grandchildren and watched cartoons on TV with them before they left for school. After that he would clip a bow tie onto the collar of a clean and freshly starched white shirt, then take the 'N' train into Manhattan where there was Lefty at the newsstand to swap gossip with, and Rupert who shared his passion for baseball, and of course Tom and Uncle Jack. His own dusty office held little interest for him: a desk cluttered with unimportant papers; a telephone that never rang; a file cabinet full of yellowed pieces of sheet music, lists of names of people in the business—most of whom were now dead, and scrapbooks filled with old newspaper clippings. He preferred to spend the better part of the day in Anderson Personnel—reading, smoking, chewing his mustache, and droning on until mid-afternoon when he and Uncle Jack went out for a drink and checked on their bets at the OTB parlor.

Later he would return to his daughter's house for a long, snoring nap before dinner.

Just then they heard the chains of the elevator rattling, the sound of its door sliding open, and Rupert's singsong dialect.

"Say Jackie boy, what's the good word?" Louie called out when Uncle Jack walked in.

"Hey Louie. How was Puerto Rico?"

Tom usually ignored nearly everything Louie said and had paid scarcely any attention to him when the he talked about going to Puerto Rico a few weeks ago. But he remembered now the glossy picture postcard depicting a grove of palm trees on a white beach washed by the turquoise sea that he had found lying on the floor one day with the rest of the mail. Tom had thrown it away without bothering to read it.

Smelling of alcohol, Uncle Jack hung up the wool overcoat. He handed a pack of cigarettes to Tom who noticed that it was already open and more than a few were missing.

"And the *Journal?* Uncle Jack."

"Damn it Tom, I'm sorry. Lefty and I got to chatting and I forgot all about it."

"That's all right. I think I'll be heading out to grab a bite to eat. I'll pick it up myself. Would you mind typing up some business cards while I'm out Uncle Jack? I bought some of those little pocket calendars at Woolworth's and a new typewriter ribbon. It types red and black."

"You call those goddamned things business cards?" It never took much to get his uncle started, especially after a couple of drinks. He turned away from Tom and now addressed Louie. "I tell you Louie, I bet you can remember when we had real cards printed up in a shop by a professional printer."

"Uncle Jack, don't get yourself all worked up."

"I'm not worked up. I'm only saying to Louie here—"

"Louie has heard it all before Uncle Jack. Please, just a few—"

"All right, all right. Whatever you say . . . you're the boss."

Tom put on his overcoat then lingered in the doorway for

a moment glaring at his uncle.

"I'll get to it in a minute Tom. Let me talk to Louie first. He's my friend you know." Uncle Jack sat back in his chair and exhaled sharply. "So go eat your lunch for Christ's sake. I said I'd do it."

Tom left the two of them in their usual places. Louie by the window leafing through the paper, reading aloud, airing his opinions on everything. Uncle Jack at his desk, rubbing the whiskers on his chin, looking impatient for Tom to leave.

*

A damp swirling March wind blew off the harbor waters and whistled through the narrow streets, creating here and there along the sidewalks little whirlwinds of paper and debris. Tom buttoned his overcoat to the collar and shoved his hands deep into his pockets.

With a copy of the *Wall Street Journal* tucked under his arm, he walked up Broadway under the bright mid-day sun until he arrived at the Exchange Deli & Grill, already crowded for lunch, where a small handwritten sign hung in the window announcing the *Thursday Special—$2.99.*

He squeezed himself onto a stool between patrons at the busy counter. Sonny, the owner, who was Cuban—"Hi-ya Sonny"—was shouting as usual at Frank, the fry-cook, down the length of the counter. The waitress, Mary—"Hi-ya sweetheart"—was all over the room taking orders, figuring checks, clearing tables, serving up platters of food as fast as Frank turned them out.

"Hello Mr. Anderson," she said. He had once asked her to call him Tom, but she never did. "You want the Special?" A cup of coffee appeared in front of him as he nodded.

"I NEED A SPECIAL FRANK . . . Soup today is Lima Bean Mr. Anderson, how about it? Still your favorite? WITH A CUP OF LIMA, FRANK!"

Twelve o'clock noon. So many customers coming and going. The grill was covered with more than a dozen hamburgers frying, their heavy, meaty smell hanging in the air. Frank's enormous hands worked unceasingly, but delicately—first chopping an onion then slicing a tomato, flipping the hamburgers and pieces of bacon, ladling soup out of a steaming pot, folding an omelet while it still bubbled in the center. Rapidly he prepared a turkey sandwich and arranged it on a platter with a pickle and a dollop of coleslaw, then barehanded scooped up some French fries and shook off the grease. Meanwhile, Sonny, always smiling, overseeing everything, answered the telephone, handled the take-out orders, and worked the cash register.

"Market Has Active Day . . . " Tom read, skimming the front page of the *Journal* . . . "Uncertainties Loom in Wake of Deficit." He read no further. He wondered what Mary did at the end of the day, where she lived—Brooklyn maybe—and whether she would like to see him sometime.

"Say Mr. Anderson, you got a minute?" Tom looked up at Sonny leaning over the counter with a serious expression on his face.

"Sure Sonny. What is it?"

"You remember my delivery-boy Manuel don't you? You know, Manny?"

"Sure . . . Manuel . . . Manny . . . How is he? Where is he? Is there a problem?" Tom felt his stomach tightening as he glanced around the room.

"Manny is fine. I gave him a few days off because he got married and brought his wife up from Puerto Rico last week."

"Well that's great. Manny's married you say." Tom sipped his coffee and his stomach relaxed.

"You sent him over here last year and he's a good boy. He's done a real good job. He's got a good *cabeza* you know."

Tom smiled a business smile and nodded. He tried to catch Mary's eyes when she brought him his soup.

"But I think he ought to start trying to find something else because I can't pay him that much for just deliveries. So I was wondering if you might have something or know about something that would be good for him, good for a married man."

Tom brooded for a moment and Sonny turned toward the grill. "Need that Special, right now Frank!"

"Special's working Sonny . . . " Frank never looked up.

Tom tasted his soup.

"I hate to lose Manny. He's like a little brother to me and I want to see that he does good. And maybe you got someone else who can come over here to take his place."

"Sure thing Sonny. I'll check over some of my files and see what I can do."

"Thanks a lot Mr. Anderson. I really appreciate it."

Before Sonny could shout again Mary brought a grilled cheese with bacon and tomato sandwich. Tom avoided her eyes. He ate in silence while Sonny stalked the other side of the counter and the din in the small restaurant increased.

*

Later on the street, Anderson did not take a direct route back to his office. He walked down Broadway, progressing slowly along the bustling sidewalk. He paused in front of Trinity Church where a magician was performing before a crowd that grew and grew until it blocked the sidewalk and spilled over onto the street. The magician never spoke during his act, communicating instead by means of gesture and pantomime. With a flick of the wrist he made a lighted cigarette that he had obtained from a woman in the audience seemingly disappear into thin air. Then, with a theatrical gesture, he stuck his hand deep into the woman's coat pocket, rummaged around for a few seconds, and withdrew it slowly—the still burning cigarette now between his fingers. He tied a series of short pieces of rope together and pulled the pieces through his cupped hand so that they were miraculously transformed into a single, unknotted strand. Tom watched him deal a deck of cards into a silk hat which he then covered with a large red handkerchief. After several exaggerated flourishes with his hands moving through the air, all the while maintaining an unchanging, deadpan expression, he removed the handkerchief and retrieved from the hat a tiny toy rabbit. The crowd gasped and laughed and applauded. When the magician next took up the hat and held it out for money, Tom wandered away from the scene and into the churchyard and prowled among the old grave markers.

At first the weather-beaten stones with their often-illegible engravings appeared to him to be little more than naturally occurring eruptions through the cold, frozen ground. He thought momentarily of his father's grave in Greenwood Cemetery in Brooklyn but could not remember the last time he had visited it. And now that his mother was buried in Florida beside her second husband—a man Tom hardly knew—who else would ever visit it? Uncle Jack? Mickey? There was no one but Tom.

He no longer looked at the grave markings, averting his eyes even as he moved away. He stopped suddenly upon rounding a corner of the soot-blackened church. Beyond some barren tree limbs and behind a cluster of low buildings, a portion of the south tower of the World Trade Center sparkled like white marble high overhead.

He went back to the front of the church, passed through a pair of double doors, and stepped inside. He peered into the nave towards the altar. A service was underway and several people were filing towards a priest who was administering Communion. The priest's face moved above the line of bowed heads, murmuring a phrase which Tom could not quite hear. He had an impulse to move closer but felt self-conscious and suppressed it. He took a seat in a pew and watched from the rear. The last time he had been at any type of a church service was for his father's funeral; before that was when Mickey had been baptized in a Lutheran church in Brooklyn because Sadie had insisted upon it, though neither she nor anyone in her family attended the church or were members. And now Mickey was living on a commune in California. Tom could not understand that. He pictured his son in saffron robes and with a shaved head, crawling on his hands and knees every day to kiss the feet of some swami. No he could not understand at all.

Sitting back, he closed his eyes and listened to the priest and to the shuffling of footsteps until the mass was over. When he got up to leave he saw the priest standing in the front doorway of the church trying to greet everyone and shake their hand as they left the service. Unsmiling, Tom hurried past him and through the double doors.

He crossed Broadway and walked along Wall Street. As he was turning to his right, headed down Broad Street, he heard a commotion across the way and saw another crowd gathered in front of the steps of Federal Hall. People were laughing and shouting and heckling a stern-faced man in a black fedora and a long black overcoat unbuttoned in front, revealing a clergyman's collar. In a stentorian voice he was crying out above the chorus of jeers—"O ye viper's brood. Mine is the voice of one crying in the wilderness! I am here to warn you to flee from the wrath that is sure to come . . . "

"Fuck you pal," said a voice in the crowd.

The preacher held a Bible out in front of him and shook it as if he wanted to strike someone with it. He shouted once more, still louder, until his vocal chords were straining and his voice became hoarse. "Even now the ax is laid to the root of the trees, and every tree that does not bear good fruit is to be cut down and thrown into the fire that will burn with the unquenchable fire." And then he stopped shouting and looked at his wristwatch. An expression of what seemed to be immense satisfaction appeared on his face. He suddenly announced that he was leaving but promised to return again tomorrow at the same time. He plunged into the crowd which parted to let him pass and was still laughing and heckling him as he continued up Nassau Street. Tom had little interest. He had heard it all many times. The preacher always preached the same hellfire sermon and the reaction was always the same.

Keeping his *Wall Street Journal* tucked under his arm, Tom entered the New York Stock Exchange and rode the elevator to the third floor. Instead of turning toward the visitor's gallery after getting off the elevator, he went the opposite way down a hallway and into the men's restroom. He found an empty toilet stall, closed the metal door, and latched it behind him. He much preferred the public facilities here to the bathroom in the Maiden Lane office building where there always lingered the smell of stale urine in the air, was seldom enough heat or hot water, and discarded paper towels littered the floor. Every day during the lunch hour as a part of his routine, he came here to move his bowels, to read the paper, to be alone.

Later he stood in front of a mirror combing his hair. He stared at his reflection. In the brightly lit restroom his face looked waxen and his oily blonde hair with now more than a few gray flecks stuck to the sides of his head. Around his pale blue eyes lay folds of wrinkles and dark half-moons hung from beneath his lower lids. On his chin were two small, crosshatched shaving scratches from this morning, which the wind had slightly irritated. He washed his hands and then held them dripping under the hot air machine to dry. He began to daydream about learning to play golf and acquiring a suntan in the Caribbean. Puerto Rico couldn't be that expensive if Louie had gone there. He imagined it would make quite an impression on Mary if he were to disappear for a couple of weeks, then show up for lunch one day—"Where'ya been Mr. Anderson? On vacation?"—all relaxed and sporting a suntan. Perhaps he might even ask her to go with him, next time . . . some time . . . if only she would call him Tom.

He folded the *Journal* so that the masthead was visible as he strolled out of the restroom and ventured toward the visitor's area. He passed an exhibit with a push-button panel of multilingual tape recordings explaining the functions and operations of the stock market. A group of tourists were gathered around a woman employee of the Exchange who was demonstrating a computer terminal which instantly displayed the latest prices of any listed stock. Tom ignored all of this and continued out onto the glassed-in walkway that overlooked the trading floor. Below him he saw the familiar but incomprehensible confusion and pandemonium of the brokers as they rushed and milled about, buying and selling, their voices shouting all at once and producing an uproar that seemed to grow louder and louder even while he stood there listening. He wondered if there was anyone working below who had been recruited by Anderson Personnel in the old days. Perhaps if he possessed a better understanding of the relationship between the commotion he was now witness to and the charts and lines and rows of figures that were published in the newspapers, or perhaps if he were to study more carefully those exhibits outside, he might one day be in a position to once again do business with the New York Stock Exchange.

Something strange appeared to be developing on one part of the floor. The traders were swarming and surging and an outcry arose until the noise coming from below no longer sounded to Tom, as it usually did, like the monotonous roar of waves breaking on the shore. It had a wrenching, human quality to it that was like a cry of anguish. It was complete chaos down there—the traders were shrieking, almost howling at one another. Tom grew alarmed. What was happening? He looked around at the others with him on the walkway but they all seemed to be quite undisturbed. It was as if something terrible were being revealed only to him, something nobody else could comprehend. He rushed inside and interrupted the woman employee who was still talking to the tourists. He asked her what was wrong. Had something happened to cause such a panic? But she just smiled and told the group that she gets the same question every day when people watch the operations on the trading floor for the first time. When Tom tried to tell her that this was not his first time, that he had never witnessed anything like this before, he felt everyone stare at him as if he were the cause of the commotion. The woman continued to

smile and resumed talking to the group. He said no more and
slipped away and left the New York Stock Exchange.

Once more on the street, still clutching the copy of the
Journal, he started up Broad Street toward Maiden Lane. The
crowd that had been listening to the street-preacher had long
since broken up. But all about him people were pressing and
hurrying and he had the thought that the turmoil on the floor
of the stock exchange was spilling over onto the street. He
knew he should get back to the office. He caught a glimpse of
the World Trade Center on his left and for several moments
stood on the corner trying to recall exactly what it was at the
office he had to take care of. No doubt Uncle Jack would not
have bothered to type up the business cards as he had asked
him to do. Tom felt disoriented, and then had a sudden urge.
With an air of determination he began walking, instinctively
almost, in a direction leading away from the Maiden Lane
building.

He crossed Broadway again just above Trinity Church and
continued west on Thames Street and then onto Albany Street.
Turning right on Washington Street he stopped and stared at
the massive south tower of the World Trade Center looming
directly ahead. He had never been so close to it though his
office was hardly more than a quarter-mile away. And now it
was exerting an irresistible attraction on him, compelling him
to move closer and closer, until he had the perception of being
almost sucked in through the revolving glass door.

In the vast lobby, between a high arching wall of glass and a
long bank of elevators, all sounds were muted by an expanse
of plush purple carpeting that spread in every direction. Tom
was uncertain of what to do next. He had taken a few tentative
steps inside, hoping he wouldn't bump into Rosenberg, when
he noticed a sign for the observation tower. He rode an
escalator to another level, followed some more signs, bought a
ticket, and joined a line waiting for the elevator. He thought
once again of the office and looked around for a telephone,
but just then, behind him in line, a group of tourists arrived,

accompanied by a tour leader who spoke to them in Spanish. A pair of metallic double-doors opened in front of them and a bored guard took their tickets as they passed through the turnstile and got onto the elevator.

It was a rapid ride. A tape recording came on and a raspy voice with a heavy Brooklyn accent provided them with facts and statistics concerning the World Trade Center to ponder. The voice on the tape closed by saying, "The observation deck of the World Trade Center is as close to heaven as some people ever get . . . " which caused several people in the tour group to laugh when the guide translated for them.

Tom's ears were slightly sore when the elevator stopped. The doors opened and a gust of wind blew in. He filed with the others through a narrow corridor that immediately widened into the enclosed outer perimeter of the building. He became somewhat dizzy as the city came into view before him. He peered through a window that ran all the way down to the floor. He went down some steps that took him closer to the window and became even more dizzy as he allowed his gaze to fall until he was staring past the tops of his shoes at the shadowed streets more than a hundred stories below. Stepping backwards, he stumbled on the steps. He grabbed a handrail and caught his balance but not before he had the sensation that he was falling through the air. He moved away from the windows and walked around the building's perimeter on a counter-clockwise course paralleling the windows which gave first to the north and Midtown; then to the west, past the Hudson River towards New Jersey. He continued around another corner where he came upon an escalator going up to the very roof of the building.

As he neared the top of the swiftly ascending stairs it was as if he were being hurtled from the last step onto the outdoor platform. The wind chilled him in spite of his coat. The sunlight made his eyes ache and he had to squint and use his hands to shield them at first. But he soon was no longer dizzy or disoriented. Outside now, from this perspective, the city was at once less overwhelming and oppressive: like nothing more than a panoramic exhibit on display in an enormous open-air museum. Even the towers of Midtown had the serene and majestic air of distant mountains about them.

The sough of the wind filled his ears and banished all other noises of the city. Tom surveyed the harbor to the south, dotted with islands and boats of various sizes. The boats appeared to be as motionless as the islands, floating like dead fish on the oily waters. Their movements became perceptible only when he was able make out the tiny, white feathery wakes trailing behind them. He beheld the graceful span and pale blue towers of the Verrazano Bridge and gazed beyond the Narrows and upper bay, where the open sea began. He watched a large ocean-going passenger ship as it sailed out of the harbor and under the bridge, and as it grew smaller and smaller in the distance.

A faint roar from a jet engine next arrested his attention when he caught sight of a 747 which had come out of the sky in the west and was veering north above the Hudson. He could distinguish more than a score of planes and helicopters soaring and hovering in the wide skies over the city.

Tom put his hands behind his back and took a deep breath. He moved to the other side of the platform and looked eastwards, past the low, brown huddle of buildings of downtown Brooklyn. He saw above the flattened expanses of the borough the literally hundreds of church spires which resembled thorns piercing the fabric of the sky. The Spanish tour group was suddenly beside him, all of them talking, pointing, and snapping photographs. He heard a word, it sounded like "sea-yellow", being repeated over and over, and he wondered what it meant.

He stared once more toward the open sea. The large ship was now a faint glint on the precipice of the horizon. He walked around the platform to the down escalator and began his long descent.

*

"Seems as though you have company, Mr. Anderson," Rupert was saying as he took Tom up to the fourth floor.

"Eh? What's that?" Tom answered distractedly.

"Just took the young man right up there to your office. He was askin' which was yours and I showed him."

"When was this?"

"I'm supposin' it was no more'n ten minutes ago. Here you are Mr. Anderson. Now you have a nice afternoon."

Tom hurried into the office where his "client" was waiting on the backless bench beside the coat rack. Uncle Jack was nowhere about, but Louie was still sitting beside the window reading the paper.

"Mr. Anderson?" The boy got to his feet. "The other gentleman said he had to step out but that I should wait for you. My name is Michael Bingham."

"Just one minute Mike . . . take a seat there and I'll be right with you."

Tom hung up his overcoat. He went to his desk, opened a drawer, and searched for a pencil. He tried to find an application form in the file cabinet but there were none. The last one had been used for that Martinez guy he'd sent to Rosenberg last week. He had asked Uncle Jack day before yesterday to go to the copy shop and have some more Xeroxed, had even given him the money for it, but in the meantime they both had completely forgotten about it. He found an empty file folder and some typing paper and decided it would have to do.

"Okay Mike—you want to come over here and have a seat. I'll need a little information. It won't take but a minute. I'm Tom Anderson."

The boy was across the room in three loping strides and offering his hand. "Pleased to meet you Mr. Anderson."

He was thin and very long-limbed. His youthful face reinforced an impression of almost adolescent awkwardness.

He had short brown hair and wore it parted neatly on the side. His affable manner as well as his clothing—neatly-pressed corduroy slacks, penny loafers, crew-neck sweater, and suede jacket—suggested to Tom that this was not the usual type who applied for messenger jobs. Michael sat down, crossed his legs, and let his long arms dangle at his sides. He had a spiral notebook with him which he rested on his lap.

"Did you every play any basketball Mike?" Tom always used that one on anyone over six feet. Again, something he'd picked up from his father.

"Not much, Mr. Anderson—mostly soccer."

"Soccer? Oh yes soccer. Interesting game soccer." Tom had never seen a game of soccer in his life. "All right Mike, now tell me about yourself and what kind of position you think you might be interested in." Tom assumed his smooth, business-like manner and spoke in a friendly and reassuring voice. He sat with pencil poised over the blank sheets of paper.

"I saw your sign downstairs for messengers. I haven't been in New York City for very long. I was in school . . . until last year . . . and have been doing some traveling in Europe and California since then . . . "

"Traveled abroad you say?" Tom interrupted. "That could be very useful for some of the positions we have because we deal with a lot of import-export companies." Tom cleared his throat. "Do you know much about the import-export business?"

"No not really. I haven't really worked anywhere before. I was in college. I was majoring in French at Yale but—" he stopped talking abruptly and seemed unsure of what to say next. He uncrossed his legs and the spiral notebook fell to the floor. He hastily retrieved it, opened it, and handed to Tom what he said was his résumé. "I didn't get a degree or anything. I decided to take some time off and look for a job . . . " His voice trailed away as Tom glanced over the handsomely typed document. He became intrigued when he noticed that Michael had lived for several years in South America.

"Do you speak Spanish Mike?" Tom recalled the word—

what was it?—"sea-yellow?" and wondered again what it meant in English.

"Yes some. But I'm better in Portuguese."

"Portuguese?"

"Yes, because I grew up mainly in Brazil. My father worked there, in São Paulo, until his company transferred him back to Connecticut."

"Oh yes, yes, I see. Portuguese." Tom coughed dryly. He appeared to examine the piece of paper more carefully. The interview was becoming more and more interesting. He considered asking Michael if he knew what "sea-yellow" meant.

"And I'm studying French in school, the literature I mean, that is I was, before I took a leave of absence . . . unofficially."

French? At Yale? Tom leaned back in his chair looking very pensive. He was actually quite confused. He had scrawled some words on the blank sheet of typing paper. Brazil . . . Yale . . . Mike . . . French . . . Portuguese . . . Spanish . . . Sea-yellow.

After a long pause. "So you'll be going back to school?"

"I don't know. I mean I haven't decided. It depends on what I'm doing here in the city. What kind of job I find. I want to get an apartment of my own." He lowered his eyes and when he finished speaking his face began to color.

Another long pause. "Well I always say you can't learn about the world out of a book. The world is full of people, not books." Tom spoke smoothly again. "You say you're new to the city? How well do you know your way around?"

"My sister lives uptown, East Eighty-second, near the Metropolitan Museum, so I know that area. And the Village I know fairly well. I'm still learning my way around the Financial District."

"Could you find City Hall? The stock exchanges? The Battery?"

"Oh yes, yes, sure."

"And the World Trade Center?"

The boy happened to look out the dirty window behind

Tom's desk and see the enormous form of a white skyscraper interposed upon the bright, cloudless blue sky.

"Yes sure, the World Trade Center too."

"Well Mike, if you'll just give me your address and phone number I think I have something you will want to check on. I'm sure you'll pick it up very fast."

"What kind of salary would I receive Mr. Anderson?"

"These jobs usually pay around eighty dollars a week."

The boy's expression became immediately crestfallen. "Oh I was hoping for a little more. Do you have something for around one hundred a week?"

The office door was suddenly thrown open and Uncle Jack burst in. The faint sound of a running toilet could be heard from down the hallway. He sat down at his desk without a word and started reading a copy of the *Racing Form*. Louie shuffled his feet and re-lit his pipe. Tom had forgotten he was even in the room. He had finished with his newspaper and was staring idly out the window. Tom glanced at his uncle before resuming.

"Nothing right now—nothing that really suits you. I suppose you can discuss the salary with them when you get there. It's my understanding that eighty dollars is more or less the going rate."

Michael nodded. He could not hide his disappointment or his obvious unease. But Tom ignored this and remained solicitous. "Why don't you talk to this fellow Rosenberg at the World Trade Center. Let's see how it goes." Tom wrote Rosenberg's address on a sheet of typing paper. He took out his wallet and searched unsuccessfully for one of his business cards.

"Uncle Jack? Would you have a card we can give Mike here?"

The old man looked up from his desk. Without a word he opened a drawer and produced a card. He held it out for Mike who rose and walked quickly across the room. When the boy took the card, Uncle Jack suddenly seized him by the wrist.

Leaning forward and knitting his brows, he spoke softly so that Tom could not hear.

"I just wouldn't expect too much if I were you son?"

Michael recoiled as the old man relinquished his grip.

Tom rose and crossed the room and was now escorting his new client to the door. "You've got my card and here's a dime. Give me a call after you talk to Mr. Rosenberg and let me know what happens."

"Yes sir, I'll do that. Oh, I need my résumé, too. It's my only copy." The boy seemed much relieved that the interview had ended and he was at last able to leave. It wasn't until Tom was back at his desk that he realized he'd forgotten to get Mike's home address and phone number. But no matter, he'd get it from Rosenberg later.

He dialed the number of the Ace Messenger Service.

"Hello Art. Anderson here. Listen Art, I've just sent a boy over to see you. I know what you said Art . . . I hear you . . . That's right . . . I think you're really going to like him. Give me a call later . . . That's right Art . . . Know what you mean . . . Right . . . Okay Art . . . Good-by Art."

"Well I guess I'll be shoving off." Louie stood up, stretched his legs, and yawned. "Either of you boys got time for a quick drop down on the corner. Need something to keep you going on a cold day like this."

"No thanks Louie, not today. Maybe Uncle Jack can make it."

A look of suspicion clouded his uncle's face. He and Tom exchanged stares. The old man had been waiting all afternoon for his nephew to mention the business cards and this had caught him unaware.

"Sure Louie, just a quick one, and then I'll be shoving off myself. Not much to keep me tied down today."

The tedious fiction that the two of them enacted every afternoon for Tom's benefit was not having its usual effect. Tom was even whistling as he sat at his desk and gazed out the window. This seemed to annoy his uncle all the more.

Uncle Jack put on the rumpled trench coat and waited by the door while Louie went across the hall to his office to get his coat and lock up. He stared again at Tom.

"Say Tommy—"

"Yes Uncle Jack?"

"I'll type those cards tomorrow. First thing."

"It's all right Uncle Jack. I have some time this afternoon and I can do it myself. Have a good evening." Tom spoke smoothly. He was smiling a business smile. After the old man had closed the door behind him it was suddenly thrown open and he stalked back into the room. His shoulders were hunched up and his unshaven chin was tucked onto his chest. Tom thought for a moment that his uncle had something else to say, but he just went straight to his desk, picked up the *Racing Form* and was gone again, slamming the door behind him this time.

Tom thought about Mike's résumé once more. Rosenberg was certainly going to be surprised that someone like Michael should have been sent over by Anderson Personnel. But he had better get used to it. Because it had occurred to Tom while he was speaking to Rosenberg, suddenly, and with such absolute clarity, that what he had to do now was attract more young men like Michael—maybe he had friends—into the office. He began mentally to compose a new classified ad which would run every day in the *Times* not under Messengers but instead under College Grads. Or if not that exactly, something to do with college. Bi-lingual or Tri-lingual might be good. Portuguese eh? And French as well. That would put Rosenberg in his place. And when the time was right, Anderson Personnel would eventually drop these small-time accounts with messenger services and coffee shops in lower Manhattan, and he could walk into any bank or brokerage house or insurance company, or even the New York Stock Exchange, and go after business.

Anderson sat smoking cigarette after cigarette in the silent afternoon gloom of his office. It now seemed so simple to him—

the answer that had been there all along. It had taken someone like Michael to open his eyes.

He would have cards printed up in a real printer's shop. Cards that read **ANDERSON PERSONNEL . . . SERVING THE FINANCIAL DISTRICT FOR OVER 40 YEARS . . .** or something to that effect. And he would no longer have to worry about losing the lease on this office because as soon as possible he would rent space in some place like the World Trade Center.

And what about Uncle Jack? Tom now had a legitimate excuse to get rid of him. It was time for him to stop hanging on. Let him stay here with Louie, playing the horses and reading the *Racing Form* until the wrecking ball came. Tom would have his own secretary and new office furniture.

The phone rang. Rosenberg? So soon?

It was Sadie.

"We've got him Tom. The man we sent found Mickey and got him away from those people. Leonard and I are flying to Los Angeles tonight to bring him back."

"Why should he come back Sadie? He won't come back unless you force him to."

"He'll come back Tom, because he loves me. He knows how much I've done for him . . . "

"Then why was he out there kissing the feet of that swami in the first place? Answer that one Sadie?"

"You answer that one Tom! It's because of you that he was with those people."

"Sadie, I told you I haven't seen him in nearly a year. You've really lost it this time."

"Look Tom, I've said all I'm going to say to you about it, except that when Mickey gets back I want you to stay away from him. No calls, no visits, no letters. Do you hear me Tom?"

"No I don't hear you Sadie."

"Oh yes you do hear me Tom. I'm leaving now. I've got a plane to catch. Good-by."

Tom lit another cigarette and waited for the phone to ring one more time.

*

After passing through the deserted lobby of the office building on Maiden Lane, Michael Bingham went out the door and turned to his left and headed east, in a direction away from the World Trade Center. He walked to the corner and entered O'Brien's Authentic Irish Pub where there was a steam table in the front opposite the bar. He was very hungry and he ordered a hot roast beef sandwich served open face with mashed potatoes, gravy, and string beans. He stepped up to the bar and ordered a ginger ale to go with it, then took a seat in the corner of the darkened room and began eating.

From the bar came the noise of several men laughing. They were smoking and arguing good-naturedly with the bartender who had a purring brogue and who regaled them with joke after joke.

ANDERSON PERSONNEL—OVER 40 YEARS OF EXPERIENCE

As he ate, Michael Bingham studied the little dimestore pocket calendar with the typewritten message on the back.

DO TELL YOUR FRIENDS ABOUT US!

A few moments later he saw that the two old-timers from the personnel agency had just come in. Their backs to him, they were bent over almost prayerfully before the shots of whiskey on the bar in front of them. But their presence made him uneasy. He got up suddenly without finishing his meal and hurried out the door without anyone noticing. Or so he thought.

Because Louie had noticed him from the moment he and Jack had entered—and he observed him now outside on the sidewalk, looking first up the block then down, and tearing up a small piece of paper, the scraps of which he tossed into the air so that they were caught in the wind and blown away. After the boy disappeared, Louie lit his pipe and sipped his whiskey and said nothing.

*

Tom Anderson kept all the lights on in the office but the room grew more and more dim as the afternoon waned outside. He was becoming impatient and could not wait much longer before he would be leaving for the day.

When the phone finally rang he jumped to his feet before picking it up. It was Rosenberg. At last.

"Anderson!" he was shouting, "Anderson! We're finished. If I can't rely on you anymore than I'm getting my messengers somewhere else. This does it!"

"Wait a minute Art. How about the one I sent over this afternoon. The kid from Yale. No problems with him, right?"

"From Yale? What in the hell are you talking about? Is that supposed to be some kind of a joke or what? Look Anderson—nobody came over from your office today. And I made it clear I wanted someone this afternoon."

"But the kid was perfect Art. He had first-class credentials. He speaks French. And Portuguese. And Spanish. He's traveled in Europe. He's—" Anderson realized how ridiculous he sounded.

The damned kid hadn't even showed up.

"Anderson . . . Anderson . . . !" Rosenberg's voice was a faint clicking noise inside the receiver in Tom's hand. "One more chance Anderson. One more! And that's it. If I hadn't known your old man I would have dropped you a long time ago. Tomorrow. By nine o'clock or we're finished. Do you hear me Anderson?" The clicking noise abruptly stopped.

Tom hung up the phone. "I hear you Art," he mumbled. He slumped in his chair. He gazed out the window.

The sun was hanging low in the west. At the foot of the twin towers, beyond the shafts of shadows cast by the low buildings flanking the narrow street, a great pool of golden dusk light had formed.

Tom did not stir when he heard the elevator door open in the hallway, the sound of Rupert's voice, or the approaching footsteps. But after the loud knock he looked around to see a young Hispanic man standing in the doorway.

"Mr. Anderson? It's me—Manuel Lopez. Manny? Remember me? Sonny, he sent me. About a job."

Tom Anderson turned slowly in his chair and saw through the dirty window a long white ship floating in an empty turquoise sea somewhere off the coast of South America.

JULIA

Always the two of them, at the same table in the employee's cafeteria, every afternoon. They worked in different departments, that much I knew, and perhaps there never arose the opportunity for any type of official contact—an exchange of memos, a business-related phone call or conversation, a document to be signed, that sort of thing. Ours is a very large company after all. Nevertheless, there in the cafeteria, it was always the two of them, together. Everyone noticed.

It was her laugh that invariably attracted people's attention at first. Quite often I would have taken a seat in the cafeteria, begun to eat the sandwich my wife had made for me that morning, opened my book, or even gotten so far as lighting my after-lunch cigarette without noticing them. And then, from their corner of the dingy room, her laugh would explode like the sound of a car backfiring. At this point everyone's head turned and I would glance over and note their presence if I had not already done so. By now the initial explosion was over. She would give the appearance of barely being able to suppress a loud guffaw. He, meanwhile, having trouble restraining his laughter, succumbed finally to a series of snickers and dry-throated chuckles with a look on his face that mixed intense amusement with the pain of having to hold things in. They took turns tapping their cigarettes into the ashtray while she shook her head in seeming disbelief at something he had just said, and he, still chuckling, was nodding. Things would then quiet down. Everyone would resume with their conversations or their reading or their lunch or whatever, until five or ten minutes later, when her laugh would explode and there would again be the guffaw, the snickers, and the dry-throated chuckles.

There were occasional variations. Sometimes after the initial explosion she positively howled, while he, overcome with it all, would let loose with his own ringing laugh. They both at times would rest their faces in the palms of their hands, carried away completely by their mirth, often to the point of having to wipe away tears.

The obvious question was—what's so damned funny? When I sat close to them, sometimes at the very next table, I could never quite hear what they were talking about, but I was able to notice what they were reading. She always brought with her a newspaper opened to the crossword puzzle page; while he customarily toted with him one thick work or another of serious literature, very unusual fare in an office setting. For a while it might be plays by Shakespeare or a copy of *Paradise Lost* or *The Faerie Queen*. I'd taken a few literature courses in college, had even considered English as a major, so I recognized many of the titles immediately. Often though he would be reading novels or poems or essays by writers I'd never even heard of. But the closer I sat to them the softer their voices became. And then for long stretches they would fall silent. She would busy herself with her crossword puzzle and he would be absorbed by his reading. No one at those times paid them the slightest attention. But sooner or later, a witty remark would be made, her laugh would explode, and the whole process repeated itself.

I occasionally saw them in the offices and around the building. He was slender, had slightly rounded shoulders, and would glide along as he walked without seeming to lift his feet.

His hair was cut short and he wore thick, heavy-framed eyeglasses. And he dressed well, usually quite fashionably. She was a heavy woman and did not dress well at all. She wore mostly baggy trousers and wrinkled sweatshirts or turtlenecks. She might have been considered more attractive if she had given some thought to her appearance and did not go around with such a sour expression on her face all the time when she wasn't sitting with him. But not once—and I suppose it is odd—did anyone recall seeing the two of them together except during their usual lunch time meeting in the cafeteria.

The cafeteria was a rather unpleasant room. No matter how many fresh coats of paint were applied, or how often, after a few weeks, after another layer of cigarette smoke had permeated the walls and ceiling, it always regained its usual dinginess. It wasn't really a cafeteria either. At one time, a pair of smiling blue-haired ladies in white aprons had served hot food, sandwiches, snacks, and beverages. But during a period of belt-tightening by the company, after it had merged with a larger concern headquartered in Chicago, the ladies were let go. The low counter that had been used as a serving table was removed and replaced by a refrigerator that gave off a strong, musty odor whenever its door was open. No one ever bothered to clean it or defrost it either. The room was still referred to as the cafeteria, but actually it was just a place where people would bring their lunches from outside. There were two parallel rows of tables—one along a wall, the other row alongside a bank of windows that looked onto a parking lot. The room was always crowded between noon and two o'clock, so there were days when I preferred to take a late lunch in order to have a table to myself. On those days too I would often encounter them there, so that by 2:30 we were the only ones in the room. The only sound was of the radiator hissing and popping in the winter, or during the summer, the rattling noise of an old and inadequate air conditioner. Invariably she had with her the newspaper crossword puzzle, and he was engrossed in his thick works of serious literature. And then, at least once—there it was—the explosive laugh, the guffaw, the snickers, and the dry-throated chuckles.

When I started to work for the company, I had figured I would stay there for a few years, get some experience, and then be able to try something else. But after I was married and after our first child was born, and a few years later a second, and then shortly thereafter the third, I found it hard to leave. The pay was adequate and the benefits, such as for health and dental care, were actually quite generous. That's an advantage of working in the insurance field. And after seven years I had accumulated enough seniority to be eligible for three weeks annual vacation. I liked my job and got along with everyone I worked with and worked for. By my ninth year I had risen to a supervisory position in the underwriting department. I was a part of middle management. I had my own partioned-off workspace, a secretary, and a half dozen people reporting directly to me. I realized that if I remained with the company this was probably as far as I would ever get unless I got more education and a professional license. But with responsibilities entailed by having a family there was little I could do. I couldn't go back to school. Certainly I could have looked for another job with a different company. But I've long recognized in myself a sentiment one might call loyalty which always came into play whenever I contemplated changing jobs, even after the company had long since merged with the one headquartered in Chicago. Perhaps it was simply inertia. But all things considered, I was not at any time consciously unhappy with the ways things were going for me in life.

One Friday afternoon in late spring or early summer, shortly after I had attained my supervisory position, I went to the personnel office to speak to them regarding processing applications for the position of a new secretary for me. My previous one quit after getting married and had moved with her husband to another city. When I arrived in personnel I saw that a party was under way. Everyone in the room was smiling and chatting and offering toasts with upraised plastic cups filled with champagne. On a table was an array of sandwiches, a cake, and several wrapped packages. In the center of the group stood Jeff. I had by now learned his name, as well as the fact that he worked in personnel. When he wasn't being toasted he was busy answering friendly questions from all sides.

The head of personnel noticed me and came over to me. I gave her the papers she needed and told her I hoped someone could be found as soon as possible, perhaps by the end of the following week. I asked her about the party and she said it was for Jeff. He was leaving the company. I mentioned that I'd seen him around without ever getting to know him. She told me that Jeff had been studying for a Master's and then Doctoral degree for the last several years, part-time, at night, on weekends, and had finally finished his course work and passed his oral examinations a few weeks before. He'd been offered a teaching job at a small midwestern college for the fall. He would be leaving town for good next month to do some traveling in England while doing research on his dissertation topic—a seventeenth century English poet whose name she didn't remember—before starting his new career. Today was his last day on the job. The group watched as Jeff opened his gifts and the personnel head seemed anxious to get back to the party. I, of course, was uninvited and felt a little uncomfortable. Since my business was finished I left the room while Jeff was speaking and thanking his co-workers for their support and encouragement.

So this explained the books he always read. So many years to have stuck with it while working full-time was truly a remarkable achievement. This certainly proved that there is life outside the company for some people. Though I hadn't noticed her at the party, I assumed his friend from the cafeteria would be leaving also, as if the two of them were somehow dual aspects of one essential unity. It even occurred to me that now I wouldn't have to listen to that laugh of hers anymore.

A few days later I received a note from personnel that said they were recommending someone to be my secretary who was in-house and requesting what amounted to, salary-

wise, a lateral transfer. I didn't recognize the name. But
when she came by for an interview the next day, it was her.
Of course, she wasn't leaving. Her name was Julia. She had
made no attempt to improve her appearance for my benefit:
a baggy pair of corduroy jeans, a rumpled sweater, her hair
in need of brushing. I was put off by this, and because of
having heard that explosive laugh so many times. I decided
to inform personnel that she wouldn't do and that I wanted
them to keep looking for other candidates. But her work
record was impeccable. And when I spoke to her current
chief in the accounting department he said he was sorry to
be losing her. He already assumed she'd been offered the
job. Though she wasn't that popular with her co-workers,
from his perspective she was an ideal employee. She worked
hard, seldom called in sick, and was always willing to put in
extra time on a Saturday or stay late in the evening if the
situation demanded it.

I decided to give her a chance on the basis of this
recommendation, and she began reporting to me the following
week.

Her job performance was outstanding, no question about it.
She was certainly the most capable and efficient secretary I have
ever had. Her appearance did not change however. She still did
not dress well, and she chain-smoked the entire day which
bothered many of her co-workers. But it wasn't her appearance
or the smoking so much as her aloof attitude that caused a certain
feeling of constraint to grow between her and the rest of the
department. For example, once a month I liked to take everyone
who worked for me out to a nearby Italian restaurant and treat
them to lunch. We usually ordered a couple of large pizzas, a
pitcher of soda, and one of beer. Everyone enjoyed it and looked
forward to it, except for Julia. She never went with us, saying she
didn't care for pizza, had too much work to do, or preferred to
eat the sandwich she'd brought from home.

After I became a supervisor in middle management I rarely
went down to the cafeteria. Most days I ate lunch at my desk

while reading the paper or catching up on correspondence that needed my attention. But one day when my wife was sick and not able to fix me anything I headed for the cafeteria to purchase a sandwich and a drink from the vending machines there. These amenities had been recently introduced by the parent company in Chicago, replacing the old dirty refrigerator. I even took a book with me, just like in the old days. When I walked into the room it was as dingy as ever and very crowded. I saw Julia sitting alone with the remains of her lunch beside her and the newspaper opened to the crossword puzzle section. There were no other empty tables so I asked if I could join her. She said she was just leaving but I told her I wanted to talk to her before she did so.

While I ate a sandwich she lit a cigarette and waited impatiently for me to say whatever I was going to say. The groaning air conditioner labored in vain to cool the room. No doubt she expected me to bring up what was happening in the office between her and the others, or once again to invite her out to lunch with the rest of us. But what I actually wanted to discuss was something else altogether, something I hadn't even considered until I had walked into this room and discovered her here. What I wanted to know was what she and Jeff had talked and laughed about all the time when they used to sit together. But I never got to ask her that. As soon as I mentioned his name she began stubbing out her cigarette and seemed very uncomfortable. She pretended to barely remember him.

"Yes Jeff," I insisted, "you two certainly appeared to to be enjoying yourselves in those days."

"Oh he had a lot of problems—personal problems—he used to talk to me about them. He was gay you know. He always had a crush on somebody. One time he found a couple of gray hairs in his head and he dyed his hair red so he wouldn't look too old for some guy he was trying to impress. But it turned out the guy was only a year or two younger than he was. Jeff was constantly involved in situations like that."

"Well I never really knew Jeff. I had heard he was gay, but it was none of my business."

"Yes and now he's gone off to Wisconsin or Michigan or someplace and no one ever hears from him."

"But I thought the two of you were such good friends, that is—"

"The two of us?" She acted incredulous. "No, not really. We had nothing in common."

I could tell she didn't want to talk about it anymore. She excused herself suddenly and left a half-crushed, still-burning cigarette stub in the ashtray which I had to put out myself. I tried to recall exactly what her laugh had sounded like. I hadn't heard it for a long while.

Perhaps at that time in my life I really should have tried to look for another job and put institutional loyalty out of my mind. I knew I was going no further here and that there was little I could do to bring myself to the attention of the company's top people in Chicago. But I won't complain. Even if my life was not particularly exciting, my children were growing up well and my wife was able to go back to work which certainly helped us out financially. And if my job was not particularly interesting or challenging, I at least had the confidence that I was experienced and competent enough to handle any problems that might arise.

One day several months later Julia called in sick with the flu. Nothing seemed unusual. I spoke to her myself and she said the doctor had told her to rest in bed for at least five days. I asked her if she would be all right and she assured me she would. It was an inconvenience and I knew the others in the department would be resentful at having to fill in for her, especially since she had by far the heaviest workload. But I supposed we would get by. It was during the lunch hour, and as usual I was eating at my desk, when I read that Jeff had died. The account in our local newspaper said he had missed the beginning of classes for the second term at his college and that no one in the English department knew why. The police had gone to his home and found him dead, purportedly from a mixture of alcohol and drugs. They had discovered several empty vodka bottles as well as vials of various types of prescription sedatives and tranquilizers. A spokesman for the police stated that it was impossible for the medical examiner to conclude if his death was accidental or a suicide. The article said he was very well liked by his students and that his recently completed dissertation on the English poet Robert Herrick was going to be published as a book. Jeff was originally from a suburb of Chicago and that's where the funeral was to take place.

I thought no more about it until the next day when I was wondering how Julia was doing and if she had heard the news. I was expecting her to telephone me each day of her absence but she apparently felt that by telling me she was going to spend the next five days in bed she didn't have to keep in touch. I asked someone in personnel to call her and later was told there had been no answer. I got her number and called it repeatedly myself that afternoon. Still no answer. I was worried. I even called that evening from home a couple of times. I grew more worried. I could hardly sleep that night and in the morning I awoke with a horrible thought. It was obvious that Jeff's death must have been suicide. I remembered how uncomfortable Julia seemed the day I mentioned him in the cafeteria. I had since wondered why she at first attempted to diminish the nature of their relationship and pretended almost not to know him, but then revealed how he used to confide in her. There was definitely some sort of mutuality I concluded. There had to be. And then I remembered, vividly, the sound of her explosive laughter.

I tried once again to reach her by phone before leaving my house. I wondered if I shouldn't notify the police. I decided to wait before doing that and to go to her apartment myself. I now had a wrenching feeling in my stomach. I was afraid of what I might find.

I rang her bell several times but no one came to the door. I ran to the apartment of the building superintendent. I asked him if he had seen her recently and he said he had seen no one coming or going for a couple of days, and not noticed any lights on at night either. My questions and my manner made him suspicious.

"Are you the police," he asked.

I don't know why but I said yes I was from the police department. I told him she wasn't in any trouble but that a friend of her was and I needed to talk to her.

"Perhaps if we went into the apartment it would help us locate her."

But I really didn't want to go in there by myself.

The superintendent produced a passkey and we entered. I prepared myself for the inevitable. The messy apartment. The overflowing ashtrays. Clothing strewn across furniture and piles of magazines and newspapers on the floor. And in the bedroom—

But surprisingly the apartment was neat and clean. It looked freshly dusted and vacuumed. The bed was made. The sinks in the kitchen and bathroom had been recently scoured. I realized how wrong I had been about her and how absurd were the presumptions I had made concerning her relationship with Jeff. I was ready to leave but the superintendent pointed to a door I thought led to a closet. "It's a two bedroom apartment," he explained. He opened the door and the smell of paint escaped into the air. This second bedroom was a studio and in it were dozens of paintings, some completed and some uncompleted, mounted on easels or standing against the wall. There was a low worktable in the middle of the room upon which sat a canister full of brushes, a palette, and tubes of paint. A pair of casement windows were opened slightly to allow the room to ventilate. Apparently Julia was a portrait painter in her spare time. All of her paintings were of human subjects. Most of the people I didn't recognize, but I saw a couple of self-portraits of her, in each of which she wore a flowing red dress. And hanging on a wall there was a portrait of Jeff—he appeared to be snickering and she had captured the expression in his eyes that made him seem as if he was in possession of an amusing secret. And in the corner I even saw one of myself. I was dressed in a drab gray business suit and staring out at the viewer with a severe look. The head and shoulders were mostly finished, but she hadn't yet decided on a background. I wanted to stay longer now and study these paintings but the superintendent was getting suspicious. He hadn't noticed that I was the subject of one of the portraits, but I certainly wasn't acting like a policeman either, confused as I was. So it was best to leave as quickly as possible.

I arrived late at work that day and didn't try calling her again. When anyone asked I said she still had the flu and would be back the next week. I bumped into her old supervisor from the accounting department and he asked me if I had heard about Jeff and did I know how Julia had received the news. He told me that he had heard from some of Jeff's friends in personnel that he had been depressed following the death of a lover from AIDS, and that most likely Jeff had learned that he was HIV positive himself. He asked again about Julia. I said she was doing all right. I tried to change the subject. I was at a loss at what to say.

On Monday of the following week she was back at work. There was no noticeable change in her manner. She was always so reserved and businesslike. She said nothing more to me concerning her absence. The subject of Jeff's death never came up. I never knew if the superintendent told her that the police had searched her apartment.

Over the course of the next six months there were several changes in her appearance. She started wearing a little lipstick and makeup. Her hair was usually clean. Her clothes became more stylish, more colorful. She lost weight. She said she was exercising by walking back and forth to work, a couple of miles each way. Her disposition changed somewhat. She was friendlier and much more accessible as far as the others in the department were concerned, even if she did not join us for pizza and beer once a month. People in other parts of the building asked me what was going on, if I had a new secretary. Again, I was at a loss of words at what to say.

Then one day she gave notice that she was leaving the company. A going away card was circulated around the office and there was a small get together on the afternoon of her last day. She was characteristically vague regarding her future plans. I tried to talk to her that last afternoon and thought of inviting her out for a drink after work or asking if I could call her after she left. But somehow the opportunity never presented itself. She was talking to everyone at the same time, making jokes and small talk, though she didn't laugh.

A few weeks later I did try to call her, after thinking about it for a long time. Several times I picked up the phone at work and dialed her number up to the last digit. I would keep the phone in my hand until I was automatically disconnected and a beeping noise began. I would then replace the receiver. Finally, when I did dial her entire number and let it ring, I got only a tape-recording that told me the number had been disconnected.

After she left I was not able to immediately replace her. The company headquarters in Chicago had initiated another cost-cutting campaign and one way of implementing it was to let certain positions, clerical and secretarial positions especially, go unfilled for up to a year. This caused quite a strain for everyone who reported to me and I had to determine how to most fairly and efficiently divide up her workload. It was difficult but we got by.

I did speak to her former supervisor from time to time who learned things second and third-hand as he said. He told me she had gone to Chicago and studied painting at an art school. While studying there she had taken up with an older man on the faculty—he was Russian or Polish—something Eastern European. They had married eventually. He was a prominent sculptor and she was pursuing her career as a painter. I wondered if she would ever return to her hometown and show off her work. I wouldn't have minded owning one of her portraits. Or seeing her again. Or hearing her laugh.

Time passed. Years went by in fact. And we never heard from her. Even her former supervisor in accounting had no further information.

*

It was after I had reached a milestone of sorts, twenty-five years with the company, that I received some sort of recognition from the Chicago headquarters. It wasn't really anything specific to me. I got an invitation to come to Chicago in June and attend a middle-management seminar as well as a dinner honoring senior employees of the company from all over the country. In addition to the seminar and the dinner there would be the chance to see the company's new corporate offices which were now located just outside of Chicago in a suburban setting not far from the home of the President and CEO. There would also be sightseeing excursions and a chance to attend a Chicago Cubs baseball game. Everything, including airfare to O'Hare Airport, would be taken care of by the company.

I decided to go. Since my wife would have had to pay for her ticket and because Chicago was probably the last place she would ever want to see, except for New York City, I went alone. I had a pleasant flight and was met at the airport by a limousine driver. He was waiting near the luggage carousel holding a homemade sign with the company's name written on it. He welcomed me to Chicago and helped me with my suitcase. It was a thirty-minute ride to the downtown hotel on Michigan Avenue. My room was small but comfortable and I had a view of the park across the way. I ordered lunch from room service and waited. I noticed a phone book sitting on the table beside the phone. I opened it and flipped randomly through it. I looked to see if there was anyone with my same last name living here in Chicago. I found several entries. And for no particular reason I looked under Julia's name and was surprised to find a listing. I had no idea if this was really her. I dialed the number, up to the last digit, and then after a few seconds I hung up.

My lunch arrived and I sat beside the window eating and gazing out at the bright sunshine on Grant Park. It was the middle of the day and the streets and sidewalks were very busy. My itinerary was tight. Tonight would be the banquet in the hotel. Tomorrow morning we would travel by bus to visit the company's new headquarters in the suburbs, attend the seminars, be back at the hotel in the afternoon, do some sightseeing if time permitted, and then travel as a group on public transportation to Wrigley Field for the baseball game in the evening. The phone rang while I was eating. It was a woman from the company inquiring if I had arrived safely and reminding me that it was all set for the banquet in the evening. After I spoke with her I once again dialed the number listed under Julia's name. It rang several times and then there was a recorded voice from an answering machine on the line. It sounded like her voice. It could have been her voice but I wasn't sure. I was about to hang up before the beep when a man's voice came on the line—not a recording.

"Hello, hello, I am very sorry I did not get to the phone in time. You wish to speak to Julia?" It was a deep voice and it definitely had an accent.

"Yes, I think so, I am an old friend of hers. I knew in her hometown many years ago. I was her boss. I don't know if she still remembers me."

There was a long pause. I thought I heard the man's voice speaking to someone else. He came back. He seemed distracted. "My wife is not here. She is at the gallery preparing for her exhibition. You can reach her there."

"Oh that's all right it's not that important. I was only calling to say hello. I'm sure she's busy. She's having an exhibition you say? Of her paintings?"

Another long pause. Again I could hear him speaking to someone about a different matter altogether. "I am sorry—

you said you are a friend of hers. You are calling in connection with the exhibition? You are a critic? You are in the business maybe?"

I was going to apologize and hang up, saying it was all a misunderstanding. But he spoke once more.

"Please tell me your name again. I am sorry. We are very busy. You can perhaps come to the opening tomorrow night?"

"Oh I've just arrived in Chicago. I haven't seen her in years . . . "

"Your name please. I will put it on the guest list. I'm sure Julia will be delighted if you are able to attend. Cocktails will be served. Please come between six and eight o'clock." I wrote down the name and address of the art gallery.

I couldn't tell if he was sincere or merely being polite in order to get off the phone. But I was certain that he would put my name on the guest list.

The company banquet that evening was a pleasurable affair. There were twenty of us from around the country who had been flown in to be honored, as well as another dozen employees from the Chicago headquarters who had also reached the twenty-five year mark. Several of the top executives from the company gave speeches and we were each presented with an engraved plaque with our names, the company's logo, and the phrase "A Quarter-Century of Dedicated Service" inscribed on it. After the banquet I went back upstairs to my room. A number of the honorees were heading for the hotel bar but I wasn't interested in that sort of thing.

The following morning we rode a chartered bus to the suburban headquarters of the company. It was a long two-story building sheathed in dark reflecting glass. It was set well back from the road and surrounded by a broad expanse of grass and trees. The parking lot was around back and could not be seen from the road. The facilities inside were very modern and efficiently laid out. We saw a room full of computers that processed all the information that was sent here from the company's branch offices and independent agents around the

country. We were met by the same top executives who'd had
spoken at the banquet last night, and we even had coffee in
the office of the President of the company. His was a large
office on the second floor with an enormous window that looked
across the grounds towards a stand of trees. Later we had lunch
in the employees' cafeteria. It was a large bright room on the
ground floor. There was a serving line for hot foods, a deli
sandwich section, a salad bar, as well as a selection of deserts
and a yogurt machine that dispensed a different flavor every
day. On the walls were various types of artwork—modern
paintings and some American Indian-style woven rugs. Two
large sliding glass doors opened onto an outdoor terrace where
there were tables and chairs beneath striped umbrellas where
you could have your lunch or take your coffee break in the
warm weather. Since we were guests, these tables were reserved
for our group.

After lunch we were taken inside to the company
conference room for our seminar. A consultant spoke to us
about the latest trends in management and how we should
devote more time listening to the problems and suggestions of
our staff. Afterwards, we once again boarded the chartered
bus and were driven back to Chicago. We would have the
afternoon free to sightsee. There were several tours available
at the hotel. Some in our group planned to spend the rest of
the afternoon in the hotel bar before getting ready to go to
the baseball game. I decided to walk over to the Chicago Art
Institute which was not far from the hotel. But when I arrived
it was not open. There was a sign in front that said due to
financial problems the Institute was closed an additional day
each week. This happened to be the day.

I walked around the park for a while and sat down on a
bench across the way from my hotel. I really didn't want to go
to the baseball game. I was thinking of Julia. All day long I had
been thinking of her. I wondered if she remembered that the
insurance company where she used to work had its
headquarters in Chicago. I wondered about her paintings and

if the one of me would be on display at the exhibition. I didn't know much about these things. Perhaps she'd had any number of exhibitions and showings in her career. It had been so many years. I wished we had kept in touch.

I didn't want to return to the hotel that afternoon because I didn't want to bump into any of the others and have to explain why I wasn't attending the baseball game. I wandered around and looked at buildings on the Chicago Loop and stopped in a couple of bookstores and the Marshall Fields department store. I didn't buy anything. I was just browsing. I ended up near the restored Union Station and admired the massive marble columns, the vertical light streaming in, and the hurrying crowds. I walked outside and crossed a bridge over the Chicago River and found myself at the base of the Sears Tower, the tallest building in the world. I wanted to go to the top of the building, to its observation deck, and see the rest of the city and Lake Michigan. I realized I hadn't seen the lake at all since my arrival. But there was a sign in front of the elevator that said the observation deck was temporarily closed while it was being refurbished.

I had tired myself out by now and decided to go back to my hotel after all to rest and change clothes before going to the art gallery. As I hurried past the hotel bar I spied the others from my group sitting around a couple of tables they'd pushed together. They were no doubt all relating their combined experiences after twenty-five years of working for the company.

I opened my window and let the fine cool air blowing from the direction of the lake into my room. I took off my shoes and lay down on my bed and thought once more about Julia and when she had worked for me. I thought about Jeff too for the first time probably since right after his death. How wrong I had been about the two of them. How foolish to have thought they had some sort of relationship outside the office, such that after his death, his suicide, she was going to take her life as well. Where did I ever come by such a notion? Isn't that what happens in Romeo and Juliet? Or in Japanese *kabuki* dramas?

I dozed off. I dreamed of Julia. At the time it seemed like something I'd dreamed before, a recurring dream. But I've since learned that such dreams aren't really recurring dreams at all. The sense of familiarity is actually a part of the dream. She was wearing a red dress and smoking a cigarette. She was sitting in the old cafeteria with Jeff. But suddenly Jeff was gone and then so was the cafeteria. There was just Julia and she was now in the office of the President of the company at the suburban headquarters. He was seated behind his desk and she was standing beside an easel painting his portrait. All around on the walls of the room were the portraits she had painted, the same ones I had seen that day, long ago, in her apartment. And most prominently displayed, right behind the desk of the President, so that if he spun around in his chair 180 degrees, he couldn't miss seeing the one of me.

But he continued sitting and facing her as she painted. He spoke. It was the voice of the man on the phone, her husband. He said something I couldn't quite understand and then there was the laugh, her laugh, and the explosion. He smiled and snickered while she kept laughing. Just laughing and laughing. The phone on his desk began to ring but they both ignored it, so that the two of them alone, together, could continue to enjoy their private joke.

I awoke suddenly when the phone in my room stopped ringing. I hadn't heard it except in my dream, but afterwards I was positive it must have been ringing. It was probably the others calling to tell me it was time to come down and leave for the baseball game. Instead I washed my face and shaved and changed clothes. I waited until after I knew they would have gone and went downstairs to hail a cab to take me to the gallery on the near north side of Chicago.

It was a narrow storefront set in the middle of a neighborhood of other galleries and restaurants and boutique-style clothing stores. I walked right in and looked for someone to tell my name to so that they could confirm I was on the invited list. But there was no one really in charge or checking on who came and went. The room was narrow but very deep from front to back and full of people chatting, smoking, holding drinks. This was a far different group than the one I had been associated with in my company activities. There were more women, a greater range of ages, and I had never seen such unusual styles of dress except in the pages of newspapers in the fashion sections. Needless to say I felt somewhat out of place dressed like a middle manager of an insurance company in a room full of people wearing so much leather and denim. Black seemed to be the basic color. I looked around for Julia but didn't see her. Either she had not yet arrived or she was in the back behind some hidden door waiting to make a grand entrance. I looked at the paintings hanging on the wall. She was still doing portraits of people for the most part, although there was one painting of an empty room full of furniture and an open window through which the wind was blowing. This was suggested by the way a pair of curtains stood away from the window, as if billowing in a breeze.

Along the entire rear wall was a series of paintings of Jeff. Jeff in every conceivable mood. Not just laughing—but frowning, sneering, crying, and even one which was undoubtedly of him after he was dead, as he would have appeared as a corpse at his own funeral. His face was shrunken but the cheeks and lips had an artificial glow about them. He was wearing a shirt and tie but was without his glasses. The eyes were closed and the mouth was turned down. Even though the painting was hanging vertically on a wall the viewer had the sense that he was staring down at the subject. How had she achieved this? I noticed the little sticker beside the painting. It simply said "Jeff" and gave a date, a month and a year. I couldn't recall the month but the year was definitely the one in which he had died. I could not take my eyes off this painting. Until I heard the laugh.

It was Julia, standing by the front door, she had just arrived, and she was laughing. She was wearing a red dress as she had been in my dream. She was standing inside a circle of people and beside an older man with a shock of long white hair swept back. She looked maybe a few years older but certainly not ten or fifteen. She was not a slender woman, but certainly not as heavy as she had once been. Although she had lost weight right before she had left the company, I still remembered her looking as she did from before Jeff's death. Her eyes were lively and the man beside her was laughing too at something someone had said. While he was talking, she glanced around the room for a moment at everything and everyone. Her eyes lighted on me standing there beside the death portrait of Jeff. I started to say hello, to smile, to gesture, but before I could, her gaze moved on. There had been perhaps a slight hint of recognition. But she didn't really remember me. She probably wondered who I was and why I was there, and why was I dressed like a supervisor in an insurance company.

More people were arriving now and the room became even more crowded. Everyone knew everyone else. No one was paying attention to the paintings so far as I could tell. Above the din as I made my way toward the door I heard Julia's laugh once again ring out. Such a distinctive laugh she had always had.

Outside on the sidewalk there were people hurrying everywhere. All of the galleries and restaurants and shops were full of what seemed to be fashionable and attractive couples. It was a warm and pleasant night in Chicago. Perhaps I should have gone to the baseball game. I hailed a cab and went back to my hotel on Michigan Avenue.

That night in my room I was still thinking about Julia and the day I had gone to her apartment. Did I really believe that something had happened to her? Did I believe I was going there to rescue her? And in my confusion at finding the apartment so neat and discovering her studio full of paintings, I realized now, what I had neglected to ask either myself or to ask her then, was where had she been while I was there? The answer was obvious—she was here in Chicago—or somewhere in the suburbs where they bury the dead.

I began packing my suitcase. I hadn't brought much. I had
to be up early to check out and get to the airport for my
morning flight home. I reminded myself to pick up a souvenir
for my wife, even if Chicago was about the last place she would
ever care to visit or remember. Of course I had the plaque I
had received at the banquet. I would put it on my desk when I
got back to work.

*

Mine is a very loyal staff. I am considered a good boss to
work for. I know the job and I know my people. I never stay
past 5:30 in the afternoon anymore and I don't expect anyone
else to do so either. I don't worry if I, or anyone who reports to
me, is a little late in the morning. Everyone seems content
with the status quo. There's never been any indication from
headquarters that they're less than satisfied with the way things
are going here. I no longer eat lunch at my desk. I've developed
a taste for books that I can usually only find at the public library.
Histories, biographies, sometimes a novel. I read the newspaper
at home. My children are now grown and my wife and I spend
uneventful evenings in front of the television. She knits while
I read the paper and eventually drowse off in my chair. At
work at 2:00 sharp I make my way down to the cafeteria after it
has cleared out so I can sit there and read for a while. The
vending machines have been removed and replaced by a new
refrigerator and a microwave oven. The room is no longer dingy
and no longer smells of cigarette smoke. It's been made over
into a Seattle-style coffee bar with comfortable chairs and tables
and the freshly painted walls are the color of a pink grapefruit.
Smoking has been banned throughout the office for the last
few years, the entire building in fact. This was on orders from
Chicago. We also got a quiet new air conditioner last summer.
The radiator is still the same one however, it still hisses and
pops. The weather turned quite cold recently. A Canadian cold
front moved in and some snow fell. An early winter had arrived

so the heat was turned on. Except for the noise of that radiator, after 2:00, after everyone has left, the cafeteria is a very quiet room.

CONTENTMENT

She was still an extraordinarily beautiful woman. When the painter saw a recent photograph of her that had appeared in a glossy fashion magazine he could see she still retained her delicate features and wasp-waisted figure, still wore her long dark hair pulled back and pinned almost primly in a bun behind her head. But there was another picture of her he had seen before, one deeply embedded in his consciousness and imagination, that had been the model for the portrait in oils he had labored over, had struggled with, had put everything into he possessed as an artist. It was a photograph that had been taken of the woman more than forty years before by a famous photographer in Paris while she was living there as an expatriate American and publishing her novels and poetry and exhibiting her paintings. In later years, after returning to America, the woman published volume after volume of her journals, describing in intimate detail her bohemian, Parisian milieu, her circle of famous acquaintances in New York, and the particulars of her numerous love affairs in both cities. A friend of the portrait painter, a writer, had given him copies of the journals, and it was the reading of them that further fired his imagination as he conjured up in his mind the image of the beautiful woman and the life that she led. And it was this image that he had worked on for so long to capture in his portrait.

The painter had always painted portraits of people and nothing else. He realized he was something of a throwback and that his art could be considered to be hopelessly passé. Still, he never attempted to paint anything other than portraits. Never a landscape; no still-lifes of interesting objects; nothing that could be considered to be the least bit abstract, impressionistic, expressionistic, or having anything to do with any modern trend. It wasn't that he didn't understand or appreciate the works of other artists, including some he knew personally, but for him—almost totally self-taught in the art of applying oil to canvas, and living and working in his provincial city, far from the great art scenes with their museums and galleries—the only art he could conceive of pursuing involved solely the human face and figure. And so among his small circle of fellow artists and their patrons in the provincial city, he acquired the reputation of being not simply single-minded, but nearly a zealot, dedicated totally to the pursuit of an austere vocation. But his paintings were not merely life-like, realistic portraits. They were much more than that. They were at once revealing and haunting. The portrait painter not only possessed the ability to peer deeply into the souls of his subjects, but he truly had the gift of being able to render those souls in paint. He had done so many portraits in his career—hundreds of them, of himself, of his friends, and of those who had commissioned him. But this portrait, the portrait of the beautiful woman, the woman with the delicate features, the milk-white skin, the almond-shaped eyes, the trace of a widow's peak, this portrait he considered to be his masterpiece. And because this image of the woman had for so long obsessed him, she was, he realized, the woman he loved.

He decided he would go to her, to seek her out in New York where she had lived for several years. He would go to New York with his painting and somehow arrange to meet her and show her the portrait. And then, he reasoned, he would become if not an important part of her life, at least a personage in her journals. His imagination, his talent, his vision of her, and his love were going to carry him far from his provincial city and his limited circle of friends.

He had loaded the portrait into his car. He was going to drive to New York and not let the painting out of his sight. The day he was to depart, or rather the evening, he locked up his studio. He planned to leave as soon as it got dark and drive straight through during the night in order to avoid the sweltering summer heat. But first he stopped by the house of his friend the writer. He wanted to say good-by and leave him with the key to his studio. Because it was the writer who had showed him the photograph of the woman and given him copies of her journals, and because the writer had read all of her works, it was only to the writer that the painter could confide the depth of his passion and reveal the degree of his obsession. In the writer's living room they began to talk. He told the writer he felt he was at last able to climb out of an abyss that his vocation and his isolation had led him into. He had literally painted his way out of it. As often happened in their conversations, they each set the other off like a bomb. The writer had opened a jug of *Chianti* to fuel their minds and further free their tongues. More wine, more words, more tender emotions and grand ideas flowing. They talked about the beautiful woman, about their mutual friends in the provincial city, and about distant great cities, especially New York and Paris. Not wanting to leave it in his car as night had fallen and so that the writer could view it one last time, the painter brought the portrait inside and set it up on a low coffee table with the back of the canvas resting against a wall. They continued to talk and consume glass after glass of red wine. They were now like brothers in spirit. But like brothers there was a certain contentiousness between them that could assume bizarre and excessive dimensions.

The writer lit a cigarette and grew quiet while listening to

the painter. Suddenly he became belligerent. He belittled the
painter and scoffed at his passion. He said that the woman had
never been much of a writer. She wrote precious, insufferably
florid prose; her poetry was worthless—nothing but strings of
pretty images that amounted to nothing; and her journals were
simply idle self-serving gossip concerning the meaningless
goings-ons of a bunch of metropolitan poseurs and dandies.
He told the painter he was not climbing out of an abyss but
falling deeper into it. In his drunkenness he harangued and
taunted the painter, who in his drunkenness felt his temper
snap. So just like brothers they began to scuffle. At first it was a
comical, free-swinging affair with neither of them really landing
any serious blows, until the writer, rising from a low crouch
and swinging from his heels caught the chin of the painter
with a ferocious uppercut. He was reeling from this blow when
the writer stepped forward, planted his left foot, and tagged
him with a perfect one-two, left-right combination that split
the painter's upper lip and knocked a tooth loose. This caused
his mouth to fill with blood. He fell backwards, over the coffee
table, and landed with his entire weight against the portrait.
The legs of the coffee table gave way and the painter crashed
to the floor, ripping the canvas lengthways as he did. He was
bleeding copiously from the nose and mouth. He lay facedown
with his head directly above the face in the torn painting. He
was only semi-conscious at this point. And then he started
wretching and vomited up all of the *Chianti* he'd consumed
over the course of the last two hours. Finally, completely
exhausted, drunk, and beaten-up, all he could do was to roll
over on his back and to fall into the sleep of the dead.

When he awoke after what seemed an eternity he didn't
know where he was. New York? Paris? He tried to focus on the
room he now found himself in, or the pain he felt in his mouth,
or the sour smell that pervaded everything, on something
tangible. But it was futile. His perceptions were haphazard and
his thoughts scattered and unformed. He turned over on his
side and then he did see something he recognized, or almost

recognized: broken and torn and lying in a puddle of reddish vomit and blood.

The painter got to his feet and staggered through a door and into a kitchen and through yet another door. He was standing now in the small backyard of the writer's house. And there sitting in a chair was the writer himself, drinking a cup of coffee and reading a book. The painter staggered further out into the yard and sat down heavily on the ground. The writer was suddenly kneeling down beside him, ministering to him, examining his cuts and bruises. The writer went inside the house and got a cool, wet towel which he used to wipe off the painter's face. The writer went inside again and this time returned with a clean shirt for the painter to put on and had also brought him a cup of coffee.

After the coffee the painter's mind began to clear somewhat. The pain was still present but it also was not present, or at least irrelevant. The writer asked him if he was hungry and would he like some breakfast. The painter became aware of just how hungry he was and remarked that he'd had nothing to eat the night before. The writer told him to wait here in the yard and went inside the house once more.

The painter lay back on the cool grass and looked up towards the sky. He saw the morning sunlight filtering through the leaves of an enormous oak tree that towered overhead. He stared at the top of the tree and listened to the branches creaking and leaves rustling in the slight morning breeze. He heard also the sounds of birds singing and caught a glimpse of a starling flitting from the treetop to the rooftop of the writer's house and then onto a telephone pole next door. The scent of a flowering lilac bush penetrated his swollen and blood-clogged nose. He closed his eyes and thought of his small circle of artist-friends, and of his closest friend, the writer. He thought of his life in this provincial city and what it meant to be an artist far away from the galleries and museums of the great cities. He realized he was not going to New York and that no one in Paris would ever see his paintings. He knew he'd never have a rendezvous with the beautiful woman, who was still such beautiful woman.

He opened his eyes. There beside him was a plate of scrambled eggs and buttered grits and sliced, fresh tomatoes. He stared again at the top of the enormous oak tree and its wide, spreading branches. It was such a splendid morning, he reasoned, lying there with the warm sun reaching down to him—a splendid morning not to be in New York or Paris and not to be in love with any beautiful woman.

.

MORIR SOÑANDO

I had been working late that night so around nine-thirty I put on my coat and scarf and walked out into the cold December darkness and headed for Rosita's, a little Cuban diner on upper Broadway that stays open twenty-four hours a day. As I approached, I saw glowing through the steamed-over front window the familiar sign with the tiny, pink neon rose blinking off and on and dotting the "i" in Rosita. Inside, the small main counter with room for only seven people was completely occupied. I had to sit by myself at the opposite counter, which is smaller still, with a very narrow top, and which runs along a wall where there is often a cockroach to be seen exploring the cracks in the paint. Halfway up the wall hang plastic reproductions of the flags of Cuba, Puerto Rico, and the Dominican Republic. Posted just above the flags is the handwritten list of the various flavors of *batidos* served here. One flavor in particular, *Morir Soñando*, a concoction of orange juice, milk, crushed ice, and sugar, I often order during the summer, savoring as much the saying of its whimsical name as the sweet, cold, exotic taste.

I was very hungry and ordered a complete dinner: the daily special—something called *biftec palomilla* which came with yellow rice, black beans, bread, and salad; on the side I ordered a dish of fried sweet plantains. I gave my order to Rosita herself, a plump Cuban lady who runs things during the day but whom I was surprised to see still working so late. When I asked her what *palomilla* meant in English, Rosita, usually unfailingly pleasant, seemed preoccupied. She shrugged and said "*Palomilla es palomilla* . . . I can't explain in English. Is very good. *Carne*. With onions."

Some regulars from the neighborhood were clustered at the end of the main counter nearest the kitchen. They were drinking coffee and chatting in Spanish with the cook who was known as Maestro; with the dishwasher, an old man with a perennial, toothless grin whom everybody simply called Hola; and with Carlos, the night manager and younger brother of Rosita. Maestro and Hola were leaning in the doorway that leads into the kitchen, above which hangs a faded black and white photograph of a park in Havana. The photograph, taken in the early 1950's, depicts a wide, sun-splashed plaza full of flowers and palm trees with people sitting on benches or promenading about, and a row of bleached limestone buildings in the background. Carlos, short and stocky like his sister, had grown a mustache since the last time I had been in. He was arranging a pile of fruit—pineapples, mangos, papayas, bananas—on top of a small table wedged into one corner of the narrow, rectangular-shaped room.

Also having coffee at the main counter were three guys in their early to mid-twenties, student-types. They wore the sleeves pushed up on their crew-neck sweaters and were sharing a pack of Marlboros. Next to them was an enormous black man who kept his face only a few inches above a plate of spaghetti and meatballs which he noisily shoveled into his mouth. At the other end of the counter, closest to the front door, sat a Spanish kid of around fifteen, trying to make an impression on Gabriella, the young Puerto Rican waitress who was wearing a purple sweater and gold hoop earrings, and who always has her hair done in the latest, most-popular Latin style. The kid would rise from his stool and lean over the counter while whispering to her whenever she passed in front of him or stood nearby making coffee.

I waited for my food to come.

After the enormous black man had finished his plate of spaghetti and meatballs, he muttered something to one of the student-types. I couldn't hear what he said but the three of them all looked at each other, laughed, and continued to ignore him.

Just then my food arrived, with Rosita and Gabriella bringing out steaming plates and bowls from the kitchen, setting them on the main counter, and calling out "Amigo!" to me. I transferred everything, one dish at a time, to where I was sitting and immediately got down to business with my meal—so much to eat that I had the plates and bowls spread all across the narrow counter top.

The enormous black man was now paying Gabriella. Though she was on the last part of her shift she was still full of energy and over-the-counter jokes such as "You owe $4.00. For everybody else it's $2.00. But since you are *especial* and my friend I only charge $4.00." I knew what was coming next.

"Water is free this time but next time you gotta pay. Okay?"

Unsmiling, the enormous black man got up and half-lumbered, half-staggered to one of the stools along the same counter where I was sitting and plopped himself down. He sat slump-shouldered beside the door and kept his back to me while staring out into the night where the first few wet snowflakes were appearing. From a coat hook on the wall beside him he took a shabby old overcoat and an aviator's cap and held them on his lap for a long while, still gazing through the glass door. At last he stood up and began to put on his coat, but evidently it was so tattered inside that each time he put his arm into the sleeve, his hand got caught and became entangled in the lining. He thrust his arm into the sleeve again and again but the same thing kept happening. He tried the other arm, but with the same sleeve, such that even if his hand had gone all the way through unobstructed, he would have succeeded only in putting on his coat backwards. However, he eventually realized this and resumed with his original plan.

His face was puffy and it seemed to be costing him a great deal of effort just to keep his eyes open and focused on what his hands were doing. He resembled a boxer who having been hit once too often in the early rounds of a fight was by the later rounds nearly asleep on his feet. Again he forced his arm deep into the sleeve, and then turning the coat over so that he could peer up the cuff, he searched in vain for his hand which was once more hopelessly lost in the lining.

The din in the restaurant rose higher as each of the conversations grew more animated. Cigarette smoke filled the air. No one was paying attention to the enormous black man.

He began pulling bits of paper and broken cigarettes out of the holes in his coat—he had determined that somehow this was part of the problem—and then he practically had the coat turned inside out as he tried to adjust the lining. Finally he got everything fixed just right. He stuck his hand into the sleeve and this time it emerged from the other end. Halfway home.

After another couple of unsuccessful attempts with the other arm, and I was sure his stamina was exhausted, his hand suddenly shot through the other sleeve. He made a shrugging movement and the coat was across his shoulders. He put on the aviator's cap and pulled the flaps over his ears, letting the fastening straps dangle down the sides of his face. Leaning and slouching, and without buttoning his coat, he pushed his way out the door. I thought he would no doubt immediately disappear into the night, but first he stood on the curb, the snow coming down all around him, and took a long piss right on the right-rear tire of a late-model, two door, two-tone Buick Riviera with fancy wire hubcaps. And then he did disappear— half-lumbering, half-staggering up Broadway.

The Buick belonged to Carlos who was busy in the kitchen and had not seen the enormous black man urinating on it. He came swaggering out of the kitchen smoking a cigar and fingering his mustache. While taking the money out of the cash register he asked me how I liked my steak. *"Deliciosa,"* I told him and asked him what *palomilla* meant. He said it was a special cut and patted his rear end. He put the money from the cash register into a bank deposit bag, put on a coat, and went outside, followed by the regulars from the neighborhood who stood around admiring the car which by now had acquired a thin layer of snow on top. Carlos then jumped in the Buick and drove off by himself.

Meanwhile I had finished my meal and ordered a little *café negro* to top it off. The trio of student-types paid and left but not before Gabriella went through her repertoire of jokes one more time. The Spanish kid had long since given up on making progress with her. He sat and sulked while nursing a can of Coke. Without a word he paid and left too. For a while all was quiet in Rosita's—uncharacteristically so.

But not for long.

The door flew open and in she swept in leather pants, open-toed high-heel shoes, and full-length fake fur coat. Her abundant hair fell down her back and her face was caked with make-up. She had long, fluttery eyelashes and her eyelids were shadowed in turquoise so that they matched her painted fingernails. She breezily greeted everyone as if she knew all of us and had expected us to be here when she made her entrance. "Hi—how you doin'," the woman said to Rosita and Gabriella, to Maestro and Hola, and then to me. "Good to see you." She had a low, husky kind of voice, but not at all unpleasant—and the accent was obvious—a purest Brooklynese such as one almost never hears even in Brooklyn nowadays.

"Is the boss in? I came about the job," she said to Rosita.

"No, he leave but he back soon."

"Okay I'll wait." She perched herself on the stool at the end of the main counter closest to the door. "He told me to come back at ten o'clock. Is it ten yet? I don't mind waiting."

Rosita did not seem terribly enthused with all of this. She

frowned. She drummed her fingers on the counter. She stared in the other direction toward the kitchen.

"Do you speak English? I *hablo* a little Spanish. Is this a Cuban restaurant? This is such a nice little place. I'll bet the food is good here. Do you serve Mexican food? I love Mexican food. Do you have chili? I love chili. Do you put beans in your chili? I hate beans. Excuse me, is that whiskey you're drinking?" she asked me as I finished my little cup of *café negro*. I couldn't tell if her face was that of someone old who looked very young, or someone young who looked very old.

I told her it was only black coffee.

"Coffee? Oh I'll bet the coffee is good here. So this is a Cuban place. I've never had Cuban food. Is it good? Like Mexican food? I love Mexican food." This was finally too much for Rosita who retreated into the kitchen. She hissed the words *puta* and *blanca* under her breath loud enough for Maestro and Hola to hear, which caused both of them to start winking and smirking. Gabriella however, unflappable as always, remained on duty.

"I'm so tired," the woman continued. I've been all over town today. I work for a messenger service. It's hard work. Nine to five just walking around. And some of the packages are so heavy."

"You wanna know something?" Gabriella rejoined, "I come here at noon and I gotta work until midnight."

"But I need another job. Or what I really need is one that pays more. You only get the minimum wage as a messenger. Is the boss coming back soon? He told me to be here at ten."

"He be back in a minute," said Gabriella.

"I don't mind waiting. I know he'll be back. He told me to come and see him. Maybe I should eat. I sure need this job."

"You speak Spanish?"

"A little, and I have a lot of friends who do too. I took two years in the *escuela*, high-*escuela*." Her few Spanish words floated on her Brooklynese like drops of oil on water.

"You need it here."

"Oh I'm sure. I'm sure. Say, what does that sign mean? *Batidos.* What's a *batido?*

"It's something you drink. *Muy deliciosa.* Like a milk shake. You wanna try one?"

"Oh no thank you. I'm sure it's very good—but no thank you."

"You live around here?"

"No I live in the Village. Charles street"

"You mean you walk all the way up from the Village? That's a long way."

"No, I walked all day in my work. I took the train from the Village. It's not so bad. One train brings you right here. I love the West Side. I hate the East Side. The people are all so unfriendly. Where do you live? Spanish Harlem maybe?"

"Nah I live at a hunderd thirty-five and Broadway."

"And where do you live? Here in the neighborhood?" she now asked me.

I told her I only lived a few blocks away.

"Do you come here a lot? I'll bet the food is good here. How's the coffee?"

I told her the coffee was excellent.

"Oh I'll bet it is. But I hate coffee. I drink tea. And do they serve Mexican food? I love Mexican food. You have chili don't you?" She turned on her stool towards Gabriella again. "Do you put beans in your chili?"

"Yeah we put beans in our chili."

Even though I'd had an enormous meal and coffee, and even though it was December, I suddenly felt like having a *batido.* "*Un morir soñando por favor,*" I said to Gabriella. My Spanish—adequate for ordering meals and reading the signs on the subway, but for little else—always seems to amuse her.

"Do you speak Spanish too? Everybody here speaks Spanish."

"I'm like you. I only speak *un poquito*—a little bit."

"You said *morir* didn't you. *Morir*—something. That's to die isn't it? To die—something?"

"It's *soñando.* It means dreaming."

"Oh I see. To die—dreaming . . . *morir soñando* . . . What's that supposed to mean?"

"It's just one of the flavors of *batidos*."

"It sounds so sad."

"Here you are amigo," interrupted Gabariella as she handed me my drink and a straw across the counter.

I happened to glance outside just in time to see the Buick roll into the parking space again. Carlos got out and came swaggering through the snow and through the door. He had taken only a couple of steps inside when he stopped in his tracks.

"Oh hi there! Remember me?" She spun on her stool towards him, smiling, while the eyelashes went to work.

At first it appeared as if Carlos would do an immediate about-face and go bolting out the door.

"Oh yes . . . yes . . . how are you?" he managed to stammer. His eyes darted around the small restaurant and then fastened on Rosita who had stepped out of the kitchen and stood at the other end of the counter, staring down the length of it at the *puta*. It made for a strange scene with Rosita glaring at the *puta*—the *puta* smiling broadly at Carlos—and Carlos gaping at his sister.

"I came back at ten o'clock like you said to. I've been waiting. Everyone is so nice here. This is such a nice little place."

Carlos had left his swagger behind in the snow. He walked now on tiptoe: past her, past me, past Gabriella, past Maestro and Hola, past Rosita, and disappeared into the kitchen. Rosita turned and followed him, but not without hurling a last, angry glance over her shoulder.

Carlos spoke first, his voice lowered, no doubt hoping that this would prevent Rosita from raising hers. But it was no use. Her voice, excited and high-pitched and scornful, came pouring out of the kitchen. Maestro and Hola moved away from the doorway as if there were a fire. Rosita's Spanish was gushing so rapidly that there seemed to be no breaks between the sentences, or the words even. And the only word I could understand was "*Puta! Puta! Puta!*" Each time she repeated it she screamed it still louder. Carlos could only get in an occasional "*Sí pero*"—whenever his sister paused for breath, but she would resume quickly without letting him say more.

Gabriella went about cleaning the espresso machine and washing some cups and saucers while Maestro and Hola stood by the front door and contemplated the snow. I stared at the flag of Cuba hanging on the wall a few inches in front of me and sipped my *batido* which tasted sweeter and sweeter the closer I got to the bottom of my glass. I glanced out of the corner of my eye a couple of times towards her but she had her back to me, elbows on the counter, with her face buried in her hands.

At last the shouting stopped and Carlos emerged from the kitchen. He kept behind the counter as he tiptoed towards her.

"I just find out—we no need nobody after all. I forget. My sister she hire somebody else already." Carlos's normally copper-colored complexion was now a sickly gray. A forced smile once or twice flickered across his face but vanished in an instant.

Everyone was looking at her. At first I thought she was crying—she was crying!—but then was smiling sweetly as she showed her face and wiped away the tears.

"Oh I understand. It's quite all right. These things happen. Your sister hired someone else. She's your sister huh? It's all right. It was just a misunderstanding. Well I'd better be going now. Does anybody know what time it is?"

"Ten-thirty," chimed Gabriella, breaking a long and awkward silence.

"Oh ten-thirty, yes it is late."

She inclined her head toward each of us as she slowly revolved on the stool. "Good-by everybody. It was very nice meeting all of you." She lowered her eyes and stared at the floor for a moment.

"This is such a nice little place."

And then she left.

*

Once again an uncharacteristic quiet reigned in Rosita's. Gabriella came out from behind the counter to clear my dishes and I leaned out of her way while finishing my *batido*. I got up and told Carlos what I had had and the bill came to $7.75. As he gave me my change he kept repeating for my benefit, "I forget. I forget. My sister hired somebody else already." I nodded. I laid a tip on the counter which he quickly scooped up and tossed into a cigar box full of change.

I stood by the door knotting my scarf and buttoning my coat. Carlos stood in the corner beside the pile of fruit, fingering his mustache and intently studying the faded photograph of the sun-splashed plaza in Havana. Gabriella was joking with Maestro and Hola and with another pair of regulars from the neighborhood who had come in, ordered coffee, and acted as if they were going to be hanging around for a long while. I saw Rosita's shadow move inside the kitchen.

Outside, the cold air was most invigorating and the wet snowflakes landed on my face and cooled my forehead which felt almost feverish. I walked up Broadway, half-hoping, half-expecting to see her again—sitting perhaps on one of the dilapidated benches in the center median. Though it was snowing fairly hard it was not nearly cold enough so that any would accumulate. Still, the snow was very beautiful as it floated silently down and was caught in the glow of the street lamps and the brightly colored, neon-lit storefronts. And then I did see a figure, hovering on one of the benches a couple of blocks ahead. But before I could get any closer it suddenly moved away, half-staggering, half-lumbering across Broadway, and disappeared forever this time down a dark street of tenements where only the Spanish-speaking people live.

AMERICA'S TEAM

Epstein was thinking about Texas again. Not that this was unusual. Because he had, in his mother's words, had Texas on the brain for a long time. "For most of his life, if you really want to know. I never understood," she often remarked to her friends. Thus, on a rather dreary Tuesday afternoon in November, when he found himself in a cab stuck in traffic behind a procession of horse-drawn covered wagons which were headed slowly down Seventh Avenue as a promotion for a rodeo and western show which was to open that night in Madison Square Garden, and everywhere around him the angry drivers of vehicles of every type, now backed up for blocks, were honking and cursing and gesturing furiously, Epstein regarded the covered wagons as a kind of omen. A favorable omen. The sight of the white billowing canopies and the plodding brown horses, so incongruous and unexpected on a New York City street, filled him hope and self-assurance, and led him to reflect once more upon what he was planning to do. For the first time in his life he felt that he was in charge of things—that his fate was truly in his own hands.

The reason for Epstein's being in a cab in midtown on a weekday afternoon was that he was on the way to the office of

the insurance company where his brother worked. He was on
the way to pick up the first installment of a supplementary
income check covering him for losses sustained by his business
during a recent fire. He looked at his watch. Still plenty of
time. He sat back and relaxed and daydreamed while the driver
grumbled and repeatedly blasted his horn.

*

When he was a teenager Epstein had gone to every movie
and read every novel he could get his hands on with the word
"Texas" in the title, or if the story or setting even half-way had
something to do with the Texas that existed in his imagination.
He used to make the long trip on the rattling IRT train from
his parents' home in upper Manhattan to buy the Dallas and
Houston newspapers at the out-of-town newsstand in Times
Square, and would ostentatiously open them and read them
on the return trip so that everyone in the crowded car might
notice and wonder who he was and why he was reading
newspapers from Texas. He had planned to go to college in
Texas and sent off for catalogs from such schools as the
University of Texas at Austin, North Texas State, and SMU.
But there was no way his parents could afford for him to go
away for college—his father was in failing health and Epstein
was needed to help with the family business, a laundry and
dry-cleaning establishment on upper-Broadway. So he attended
City College instead, part-time, while working full-time. He
majored briefly in U.S. history because that was as close as he
could get to anything even remotely concerned with Texas,
but he never finished school. His father died during his
sophomore year and he had to step up and put in even longer
hours, helping his mother run the business, while supporting
not only the two of them, but his younger brother, and then
Sophie, a girl in the neighborhood to whom Epstein had
become engaged.

For the next several years he had little time to indulge

himself by thinking or reading about Texas, except to follow the ball teams in the papers or watch them on TV. In the summer, whenever the Yankees or the Mets happened to be playing in the Lone Star State, the New York announcers would comment, usually in passing, upon the look of the rolling Texas countryside and the clean prosperous cities. During dull parts of a game they often engaged in long leisurely discussions concerning the hot weather, the spicy Tex-Mex cuisine, or the friendly people. To Epstein in New York it all sounded so far removed from anything he knew—an alluring but unrealizable fantasy.

In the fall and winter there was football. Epstein loved football, and he was glad that his younger brother received a partial academic scholarship to attend Syracuse University which fielded an upper division football team. But unless Syracuse was playing, Epstein only followed the teams from Texas. The Longhorns, the Red Raiders, the Aggies, the Owls, the Horned Owls, the Mustangs. So many teams that even he could hardly keep up with all of them. During the Cotton Bowl game on New Year's Day he always watched as much to see the live camera shots of the city of Dallas taken from a blimp, as the game itself. And since the late 1960's there had been the Dallas Cowboys—America's Team as even the New York papers now called them. They were his team all along. No matter how busy he was at work or how much he had to do around the apartment, whenever the Dallas Cowboys were on TV he never missed the game. Epstein considered Tom Landry to be the most intelligent man in America. He once told Sophie after Dallas had come from behind to win an unusually exciting game in the final seconds that Tom Landry would make a great general, or a great President for that matter. Sophie had not the slightest idea who or what he was talking about.

By the time of his thirtieth birthday his fascination had once more reached the point where it became a kind of spare-time passion for him. He began reading western novels again and ordered home subscriptions to *The Texas Observer, Texas Monthly,* and *The Dallas Morning News*. He had more spare-time because he was no longer supporting his brother who had not only finished college but was working for an insurance company where he quickly rose through the ranks to a well-paying, junior-executive position. The family business was doing well, so well that his mother was able to retire and start receiving her Social Security while she continued to live with him and Sophie.

Toward one thing however, he remained completely disdainful—the TV program *Dallas* which had grown so popular that even his mother and Sophie watched it the one night a week it was on, and then spent the rest of the week discussing the characters or the plot or likely developments in the next episode. In the final installment of the past season, the main character, J.R. Ewing, the obnoxious Texas tycoon, was shot under mysterious circumstances, and it was not going to be revealed who had committed the crime until the fall season commenced. In Kelly's bar too, a few doors up the block from Epstein's dry cleaning shop, that entire summer, all anyone talked about, more than baseball or politics or the events in the neighborhood, was who shot J.R.? Epstein had read in the Dallas paper, as well as in the New York papers, that the actual people of Dallas felt that the program did not present an accurate picture of what life was like there. To him it was utterly foolish how everyone in his own family and in the neighborhood followed the show so religiously. In September, when the new TV season was about to begin, it only got worse and he could hardly stand it. He just wanted the whole thing to be over with. Finally the Friday arrived, the night the whole nation had been waiting for, the night when the first episode of the new season would at last reveal who had shot J.R.

"I don't know and I don't give a damn," he had growled at his mother and Sophie at breakfast that morning as they sat there discussing it and ignoring him completely. He said the same thing to Mr. DiNucci and old Schaeffer while they stood on the sidewalk in front of his shop arguing when he arrived to open up. DiNucci's barbershop was next door to Epstein's, and old Schaeffer owned the coffee shop next to DiNucci. They too ignored Epstein as they wandered off down the street and continued their argument which no doubt would later include their customers.

That night after closing up, Epstein walked down to the corner to Kelly's where he liked to have a glass of red wine and catch a part of a ball game or boxing match before going home. A few days before, Kelly had installed a large-screen TV system in the back of his place beyond the bar. When Epstein entered he noticed a larger than usual gathering in front of the screen. Carrying his glass of red wine with him he went to see what was happening. He couldn't believe it. That damned program! The opening credits appeared on the screen and murmurs of anticipation passed through the group. He didn't bother finishing his wine. On the way out he complained to Kelly, an always smiling and ever-polite, authentic Irishman, who merely shrugged as if to say what can I do? He said that's what everyone had wanted to watch.

Epstein walked the few short blocks back to the apartment building where he had lived all of his life. It was eerie how unusually empty the streets seemed to be. Only on one block did he notice much activity—a block he usually avoided when he came to it because within the past couple of years it had become almost entirely taken over by shops and stores catering to the Spanish-speaking people moving into the neighborhood in ever-increasing numbers. He stood on the corner and listened for a while to the raucous music, all horns and percussion, pouring out of the bars. The sidewalks were crowded and bustling as they always were on a Friday night. When he entered his apartment he found his wife and mother sitting in front of the TV set exchanging whispers. The tension was building. His mother was convinced that J.R.'s wife had shot him. But during a commercial break Sophie had protested: "No! That's too obvious."

Epstein muttered under his breath. He went into the kitchen and warmed up the supper they had left for him. He brooded while he ate but soon became absorbed in reading an article on the Texas legislature in a copy of *The Texas Observer* which had arrived with the day's mail. After he finished eating he put his dishes in the sink and headed for the bedroom to lie down and continue his reading . . .

He must have fallen asleep. But surely for no more than a minute. And why was Sophie shaking him and what was she saying? Epstein grew annoyed and blurted out that he wasn't the least bit interested in who had shot J.R. But Sophie was saying someone had called from Kelly's—there was a big fire at Schaeffer's restaurant. It had already destroyed DiNucci's barbershop and had spread to our place.

He jumped up and left without putting on a jacket and hurried along the dark side-streets toward Broadway. Because one entire portion of Broadway was now blocked off by fire engines, police cars, and police barricades which had been set up to keep back the crowds, he could not immediately tell what was happening. The fire engines sat with their engines idling and their red lights whipping through the night. Firemen were everywhere, carrying axes and sledgehammers and wrestling with the hoses which shot plumes of water into a wall of flames that rose higher and higher. His shop, he realized, was behind those flames. Epstein climbed over a police barrier and tried to move closer, but he was driven back by a blast of heat from the fire and then collared by a cop who hustled him away.

"It's my shop that's burning!" he pleaded above the wailing sirens, the roar of the fire, and the shouts of the firemen.

The cop, still holding him by his shirt, screamed in his face. "There's nothing you can do mister. Nobody gets through until the fire chief say so!"

He looked on helplessly while the fire continued to burn out of control. Schaeffer's restaurant was gone and so was DiNucci's barbershop. His own place as well—and then the bakery on his other side—and the newsstand next to the bakery. Everything on that side of Broadway was being destroyed. Except

for Kelly's. The progress of the fire was finally arrested before
it reached the tavern on the corner of the block. And standing
in a crowd across the way was Kelly himself, surrounded by the
same group who had earlier been watching the large-screen
TV beyond the bar. Epstein ran over to Kelly who had a
beleaguered look upon his face. Everyone was shouting at the
old Irishman excitedly. Someone even turned to Epstein and
shrieked, "Epstein! Tell us! Who shot J.R.? The damned power
in Kelly's was knocked out half-way through the show!"

Epstein threw his hands up in disgust. He stalked away. It
was hopeless. Just like the cop said, there was nothing he could
do but watch and wait as the firemen slowly brought the fire
under control.

Later, Epstein walked home. It was a total loss without a
doubt. But he consoled himself with the thought that at least
he had plenty of insurance. It was not for nothing he had a
brother who had gone to college and become a big shot in the
insurance business. And he and Sophie had managed to save
some money which they could comfortably get by on until he
was back in business. Sophie was waiting for him when he
returned. He told her the bad news. She said the same thing,
echoing his thoughts, that at least they had plenty of insurance
and their nest egg to fall back on. To take his mind off their
troubles, she suggested that maybe after things were settled
and before he reopened they should take a trip. It was Sophie,
in fact, who first mentioned it. "Why don't we go see Texas
like you've always wanted."

"Who cares about Texas at a time like this," he snapped at
her. But that night, instead of lying in bed feeling his stomach
churn and worrying over the future as he had assumed he
would, Epstein had been able to go right to sleep. And he had
dreamed. He dreamed of wide skies and rolling plains, of oil
wells and cowboys, of cheering football stadiums. In his dreams
he conjured up a myriad of images which he had been
accumulating and carrying in his imagination for so many years.
At one point he dreamed he was in Kelly's, talking to a stranger,

when he suddenly realized it was Tom Landry discussing strategy with him about the Cowboys' next game. He then dreamed he was riding the rattling subway train to Times Square, but upon coming out of the station he found himself not at 42nd and Broadway, but standing on Main Street in Dallas staring at the front of the old Adolphus Hotel.

When he awoke the next morning at the usual time Epstein was confused. He couldn't immediately sort out what from the night before was real and what was a dream. It was all a dream he concluded and started to get up and get dressed. But no. The fire. That was real. The whole block nearly gone. But plenty of insurance. Sophie said so too. He lay back next to her and realized that for the first time in years he did not have to go to work on a Saturday morning. Something else occurred to him at that very moment—as if something had been decided for him while he was asleep, as if he were not the same person he was when he went to bed. And since everything was now so irrevocably decided, he closed his eyes and dreamed some more.

*

"Looks like we'll be moving again in a minute," the cabbie was saying. "Something to do with the rodeo at Madison Square Garden. Ought to be against the law to block traffic like this." The cab inched along until at last arriving at the building on Seventh Avenue where Epstein's brother worked.

Epstein was going to pick up the check in person because he didn't want to have to wait and worry about it getting lost in the mail. His brother had speeded everything else along—the investigation, the claim, the settlement. Epstein rode an elevator to the 27th floor and went to a reception desk to ask for his brother. He was directed down a long, carpeted hallway and found him sitting in his office which had a view looking to the east toward a crowded array of midtown skyscrapers. To Epstein they resembled a picture he'd once seen in a magazine of gigantic trees in a South American jungle contending with one another for space in the sunlight.

His brother was waiting for him. In between phone calls and people coming into the office with documents for him to examine and sign, he told Epstein, "I almost hate to give you this because I know what you're going to do. I won't try and change your mind. But you realize of course that you're making Ma very unhappy. And if you won't change your mind then just remember, if things don't turn out like you expect, don't hesitate to come back. I can help you get started again." Epstein felt he was being patronized. He sat, unsmiling, and waited for his brother to finish. He only wanted his check. He didn't appreciate the big-shot treatment or need this portioning out of guilt. Besides, Sophie was with him in this. It had not taken much to convince her.

The morning after the fire Epstein proposed his plan to Sophie and his mother over breakfast.

"What'll we do in Texas?" was his wife's first reaction.

"You're going too far with this stuff," his mother objected. "It's nuts, I tell you, nuts. It's those magazines you read. If your father were still alive—"

"Look Sophie, look Ma, do you think they don't have dirty shirts in Texas or trousers that need to be pressed? I can do the same thing there that I've been doing here for all these years. It's not like I'd be digging ditches."

"But it's so far from your brother, from me, from where you've always lived. And how will you get around? There's no subway in Texas in case you haven't heard."

"It's not the moon Ma, it's part of America. You'll love it. We'll have a car and I can drive you anywhere you like."

"The only place anybody is driving me is to your brother's new house in Riverdale. He's got plenty of room now and has been asking me to come and live with them. They shoot people in Texas! Did you know that? Someone gets shot there every twenty minutes. I know. I watch TV."

"As if they don't shoot people in New York! Half the people here are afraid to go outside at night."

"Yes but at least here they shoot you for a reason, for your money, your jewelry—and most of that is in Brooklyn. I never go to Brooklyn." An impervious, unwavering frown settled on her face.

"Oh Ma, that's just a bunch of crap on TV you watch."

"It doesn't matter. I'm not going. You go. But why don't you ask your wife? Does she have any say-so in this? What about it Sophie? Is my son crazy or is he crazy?"

Sophie had been only half-listening to her husband and mother-in-law while they argued. After a preliminary image of dirty shirts and undug ditches receded, another one formed in her mind, one consisting of enormous shopping malls and suburban blocks of ranch-styles homes with wide lawns in front and swimming pools in back, such as her husband was always showing her in his magazines. Why not? Since her own parents had retired to Florida and her sister had moved to Chicago, she was the only one left in her immediate family still in New York. For years she had been merely tolerant of what she had considered to be her husband's eccentricities, but now—was it because of that TV show?—she wondered if maybe her husband wasn't right. And if they really did have the opportunity to move, could she? Should she? Well why not. Still, it was all so much to think about. She let the possibilities tantalize her imagination, even though she was of a cautious nature.

"Well why don't we wait and see? Are you sure that the shop is a total loss? Maybe we should only plan to visit Texas first."

Just then the phone rang. It was Epstein's brother. He had talked to a fire marshal and was sending an investigator from the insurance company to the scene. He told Epstein to meet the investigator in half an hour.

Epstein put on a jacket and walked back to the burned out block. The row of storefronts was now a mass of blackened bricks while inside there was left little more than piles of wet, smoldering rubble. The sidewalks were littered with debris and shards of broken glass that glinted in the morning sunlight.

Pools of dirty water remained standing in the gutters. Along the curb in front of the burned out stores there still stood the police barricades which kept back the curious who'd come to inspect the damage. Schaeffer and DiNucci were there, just inside the barricades, staring at what had once been their businesses. Everything, starting with Schaeffer's restaurant, then DiNucci's barbershop, Epstein's dry-cleaners, the bakery, and the newsstand had been completely destroyed. Only Kelly's had been spared. And there was Kelly's, open for business, despite having no electricity.

Epstein met the insurance investigator his brother had sent, a young man with a neatly trimmed beard who was even younger than his brother was. He told Epstein he knew his brother very well and was very sorry about what had happened. "It's obvious," he said—"a total loss." He would get documents from the fire marshal certifying it first thing Monday morning. A miracle nobody was hurt. "And you're very fortunate sir, you have an excellent insurance plan thanks to your brother. We'll be able to settle this with no problems. In a matter of months, if not weeks, you'll be back in business. I'll take care of everything. In the meantime you have nothing to worry about."

Neither Schaeffer nor DiNucci were so well insured as Epstein. The three of them walked down the block and went into Kelly's. Although Kelly's place had not been touched by the fire, the old Irishman looked very sad and distressed. The bar was otherwise empty except for a pair of Spanish-speaking fellows who had apparently wandered over from the adjacent neighborhood.

Schaeffer sat in front of the beer which Kelly had provided while DiNucci and Epstein drank red wine. Epstein said nothing while the others discussed what they were going to do.

"This does it for me," Schaeffer said. "I'm sixty-six years old and don't have the energy to start another restaurant. I can retire. I've got money saved. I was thinking about it anyway before this happened."

DiNucci stared glumly at his wine. "I guess I can go work for my nephew. He's got a shop in Midtown near that new hotel on 44th Street. I suppose I'm lucky. Except now I'll have to travel forty-five minutes to work and back every day. How about you Epstein? At least you'll be back in business."

Epstein blurted out the nature of his plans and watched the expressions on their faces.

"Texas!" they cried in unison. "What'll you do in Texas?"

"Do you think they don't have dirty shirts in Texas? It's not like I'd be digging ditches."

*

After picking up the check from his brother, Epstein deposited it in the bank so that it would clear as soon as possible. In the remaining days he and Sophie were busy packing and getting their affairs in order. They had sold most of their furniture and other possessions, and were only taking as much with them as they could load in the car Epstein had rented. His mother had moved in with her younger son in Riverdale the week before. Though she missed the old Manhattan neighborhood and never neglected to say so, she was not far from several good friends of hers who had moved up to the Bronx years ago.

On the Saturday morning Epstein and Sophie were to leave, the sky was swollen with clouds and a brisk, damp wind was blowing loose pages from discarded newspapers here and there. By noon the car was loaded. Epstein handed the keys to their apartment over to Manuel, the super, who wished them luck. Epstein's brother was to have been there to see them off but he had called and said he had to go to the office and would be tied up all day. At dinner the night before in a restaurant in the Bronx with his mother and his brother's family, everyone had been in a somber mood, especially her. "You'll be back. You'll be back," she kept repeating. "I give you six months— no make that three. You'll be back."

After they pulled away and left Manuel standing in front of their old building, Epstein turned the corner and drove down Broadway one last time, past the row of burned out shops. A temporary wall of plywood had been erected along the sidewalk and where it was not already plastered over with posters for Spanish-language movies and salsa concerts, it was covered with graffiti in Spanish. It began to sleet. The streets became slick and Epstein had to go easy on the brake pedal to keep from skidding. The noise of the sleet on the roof of the car sounded like tiny stones being hurled at them.

For several weeks no one in New York heard from Epstein and Sophie except for a post card, written by Sophie, with a picture of downtown Dallas on one side, telling Epstein's family that they had arrived safely and were temporarily renting a furnished apartment in a suburb of Dallas in a complex which had a swimming pool and where all the utility bills were paid. She ended by saying that the rent was substantially less than what they had been paying in New York.

After a few months Sophie wrote again. A letter this time. She talked about the mild winter that had just passed and how spring had arrived so early. She said she was constantly surprised at how courteous and friendly the people were. Epstein had had little trouble in finding a job in a dry-cleaning establishment in a shopping center not far from where they were living. She wrote next in May, saying that Epstein had become acquainted with the man who owned not only the dry-cleaners where he worked, but several others as well. The man had asked Epstein to manage one of them for him. She wrote again in the fall and said that they were planning to buy a house in a town called Richardson, north of Dallas, and that Epstein had done so well managing the dry-cleaners that his boss had offered him a position where he would be a sort of roving general-manager for all of the man's operations in the Dallas-Fort Worth area. She mentioned that Epstein for the first time in his life would be wearing and a suit and tie to work every day and would even be provided with a car.

After the New Year, Sophie sent a card and apologized for not writing more often, but they were very busy with their new home as was Epstein with his new job. The man for whom Epstein worked was opening still more dry-cleaning shops all over northern Texas and it was Epstein's responsibility to set things up, train the staff, and oversee the operations until a full-time, on-site manager was in place. "We miss all of you," Sophie wrote, "but other than that the only thing we regret is not having come out here years ago."

Epstein had taken to wearing cowboy hats and boots in his work. Like everyone in Dallas he followed the Cowboys football team very closely and went to their games whenever he was able to get tickets. He never missed the Tom Landry Show on TV the night before a game, and he pored over every newspaper account the day after. He had put on some excess weight that he tried unsuccessfully to lose in the spring by cutting the grass and working in the yard of his new house at least twice a week. All during that spring and into the hot, blistering Texas summer, on Sunday afternoons, he would cook steaks on an outdoor barbecue grill and sit on his patio wearing only a pair of plaid Bermuda shorts, while sipping beer and listening to the Texas Rangers baseball game on the radio. One afternoon when the Rangers were playing back in New York, something about the noise of the crowd—a raucous, distinctively New York noise—reminded him of his former life, a wasted life, a life that had been spent reading magazines and novels and watching TV, only half-imagining what Texas was really like. He was sometimes surprised at how seldom he thought of his family, the old neighborhood, and his friends. They seemed so far away. As far away as Texas had seemed to him in the old days. The sound of the steaks sizzling on the grill and the smell of the smoke hanging in the humid afternoon air filled him with a feeling of utter satisfaction at how his life had turned out.

That fall, now nearly two years after they had left, Sophie invited Epstein's family out to visit for Thanksgiving and the invitation was readily accepted. Though Epstein was very busy with his work he arranged to take a few days off and was even able to get tickets for himself and his brother to the Cowboys vs. New York Giants football game which was to be played on Thanksgiving Day in Dallas.

On the Sunday before Thanksgiving his brother phoned. Epstein took the call in his newly paneled den and knew it was bad news. "It's Ma," his brother informed him. "Never been sick a day in her life. And now this. Her heart. It happened during the night."

Suddenly it was Epstein who had to make travel plans. He called his boss at home who told him to take off for as long as he needed. Epstein went to Neiman-Marcus on Monday morning right before he was to leave and bought a new overcoat. While he was there, on an impulse, he also bought an extra cowboy hat and a new pair of boots for the trip back to New York.

When his plane landed on a dreary, rainy evening he took a cab from LaGuardia to his brother's house. Crossing the Triborough Bridge he tried to look south toward the Manhattan skyline but a thick wall of fog and mist lay over the East River and obscured the view.

"You from Texas mister?" the cabbie asked him. "You look like a Texan to me, if you don't mind me saying so."

"Yes I am from Texas," Epstein replied, pleased that the cabbie would notice.

"What part?"

"Richardson—a town just outside of Dallas."

"Oh Dallas. The Giants are playing there this week. If they win they've got a shot at the playoffs. Of course Dallas is in again for sure. You know I pick up a lot of people from Texas at the airport but they usually stay in Midtown at a hotel. Not many are going up to the Bronx."

"My brother lives in the Bronx," said Epstein without elaborating.

"Oh I see. Your brother. Is he from Texas too?"

*

After the funeral Mrs. Goltz and Mrs. Mayer, two of his
mother's friends, approached him. In his hat and hand-tooled
boots he was the center of attention. "So good to see you—
we've heard so much about you from her," said Mrs. Goltz.
Doing so well and all."

"Your mother was very proud," added Mrs. Mayer as she
stared at the boots. "Yes so very proud."

Epstein had felt somewhat guilty up to this point because
he had not spoken to his mother since the restaurant the night
before he and Sophie left. And he regretted even more the
fact that now she would never come to Texas to see what he
had made of himself. But he felt absolved by the fact, as testified
to by her friends, that she had apparently come to realize that
what he had done was right and had even spoken with pride
about him to them.

He called Sophie that night and told her that he would be
back late Thursday night. The two of them could have their
own holiday meal on Friday in a restaurant. He was going to
stay and have Thanksgiving dinner with his brother's family
and watch the football game on TV. He would catch an evening
flight to Dallas after the game.

It remained cold and drizzly the entire time he was in New
York. He had little interest in seeing the city and grew restless
and bored at his brother's house. After the Thanksgiving dinner
he and his brother sat down in front of the TV. His brother's
wife brought them coffee and desert and saw that they were
not disturbed by the children. The announcers described a
perfect, fall-like day, while from the blimp there were the usual
panoramic shots of downtown Dallas and the surrounding area.
Epstein was totally absorbed by the game. He didn't speak but
his face registered the intensity of the contest. The score was
close all the way, back and forth, but Dallas got a touchdown
late in the fourth quarter and went on to win. After the game

Epstein was exhilarated while his brother remained stoical with an expressionless, emotionless look upon his face.

It was almost time to leave. His brother offered him a ride to the airport but Epstein insisted on taking a cab. "It's such a lousy night. Don't go to any trouble."

He was packed and a cab was called for. He stood in the living room in his boots and cowboy hat with his suitcase beside him on the floor. Leaving New York this time seemed to be even more of a final break with the past than before. He could think of nothing really important or appropriate to say to his brother, whom he noticed in the past two years had become a heavy smoker.

"The Giants are a good team, they have lots of young players. They still might make the playoffs," he finally said. "They just aren't in the Cowboys league yet."

His brother said nothing. He still had an expressionless, emotionless look on his face as he stared at Epstein. But Epstein paid no attention.

"That's why they're called America's Team," he declared with evident satisfaction.

His brother exhaled a cloud of smoke. He started to say something in reply, but with much effort he restrained himself. He just wanted Epstein to be gone.

A pair of headlights beamed through the gloom and pulled into the driveway. Epstein shook hands with his brother and went out. His brother watched through the window as the headlights receded, and after the cab had backed out and turned around, as the taillights became two tiny red points of light which floated momentarily in the air before vanishing.

It had begun to sleet. The noise of it beating on the roof recalled to Epstein the day he and Sophie had left New York. The cab maneuvered onto the parkway where the traffic was moving very slowly. Epstein sat gazing absently out the window. A voice cut through the static on the cab's radio and was saying something about an accident directly ahead of them that had the traffic backed up for miles.

"I think I can get around it," the driver said and quickly pulled off the parkway.

Epstein checked his watch. Still plenty of time.

He continued staring at the dark, cold, wet streets. It all seemed so familiar. Suddenly he realized where they were.

"Hey cabbie—do me a favor. Take a right at the next light and head back to Broadway. There's something I want to look at."

A few minutes later he was once again on the old block. Epstein peered at the empty sidewalks and the darkened storefronts. So they had re-built everything after all. Things appeared much the same as they had before. But as he looked closer at the neon signs in the windows he noticed that nearly all of them were in Spanish. He couldn't believe it. *Limpieza en seco* read the sign in the window of his old shop. DiNucci's was now *La Barberia*. And Schaeffer's place was still a restaurant but with the name of *Sol Caribe*. The cab stopped at a red light. Epstein was even more surprised when he saw Kelly's same old green and white sign glowing on the corner.

He told the driver to pull over. "Leave the meter on. I just want to run in and say hello to someone."

As he entered Kelly's he was greeted by a blare of horns and a booming conga drum. A Spanish salsa band was playing at a frenzied, delirious pace such as he used to hear coming from the bars on the blocks he would pass while walking home. He hesitated a moment before going in further. The bar was crowded and everyone was speaking Spanish. He recognized no one. Except behind the bar, his face slightly more sunken, the skin somewhat looser under the chin, and the thin hair now gone almost entirely gray, unmistakably it was Kelly.

Epstein walked up to the bar and stood right in front of him.

"What can I get you cowboy?"

"Say young-fellow, is that any way to treat an old customer?"

Kelly examined the face beneath the hat. Then his own face brightened into the familiar Kelly smile.

"Epstein—you! I thought you were in Texas."

"I am. I am. Or on the way back. I had to come to New York because my mother passed away last Saturday."

"Oh I am sorry to hear that. I remember her so well when she worked with your Dad. Had she been ill?"

"No, it was quite sudden. She was even planning to come out with my brother and his family to visit Sophie and me for Thanksgiving."

"Oh what a shame. God rest her soul. And how is dear Sophie? Is she here with you?"

"No, she stayed in Texas. She's just fine though."

"And your brother? Still in Riverdale? Still doing well? Can't remember the last time I saw him."

"Yes he's still in the Bronx—a real big-shot."

"Let me buy you a drink. It's red wine isn't it?"

Epstein glanced at his watch. Plenty of time. "Sure Kelly, a quick one. I've got a cab waiting outside. But make it a *cerveza*. That's beer. That much Spanish I know. That's what we say in Texas. I guess you've been learning a lot of Spanish yourself in the last couple of years. Looks like they've really taken over."

The music stopped and the room grew quieter. Then a man in a white *guayabara* shirt stood up and began to make a speech. Everyone listened intently, but Epstein did not understand a word. When the man finished there was a burst of cheering and applause and the music started again.

"Yes and they'll be taking me over soon too. I'm getting out and retiring in a few months when my lease on this place expires. Sold everything to the fellow that owns that *Sol Caribe* restaurant up the block. Schaeffer's old place. That's him that was talking a minute ago. Fellow by the name of Sanchez. He and his friends are in here celebrating."

"Do you ever hear from Schaeffer? Or DiNucci?"

"No—never. They stopped coming in right after the fire."

"I guess it would break old Schaeffer's heart to see what's

happened to his place," said Epstein, lowering his voice and disdainfully shaking his head. "It's a shame. A real shame."

"Are you kidding?" exclaimed Kelly. "Everyone in New York City has heard of the *Sol Caribe*. It's supposed to be the best Cuban restaurant in town. It got reviewed in the papers and everything. It's so popular that Sanchez is planning to turn this place into a banquet room. It'll be called the *Sol Caribe II*. There was a story in the papers about Sanchez too. He was a lawyer down in Cuba before Castro threw him out. He came to this country on a boat without a dime in his pocket. Now look at him. He and his wife do all the cooking. Food's pretty good there. I even tried it. Different all right . . . but good."

Sanchez was shaking hands all around and then he approached the bar. Short and stocky, he wore his dark hair slicked straight back. A broad smile revealed a gold-capped tooth. The clapping and the cheering and the music continued. "And you also Mr. Kelly," he said in a heavy Spanish accent, "are invited to come to the *Sol Caribe* for an *especial* dinner. I fix *paella* for everybody. Because I have been in business exactly one year, and tomorrow I become a citizen of this country. You are always so kind Mr. Kelly, to me and my family and my people. You are most cordially invited, you and your amigo of course."

Sanchez turned toward Epstein who looked at his watch. It was time to leave. He backed away from the bar, ignoring Sanchez.

"Got to run Kelly. Got to catch my plane. Nice talking to you." And he hurried out.

Crossing the bridge he again looked for the city skyline and again it was obscured. On board his plane he stared out the window at the tarmac as they taxied and then took off. The plane climbed higher and higher into the low clouds and into the night and Epstein never got a last glimpse at the lights of the city. As far as he was concerned this would be the last time he would ever return to New York. He had a beer and a sandwich for supper and afterwards reclined his seat as far back as it would go. He felt pleasantly sleepy now. As he was dozing off he re-played Dallas's final touchdown against the Giants—a long pass from the quarterback to the wide receiver who had sprinted down the field, leaving the New York players behind—over and over in his mind.

THE KING AND DADDY-O

"What will it be like when I'm a Queen, Daddy-O?"

Daddy-O was staring straight ahead at the road. He took a quick look in the rear-view mirror and glanced at Suzy-Q who sat in the back seat of the Cadillac drinking an RC Cola and gnawing on a Goo-Goo bar.

"And what kind of car is that one Daddy-O?" Suzy-Q pointed at the gray Ford Fairlane which they had just passed on the right and were leaving far behind. "I'll bet ours is faster, isn't it Daddy-O? Say it is! Say it is!" Suzy-Q scrunched down in her seat and licked the chocolate off her lips and out of the corners of her mouth. Her smile was turning into a frown as she was growing bored again. She picked up a comic book from an unread pile and leafed through it back to front before throwing it down on the floorboard which already was littered with candy bar wrappers and empty soda pop bottles.

"Can't we stop soon Daddy-O? I'm still hungry. I'm still thirsty. I have to go to the bathroom. How much further is it Daddy-O? How much further is it to the Castle?"

Daddy-O spotted a sign for the turn-off up ahead for a Gas'N Go station. Then off to the right and in the distance he recognized the familiar Gas'N Go symbol—an enormous orange star outlined in black. The enormous star seemed to be floating in mid-air and was turning around and around so that it became invisible every few seconds when if faced directly into the sun and disappeared behind the glare of reflected light that flashed out across the achingly bright blue afternoon sky.

As he approached the exit ramp, for a moment, Daddy-O allowed himself to wonder if things would have maybe turned out different if he'd had himself such a fancy sign at his own Gas'N Go station back home all these years. Nah, not really he decided. Since his was the only station on a back country road, and since most of his business came from people who were lost and tired and hungry and had used up all their gas trying to find their way back to the main highway, no one ever paid much attention to which brand he was selling or what his sign looked like. For sure it wouldn't have mattered that one time, and that one time was all that mattered. That one time which was the most important day in Daddy-O's life, and Suzy-Q's too—the day when the King himself, and his men, and the three gold Cadillacs had miraculously appeared in the driveway of Daddy-O's two-pump filling station and country store.

Daddy-O suddenly made his move. He hit the gas on the Cadillac and whipped around a slow-moving pickup truck. "Damned old redneck better get out the way," he muttered. And cutting in front of it just in time, he eased off the pedal, glided into the right-hand lane, and continued onto the exit ramp that curved sharply to the right and ended at a stop sign which he ignored.

Daddy-O took a drag on the cigarette hanging from his lip. He glanced into the rear-view mirror again, the corners of his mouth twisting into a half-sneer, half-smile. So many times he had noticed a similar expression on the King's face: on record album covers, during close-up shots in the many hot-rod films the King had starred in, and on the various box office posters and movie-stills which Daddy-O had purchased by mail from an outfit in New York City. Daddy-O owned all the albums. He had seen all the movies. He had remained loyal to the King, had never forgotten. And his collection of album covers, posters, and movie-stills had been hanging up that day, that day when the King had come to Daddy-O's.

"Look Daddy-O! It's a Gas'N Go station just like ours. Is that where we're stopping? Oh say it is Daddy-O!" Suzy-Q gripped the top of the front seat and brought herself up out of the back so that she was hanging over Daddy-O's shoulder. She clasped him and hugged him around the neck.

Daddy-O pulled into the driveway and drove past several islands of gasoline pumps to the self-service area. Suzy-Q jumped out and went straight to the Premium pump. She took the nozzle off the hook, mashed the button to re-set the register at zero, and dragged the hose to the rear of the car where Daddy-O was unscrewing the gas cap.

"Let me do it Daddy-O. Oh please let me do it. I can do it. Just like in our station."

While Suzy-Q pumped the gas, Daddy-O checked things out under the hood. Everything was just fine—like Daddy-O had known it would be.

"Here Daddy-O, you finish the gas and I'll clean the windshields."

Suzy-Q released the trigger and handed him the nozzle. She got the windshield cleaning fluid and some blue paper towels out of a dispenser hanging on a pole next to the pump and went right to work. She started in front and made her way around the car, rubbing the glass until it squeaked under the towel.

"Oh Daddy-O it looks so beautiful—your very own gold Cadillac. How I want it to look nice when we get to the Castle."

Daddy-O topped off the gas in the tank. He replaced the nozzle on the pump and checked the figures. He reached in his back pocket for his wallet and credit card.

"You go pay the man while I freshen up," said Suzy-Q as she tossed the grimy papers towels into a metal trash barrel then skipped across the driveway in her lipstick-red patent leather shoes, with her long white dress flowing behind and her curly blonde hair bouncing off her shoulders.

Daddy-O walked through the empty gas islands. In only the few minutes he had been outside the air conditioned comfort of the gold Cadillac and was standing in the blazing afternoon heat, he had perspired so much that his face was soaking wet and his damp T-shirt clung to his back. He caught a glimpse of his reflection in the plate glass window as he approached the office. Although Daddy-O was a grown man of almost thirty, he still had the lean look and cocky walk of a 19 year-old.

Inside the office an oscillating fan flipped up the ends of some papers attached to a clipboard lying on top of a glass display case full of cigarettes and souvenirs and candy bars. Behind the window stood a gangly, gap-toothed boy of 14 or 15 who stared out at the gold Cadillac through a shock of scraggly red hair which nearly covered his eyes. He was wearing a pair of blue jeans and a gray work short with an orange Gas'N Go star outlined in black sewn onto the pocket. Above the pocket was some orange stitching which spelled out the name "Dwayne".

He kept grinning as he stared now at Daddy-O and had his head cocked to one side as if trying to size him up. He looked quickly again at the gold Cadillac then turned toward Daddy-O who was holding out his credit card. The boy took it and ran it through the machine along with the charge slip. After filling in the figures and watching him sign the form, he compared the signatures carefully before tearing off the customer's copy and handing it and the credit card back to Daddy-O.

"You know," he finally said, "I hear the King has got maybe half-a-dozen gold Cadillacs just like that one out there. Down this way everybody knows about the King and his Cadillacs." The boy grinned slyly, pulling back his lips to further reveal the space between his front teeth and some white spots on his gums. Daddy-O observed the boy's blue eyes growing wider behind the fringe of red hair, and then nearly bulging out of their sockets, when he remarked, quite matter-of-factly, that that very car had once belonged to the King, who had given it to him as a personal favor.

Just then Suzy-Q came skipping around the corner outside the window and then back across the driveway to their car.

"And that little girl there is the King's fiancé, on her way right now to the Castle to get married. Maybe you heard about her . . . Say there Dwayne, would you happen to know right off hand how much further it is to the Castle?"

"You mean it's true?" You mean there really is a girl like in the song *Come Be My Angel in a Rock and Roll Paradise?* You mean the King really is going to get married again?"

Daddy-O said no more. A half-sneer, half-smile crossed his face. He pulled some cash out of his pocket. "And could you give me a pack of Winstons and a couple of dollars worth of them candy bars and some change for the soda pop machine."

Dwayne let out a whoop and slapped his thigh and began spinning around in circles. He threw back his head and his jaw went slack as if he were in some sort of trance. He moved over toward the display case, slid back the door, and told Daddy-O to just help himself. He rushed over to the soda pop machine and was feeding it change as fast as he could remove it from the coin dispenser that he wore around his waist. Excitedly, he pushed the row of lighted buttons all across the panel. He kept it up until he had accumulated a dozen or more Cokes, 7 Ups, Dr. Peppers, Root Beers, and Chocolate Soldiers, which he then gathered up in his arms, hugging the bottles to his chest, and carried out to the gold Cadillac. Daddy-O followed him to the car, opened the door on the driver's side, and tossed the candy bars and cigarettes onto the front seat. He pressed a button on the console on the armrest of the door and the window on Suzy-Q's side silently disappeared. She reached out and started taking the bottles, one by one, out of Dwayne's embrace. All at once a bottle of Dr. Pepper fell and shattered on the concrete, the sticky brown liquid splashing all over his shoes and the cuffs of his jeans.

"Don't worry about that ma'am—I'll sweep it up later. You'll tell the King when you see him that I'm one of his biggest fans, won't you please ma'am? Say you will!"

After Suzy-Q had relieved him of the last bottle, Dwayne ran back inside the office and came out with the clipboard which he thrust through the window and begged her to sign.

"That's today's sales inventory sheet, and if you would ma'am, put 'to Dwayne' on it so I can show it to Ralph. He owns the station and won't ever believe me unless I have proof that you were here. And you'll tell the King won't you? I'm one of his biggest fans. Say you will ma'am."

"Sure she will son," said Daddy-O sliding behind the steering wheel. "Write something nice Suzy-Q and sign your name— from you and from the King too. We've got to be moving along now . . . . "

Another car had pulled into the station at another island and was honking its horn impatiently.

The gold Cadillac eased out of the station but the boy remained standing in one spot, still clutching the clipboard and staring through his red hair as Daddy-O made a left out of the driveway onto the street and headed back toward the interstate.

"Oh Daddy-O I'm so happy. My first autograph. It's just like you said it would be. And I can't wait to meet the King and see the Castle."

Daddy-O glanced at Suzy-Q in the rear-view mirror. She truly did look like the Queen she was destined to become— taking swigs from a 7 Up and popping peanut M&M's into her mouth. She closed her eyes and leaned back.

"I'm so happy. Oh Daddy-O."

*

Daddy-O set the cruise control on the gold Cadillac at 90 miles per, so that it easily overtook all the other cars on the road. The sun-glistened pavement stretched out ahead of them, and the air above it shimmered with rising waves of heat.

He set the A/C on High Cool and put a tape on the tape deck entitled *The King of Vegas*. It was right after this album, and the two that had come after it, *The King of America* and *The King of the World*, recorded live at some of the King's old concerts, that the newspapers and magazines had started in with all those stories and reports that grew more and more outrageous as time went by. But Daddy-O hadn't believed them then. He had remained loyal to the King and no one but the King. And he didn't believe them now, because he knew that none of them could be true. He had seen him with his own eyes—the King!—in person—that day at his own Gas'N Go station, when not one but three gold Cadillacs had miraculously appeared in the driveway and sat there while Daddy-O pumped the gas and Suzy-Q cleaned the windshields.

And in the third car, the one with the smoked windows all rolled up, had been the King himself.

Not knowing she was being observed, Suzy-Q had nonchalantly gone about the business of wiping the windshields. After she was finished she tossed the sponge and the chamois into the bucket of soap and water and ran back into the store. After Daddy-O filled the tank of the third gold Cadillac, he asked the drivers, who had all three gotten out and were standing over by the Regular pump, if they wanted him to check things out under the hood.

"Don't worry Daddy-O, everything's just fine under the hood . . . " Daddy-O turned around. The voice had come from within the third car. As the smoked window noiselessly closed on the left-rear door, he caught a glimpse of a pair of sunglasses and the black pompadour, exactly like they were on the record album covers. And the voice. The voice he recognized instantly. The voice of the King. It had spoken to him.

One of the King's men went inside with Daddy-O to take care of the bill. He wore a red T-shirt that said THE KING in gold letters on the back tucked into a pair of skin-tight blue jeans. The King's man didn't notice, or pretended not to notice, all the album covers, the box-office posters, and the movie-stills hanging on the walls. He went to the refrigerator case and took out some 6-packs of beer which he stacked on the counter beside Suzy-Q. She put them in grocery sacks without saying anything or raising her eyes, except to steal a quick look at Daddy-O who stood in the middle of the room with an unlighted cigarette dangling from his lip and a half-sneer, half-smile on his face. Daddy-O walked over to the refrigerator case. He snapped off a single can of beer from a 6-pack, popped the top, and took a swig. He walked back to the middle of the room and stared past the King's man toward the three gold Cadillacs outside. A pair of flies that had been asleep for the whole hot drowsy afternoon began noisily buzzing around in circles inside the store window that looked out onto the driveway.

"So what brings the King out this way?" he asked in a strange, almost disdainful tone of voice.

"He's been doing a little hunting . . . a little fishing . . . " the King's man answered. He produced a crumpled hundred-dollar bill from a wad of hundred dollar bills he had stuffed in his jeans pocket. As he did so, another bill fell on the floor, but he didn't notice, or pretended not to notice.

"Catch anything?"

"Not yet . . . but maybe his luck is getting better." The King's man grabbed the sacks of beer and turned without waiting for his change. With the toe of his shiny black loafer he flicked the hundred-dollar bill on the floor to one side and continued on his way.

The flies buzzed louder and flew against the glass again and again. The three gold Cadillacs pulled out of the station, one by one, and disappeared down the road while Daddy-O stared out the window. When the King's gold Cadillac with the smoked windows was finally out of sight, Suzy-Q, without saying anything, went into the back room and switched on the record player. The voice of the King filled the store, singing one of Daddy-O's favorite songs from his very first album, *The King of Hearts*. She came back out and picked up the hundred-dollar bill on the floor. Together with the one sitting on top of the counter she put it in the cash register. Suzy-Q looked at Daddy-O who was smiling like she had never seen him smile before.

"I only wish your mama could have been here—yes I do. Then she'd know. Then she would've seen for herself." The words seemed to escape from him involuntarily. Daddy-O squeezed the can of beer and walked to the doorway where he stood snapping his fingers and swaying from side to side as if he were in a trance.

Suzy-Q ran up to her Daddy-O and gave him a hug. Daddy-O had only once before spoken to her about her mother. "Oh Daddy-O, please tell me. Tell me the story. I know you don't like to remember, but please Daddy-O. I'm 12 years old now and I want to hear it again."

Daddy-O came out of his trance and looked at Suzy-Q. The story. Yes the story. She wants to hear the story. He would have to tell her.

So while the record played and played, over and over, Daddy-O told Suzy-Q the story . . . once more . . .

But not the whole story.

He left out the part about how he used to have a candy-apple red V-8 Dodge convertible that made him famous all over the county, and how he and her mama used to drive around with the top down, playing the radio and listening to the King's music night and day. They both were great fans of the King. They owned all his records, and when all those hot-rod films that starred the King came and played at the Skyview Drive-In Theatre, Daddy-O and Suzy-Q's mama saw every one of them, often sitting through them several times. They used to park on the back row and put the top up and tip the attendant a quarter to leave them alone during the midnight feature. Daddy-O still remembered Suzy-Q's mama's smiling face, messed up hair, and soft body next to him while the sounds of the movie—roaring cars and the voice of the King singing songs like *Asphalt Romance* or *Hot-Rod Honeys*—was being piped into the car through the little round speaker hanging inside the rolled up window. Those were the days when the King was really the King and his music was brand new. And those were the days when Daddy-O acquired the nickname of Daddy-O, after one of the King's songs, *Love Your Daddy-O.*

Not only did they own every one of his records and see every one of his films, they once drove all the way to Memphis to see him in concert. Daddy-O had grown more and more tense as he waited in the darkened arena where the King was appearing. He, like the other 10,000 people attending, sat reverently in their seats as first some blinking lights came on behind, then above, and then on either side of the stage, forming the outline of the walls and towers of a castle. An enormous paper star was lowered onto the stage and backlit so that the first glimpse of the King was in silhouette. And even in silhouette the crown on his head was apparent. Suddenly everybody was on their feet stomping and clapping and shouting. A roar went up when the p.a. announcer's voice said, "Ladies and Gentlemen, presenting THE KING!!!"

The excitement of the crowd turned into utter frenzy when first the King, and then the members of the band, burst through the paper star, picked up their instruments, and started to play. The crowd laughed and cried, sang and danced, and reacted to the King's every gesture. "My god, my god, it's the King—I don't believe it!" a woman sitting behind Daddy-O cried out. Another fellow, about Daddy-O's age, became so excited that he passed out, fell forward, and rolled down the concrete steps in the aisle until he landed against the railing in the front of the section. Throughout the concert, spotlights from high above the stage would relentlessly probe the crowd and then pause for a few seconds to illuminate various pockets of the pandemonium that was mounting in the darkness under the influence of the King and his music. At one point, the area where Daddy-O and Suzy-Q's mama sat was bathed in light, and Daddy-O saw clearly the gyrating bodies and contorted faces of everyone around them. But Daddy-O just stood there. And then the music stopped. The crowd was quieted as the

King sang in a soft, low voice the opening bars of his most recent hit, *Those Stars That Shine in Heaven*. The spotlights no longer moved about the auditorium. Daddy-O thought he could almost feel the heat they gave off, as if somehow they all were being aimed directly at him. He began to snap his fingers in time with the slow cadence of the King's melody, and the crowd began to snap its fingers. Daddy-O began to sway from side to side, and onstage the King began to sway from side to side, and everyone else began to sway from side to side; and then the band came blasting in with their instruments while providing the backup vocals, repeating over and over the chorus to the song—"You are my shining star . . . You are my heaven . . . " All the spotlights were now shining on the King. Suddenly the stage itself rose higher and higher into the air toward the lights as the music grew louder and the King sang the words to the final coda—"And I'm in heaven . . . When your light shines on me . . . " Still higher the stage continued to rise until it looked like it was going to crash through the ceiling, and then the music suddenly stopped and the spotlights went out. After a minute of total darkness, during which the cheers of the audience never stopped, the house lights came on again. The stage was back on the ground. But it was completely empty. Not a sign of the King or his men or their instruments remained. The crowd was exhilarated—but exhausted. It could not even call for an encore. Besides, it was well known that the King never played encores. Everyone gathered themselves up and their things and made their way out as best they could.

Afterwards, while they were driving home that night, Suzy-Q's mama curled up next to Daddy-O and went to sleep while he kept his eyes on the road and drove. On and on. And inside the car, with the radio playing and Suzy-Q's mama by his side, it was as if the King was right there with them, singing his songs just for the two of them.

Daddy-O did not tell Suzy-Q that after her mama learned she was pregnant and they got married, she had lost interest in the King, his music, and his movies. But Daddy-O still cared, still listened to the records, still went to the movies by himself in his car when he had to. He was even able to talk his wife into naming the baby Suzy-Q, after one of the King's songs of course.

By then Suzy-Q's mama was insisting that he sell the candy-apple red Dodge convertible to raise money so that they could buy the country store and two-pump gas station that her uncle had put up for sale. At first, everything was fine. There had been so much business that Daddy-O could hardly keep up with it all. Suzy-Q's mama used to help him whenever the baby was asleep—pumping gas, washing windshields, selling groceries and beer and fishing bait to the people who stopped in. But how was Daddy-O to know that the state would build a new bridge and a new four-lane highway connecting with the interstate that would re-route much of the traffic. It got real hard for them after that. And when Suzy-Q's mama began staying in bed all the time in the room behind the store, Daddy-O became worried. He was afraid she was sick or something. She seemed to blame him for all their money problems and was even cross much of the time with the little girl. But she wasn't sick. Daddy-O found that out when he came back to the store with Suzy-Q after the two of them had been to the movies and discovered that his wife had deserted him. She had taken all the money from the cash register and left behind a note saying she couldn't stand it anymore and was running off to Arkansas.

Daddy-O felt low, real low. He didn't think he could go on. Suzy-Q's mama never even bothered to ask for a legal divorce, so after he learned that she was living with some guy in Little Rock and working as a hostess at a Steak and Ale, Daddy-O had filed for it himself. Were it not for the little girl—his having to raise her all on his own—and taking care of what business there still remained at the Gas'N Go, Daddy-O wasn't sure what would have happened.

But it was about this time when tragedy struck in the life of the King. His wife was killed in an airplane crash while she was flying to Hollywood to be with him while he was making another movie. No one had known that the King was even married before this. The movie was canceled and the King went back to the Castle which he had just had built the year before, and where he and his secret wife had been planning to live. He released an album of new material several months later, an album that he had recorded in his studio right there in the Castle and on it were some of the saddest songs that the world has ever heard, including classics like *Monday Through Friday Blues, Weekend Blues, Lost Love—Secret Love, Angel So Near.* Some of the greatest hits of all time were off that record, but it was the last studio album he had ever done.

Daddy-O owned several copies. He would play it on the stereo at night after he was closed down and Suzy-Q was asleep. Sitting in his store, in the darkness, with the only light coming from the pools of illumination the stars and moon cast down on the driveway and from the little glowing circles that his cigarette made, he listened to the King's hushed, choking voice sing of a love that was more than a love and was never to be. Daddy-O brought out his collection of old album covers, box office posters, and movie-stills which his wife had made him put away, and hung them up all over the store as a kind of shrine to the King and his lost love.

The King made no more albums. His recording company released only those three that had been recorded years before at some of his old concerts. And the King made no more movies. So when the newspapers and gossip magazines started with all those stories and rumors that grew more and more outrageous as time went by, many of his fans lost interest and forgot about him. But not Daddy-O. He still remembered. He still cared. The King was the King and always would be . . .

And so, on the day that was the most important day of his life, Daddy-O told Suzy-Q, once again, the story of how he and her mother had been secretly married, how her mother was really a movie star, and how she was later killed in an airplane crash while flying to Hollywood.

*

It was swiftly growing dark. The sun had sunk behind the tops of the fuzz-covered trees that seemed to have crawled up from out of the bogs and piney woods and now lined both sides of the highway. There were only a few other cars to be seen on the road, all of them with their headlights turned on. Daddy-O did not slow his pace at all. He had a full night of driving ahead of him if they were to reach the Castle by morning. The Cadillac ran smoothly and everything was just fine under the hood. The smoke from his cigarette was being noiselessly sucked out through an air vent. The voice of the King had never sounded so clear and pure as it reverberated throughout the plushly upholstered, smoothly contoured interior of the car. Suzy-Q sat quietly, sipping a Dad's Old Fashioned Root Beer and gazing out the window at the stars which barely managed to twinkle through the gauzy evening air. It was right about then that Daddy-O first noticed the tiny splotches the night-flying bugs were making upon impact with the windshield.

Later, a few miles past their final gas stop, Daddy-O looked in the rear-view mirror to see a spinning red light on his tail. When he turned down the volume on the tape deck he heard the harsh wailing of the siren. He slowed and pulled off onto the shoulder with the red light still hovering right behind him as he braked. Daddy-O didn't get out though, even after he was completely stopped and had mashed the emergency brake to the floorboard. He stared into the mirror and waited to see what would happen.

"What is it Daddy-O? What's going on?"

Suddenly the inside of the car was flooded with light. A spotlight blinded them as they blinked and looked around.

A voice barked at them from behind the spotlight. "All right in there—out of the car! And let me see your hands out in front of you."

Suzy-Q began to cry. "Oh Daddy-O." But Daddy-O was

whispering to her, was soothing her, telling her not to worry. Because he had the letter . . .

"Oh yes, Daddy-O. The letter. You've got it Daddy-O. Show them the letter."

Yes he had the letter all right. The letter that had arrived not more than three days after the King had been to Daddy-O's. The letter that was so important that the King had sent his man in the gold Cadillac to deliver it in person. The letter that had inspired the song that had brought the King's name back, overnight, to the top of the record charts.

At last Daddy-O got out and stood beside the open door of the gold Cadillac with his hands in his pockets. When the spotlight was shut off an unmarked patrol car and a uniformed highway patrolman waving a flashlight loomed before him. He had a moment of difficulty adjusting his eyes in the warm, moist darkness, and remained standing where he was. When the beam of the flashlight struck his face, it revealed a half-sneering, half-smiling expression.

"You got a driver's license and maybe some registration for that there car boy? You got any identification you can show me?" The voice of the highway patrolman had a menacing tone behind it.

"Maybe you got some identification you can show me yourself, besides your uniform and that pretty red-light," Daddy-O answered back.

"Now don't get smart with me Bubba. Keep your hands out in front of you and come on back here and see me. I noticed you back at the Gas'N Go and I'm mighty curious to find out how you got ahold of one of the King's gold Cadillacs."

Daddy-O walked slowly back to the patrol car. He saw that the patrolman was waving the flashlight with one hand while resting the other on the butt of a pistol slung into a side holster. He was one of the fattest people Daddy-O had ever seen. Daddy-O produced his driver's license and it was immediately snatched away from him by the hand that been resting on the pistol.

"You a friend of the King's? Or maybe you've borrowed one of his cars."

"Oh Daddy-O!" Suzy-Q cried out from inside the Cadillac as she leaned forward to turn up the volume on the tape deck. And then there was music. The song. The song that the King had composed and recorded just for her. The song that was at the top of the charts from coast to coast. Her song. Pouring out into the night.

"Who is that in there? What is this all about?"

Daddy-O said no more. He took out the letter, slowly unfolded it, and handed it over to the patrolman. It was the letter—the letter the King's man had delivered personally, along with the keys to the gold Cadillac—asking Daddy-O for his daughter's hand, and with the words to *Come Be My Angel in a Rock & Roll Paradise* set down in writing by the King himself.

The highway patrolman read the letter over using the flashlight to illuminate the single page. He looked at Daddy-O then read the letter again. As he folded it and was handing it back to Daddy-O, he began to stammer and to apologize.

"You mean it's true? That's her? In the car? Right now?"

Daddy-O said no more. He had turned around and was striding back to the Cadillac when the patrolman rushed by him and stuck his head inside the open door.

"Bless you little angel. Bless you. Everyone hoped that the King would get married again . . . that the King would sing again. And now it's true. All because of you he's really making a comeback. We all love the King so much and admire him, and now he's giving us a Queen! The Queen we've all been waiting for. Oh bless you little angel." He backed out of the car and tears were rolling down the jowls of his face. He shook Daddy-O's hand. "We've all been so worried about the King. You know what they've been saying about him for so long, but around here the King's always been the King and always will be. Oh bless you sir—on behalf of everyone. And thank you, thank you, thank you for letting your daughter marry our King and give us a Queen. Like the Queen we would've had all these years if only that plane hadn't crashed on the way to Hollywood. Oh bless you sir. Bless the both of you."

Daddy-O got into the Cadillac and started the engine while the highway patrolman stood there crying and blubbering with his hands to his sides, holding the flashlight so that it was shining down onto the tops of his shoes. Daddy-O interrupted him to ask for directions to the Castle.

"Just follow this road right there to the walls of the Castle . . . Oh bless you sir! You can't miss it . . . Our Queen! Oh we're going to have a Queen at last." And with that he staggered back to the patrol car as if he were in a trance.

Daddy-O lit another cigarette. As the flame of the match flared he looked at Suzy-Q and saw that she was no longer frightened and was smiling the smile of a Queen again. "You showed them Daddy-O. You really showed them this time. Oh Daddy-O."

Daddy-O engaged the gear and eased the Cadillac onto the highway. But when he had almost regained full speed, the four-lane interstate on which they had been traveling all the way abruptly ended—becoming instead a narrow, bumpy, two-lane blacktop road that seemed to plunge off into the darkness.

Suzy-Q screamed.

"It's stinging me Daddy-O. It's a June bug. It's a big one. And there's skeeters too. Make them stop! Oh Daddy-O!"

Daddy-O hit the row of buttons on the console on the armrest and simultaneously all the windows flew open. "Just try and shoo them out Suzy-Q." But it was useless as more and more of them streamed in.

Finally Daddy-O stopped in the middle of the road. He put up the windows, turned off the A/C, and switched on the interior light. With rolled up comic books in both hands he was thrashing and swatting wildly in every direction—smashing the buzzing insects flat against the windows, the seats, the dashboard, the steering wheel, the overhead dome.

"Get them Daddy-O. Don't let them bite me. Oh Daddy-O." The girl was moaning hysterically. Only after he had finished, his face dripping with sweat, and all over the inside of the car were the crushed bodies of the dead bugs, did Suzy-Q calm down.

"Oh thank you Daddy-O." She opened another bottle of Dr. Pepper. "You wouldn't let those mean old bugs hurt a Queen would you? Oh Daddy-O?"

Daddy-O drove on. He was tired and it was getting harder and harder to see. The swarms of insects rose in front of them like dark clouds that blotted out the moon and the stars. In the beams of the headlamps they were dancing and swooping. They pelted the car like tiny black hailstones, and Daddy-O had to turn on the windshield washer and the wipers to prevent the crust of their squashed bodies from totally obscuring his vision.

Every few miles or so they passed by what once must have been small settlements beside the road. But now they were all deserted—nothing but ghost towns of ramshackle buildings and tumbledown cabins, and not a store or filling station or even a road sign along the way. But Daddy-O didn't care. He still had nearly a full tank of gas and everything was just fine under the hood.

Suzy-Q had gone back to sleep. Daddy-O again turned the A/C to High Cool. He put on a tape and the voice of the King filled the interior of the car and steadied his nerves. He pressed the gas pedal and the gold Cadillac sped into the night.

By sunrise they would be at the walls of the Castle.

*

The King's Castle lay in a clearing on the side of a low sloping hill at the back of an isolated valley. The narrow-two-lane highway terminated at a crossing with an even narrower, gravel-topped service road that fronted the high walls of the Castle for a quarter of a mile before reaching a dead-end at the point where the walls retreated up the sides of the hill. Daddy-O heard the rattle of the gravel and felt it pounding beneath the car as he drove the length of the road, up and down, searching for an entrance to the Castle.

A bump started some of the soda pop bottles rolling around and crashing together and awakened the sleeping girl.

"Oh Daddy-O are we there? Is this the Castle? Will I be a Queen today at last?"

Daddy-O stopped the car and got out. He walked along a fringe of grass growing between the road and the high, impregnable walls. Still he discovered no means of entry.

He crossed the road and gazed up the hill trying to see inside the Castle—and it really was a Castle—with a crenellated upper wall, rounded turrets at either end, and soaring towers within, as enormous and as grand as he had imagined it to be. He called out but there was no one, nothing to answer him.

He beeped the horn of the car a couple of times then held it down for several seconds. Nothing . . .

The warm morning sun was already pouring down from what was going to be another achingly bright blue sky. Daddy-O sat in the car, peering through the bug-splattered windshield at the gray walls of the Castle. He must have dozed off for no more than a quarter of an hour behind the steering wheel, with the door propped open, exhausted and not knowing what to do next, when he abruptly came to.

He had been half-dreaming, half-remembering the night before and that spinning red light when he heard faintly at first, somewhere in the distance, the drone of a siren. But more than one, several in fact, and they grew louder and louder with every second.

"What is it Daddy-O? What's happening?"

All at once they were enveloped in clouds of dust. Then the rat-a-tat of flying gravel beating on the exterior of the gold Cadillac was pierced by the sounds of squealing brakes and shrieking sirens coming off the highway and onto the service road.

Daddy-O jumped out of the car. Slamming the door he shouted at Suzy-Q and told her to hit the automatic lock button on the console. Police cars and motorcycles now were everywhere—skidding and careening on the road and on the grass, racing up the sides of the hill. More unmarked cars appeared and turned off the highway onto the road and came to a halt. Their doors flew open and from them emerged a number of men and women who momentarily blinked and hopped about, then swarmed together as they moved past a policeman in a short-tailed blue shirt who was screaming at Daddy-O through a bullhorn.

"You there! Get that goddamned car out of the way! Right now!"

As the swarm approached Daddy-O he saw that some of them were carrying notebooks and others were speaking into microphones. Daddy-O observed a man with a movie camera strapped to his shoulder, and another one holding a portable spotlight that was flashing on. Daddy-O realized he was being surrounded by news reporters.

"Who are you? What do you know? Do you work for the King?" Their questions flew at him from every direction.

The policeman was also considerably red in the face. He came forward with his drawn gun in one hand, the bullhorn in the other, and his short shirttails flapping.

"You better get in that goddamned car and move it out of the way mister! Do you hear me?"

The swarm of reporters moved toward the policeman.

"Sheriff—Sheriff! What information do you have? What can you tell us?"

Daddy-O was stunned and bewildered. His legs felt paralyzed.

More policemen ran up and the Sheriff gathered his men together. One group of them formed a line beside the wall of the Castle, while another group followed him toward the gold Cadillac where he began hammering the glass out of the window on the driver's side with the butt of his gun.

Suzy-Q screamed and could be seen looking around in

terror. Daddy-O tried to get to the car but was repulsed by the swarm of reporters and shoved aside by the crowd of policemen.

"Who is she? Who is she? What's she doing here?"

The Sheriff reached through the broken window, opened the door from inside, and got behind the wheel. He threw the car into neutral and his men pushed it off the road. Daddy-O fought his way again through the confusion and succeeded this time in reaching the rear door on the opposite side and pulled Suzy-Q out. But she no longer showed any signs of being frightened in the least as she stood there in her long white dress and her lipstick-red patent leather shoes, with her curly blonde hair bouncing off her shoulders. She regarded everything and everyone with a strange, twisted smile on her face.

Suddenly there was a loud roar from inside the Castle that increased to a deafening intensity. Then whirring and rising high into the air—a gold helicopter that hovered overhead for only a moment before soaring away.

And once more from inside the Castle there came a grinding noise and the sound of an alarm bell, and a section of the wall which was actually an automatic gate, slowly parted until everyone could see coming out of the wide courtyard over a polished marble driveway, a procession of five gold Cadillacs.

The policemen charged forward with their billy clubs, striking everyone in their way. The Cadillacs shot through the gate onto the service road, avoiding the chaos of cars and people, and veered onto the highway.

The Sheriff and his men guarded the gate which remained open. While attention was diverted, Daddy-O grabbed Suzy-Q and put her back in the car. He leaped in and started the engine. Leaving dust and gravel in his wake, he fishtailed his way among the clusters of parked cars. Several of the reporters and policemen had to dodge and scatter and jump out of the way. When he finally did make it back onto the two-lane highway he forced still more approaching cars off the side of the road.

The front seat of the Cadillac was covered with a shower of shattered glass while broken bottles and candy bar wrappers floated in the sticky pool of warm soda pop that covered the rear floorboard. Daddy-O drove on. There was a solid line of traffic moving in the opposite direction, headed towards the Castle, but Daddy-O's only thought was to get away as quickly as possible. He knew he couldn't be that far behind the five other gold Cadillacs, but no matter how fast he went he never caught sight of them.

He tried all of the stations on the radio and every one of them was either playing the music of the King or had people on the air talking about him. No one knew for sure what had happened, except there were reports that the King had been taken to a hospital.

When he finally reached the four-lane interstate again, Daddy-O noticed that his gas gauge was nearly on empty. The road was barricaded at this point and another crowd of policemen, news reporters, and spectators had gathered. But a highway patrolman, seeing the gold Cadillac approach, waved it past. Daddy-O stayed on the interstate and continued to the same Gas'N Go station where he had bought his last tank of gas the night before.

He pulled into the driveway and parked at a side pump. He filled the tank and cleaned the windshield himself. When he went inside the office he found an old man in a dirty baseball cap sitting away from the windows where he could not see the car. The old man was listening to a radio station with the latest news of the King. Daddy-O took the restroom key off a hook without saying a word.

As he washed his face and combed his hair he stared at himself in the mirror. He had the beginnings of a black eye and a stream of blood had dried and caked around his mouth where he had been struck by a billy club. He felt dazed and weary and had a haunted look about him. What was happening?

What had happened to the King? What should he do next?
Where should he go? After all, he now had a full tank of gas
and everything was just fine under the hood. And he had the
letter. When he finished he checked on Suzy-Q who was still
asleep in the back seat of the car, and then he took the restroom
key inside.

The radio was momentarily silent but then an announcer
came on with a bulletin and read an official announcement
from the hospital where they had taken the King. "THE KING
IS DEAD. THE KING IS DEAD. DOCTORS AT THE STATE
UNIVERSITY HOSPITAL ATTEMPTED UNSUCCESSFULLY
TO SAVE HIM AFTER HE COLLAPSED AT THE CASTLE
EARLY THIS MORNING AND WAS RUSHED BY HIS OWN
HELICOPTER TO THE HOSPITAL. PRIMARY CAUSE OF
DEATH IS YET UNDETERMINED AND PENDING AN
AUTOPSY . . . TO REPEAT: THE KING IS DEAD."

"Why hell everybody knew that young fool wouldn't last
much longer," said the old man, getting up slowly to take the
key and the credit card from Daddy-O. "All that boozing, those
pills, and all those wild goings-on at that goddamned Castle of
his. If you ask me it's the worst thing that ever happened around
here when he built that goddamned place. It wasn't so bad
when he was out in Hollywood making records and movies.
Hell I was even sort of proud of him them. But after he built
that place, and after his wife was killed, they practically turned
the whole goddamned state over to him. Like he was some
kind of god, even though he never made any more records or
gave any more concerts. A legend in his own time they said. A
great big bullshitter, I say."

Daddy-O didn't say a word.

"And you probably heard about those gold Cadillacs of his
I bet. It's true he had his own underground gas tank and his
own mechanic up there with him who didn't do anything but
take care of those goddamned cars. Well that same fellow used
to drop in here sometimes to order some parts or have a flat
fixed, and he told me how it was. He said the King had come

close to dying several times over the years—from drugs, from alcohol, or a combination of both—and he even tried, more than once, to kill himself. This fellow said sometimes the staff would go for days without ever seeing the King because he had locked himself up in his room and wouldn't eat or speak to anybody. After so many times of having to break down his door and finding him unconscious and half-dead, they finally brought a doctor up there to live full-time and take care of him. Guess even he couldn't save him this time. No sir, mighty peculiar customer was that King of ours.

"But the silliest goddamned thing is this story that's been going around lately about the King getting married again. They said the King even had his new wife all picked out and that she was coming to the Castle in one of his gold Cadillacs. But you tell me mister, what kind of a woman would want to get mixed up with a character like the King. Why she'd have to be half-silly herself. But it don't make no difference anyway I guess—the King is dead and that's that."

All the time he talked, the old man was busy with Daddy-O's credit card, running it through the machine and filling in the figures. His dirty baseball cap was splattered with oil and grease spots, but on its crest was the familiar orange star outlined in black. After Daddy-O signed the slip, tore it off, and got back his credit card, the old man looked out the window and spied the gold Cadillac.

"Hey there Mister!"

Daddy-O was out the door and hurrying across the driveway while the old man shouted and came shuffling slowly after him. And he was in the car and pulling out of the station before the old man could say another word.

*

Suzy-Q sat in the back seat staring straight ahead with the same strange twisted smile on her face while Daddy-O drove. They traveled straight through like they did the day before, stopping only at Gas'N Go stations every couple of hundred miles along the way. Daddy-O turned off the radio because it was full of the same voices, repeating the same stories about the King. He shut off the A/C and let the hot, humid wind blow on them through the broken window. He didn't smoke or put on any tapes or allow himself to think of anything, or anyone. He just kept his eyes on the road. And drove. On and on.

They made good time returning and arrived at the two-pump filling station and country store around 4:00 in the morning. Daddy-O parked the car in the driveway beside the same pump where he had filled up the three gold Cadillacs that one day. Suzy-Q had slept almost the entire time since it got dark. He lifted her and carried her inside and she held him around the neck. She awoke briefly, when Daddy-O laid her on her bed and stood over her. For the first time he noticed that her dress was torn in several places, and that her arms all up and down and her forehead were red and swollen with bug bites

"Oh a Queen—I am a Queen at last," she was muttering. "You there!" she suddenly cried out, "Go to the King and tell him the Queen is waiting for him." The strange, twisted smile reappeared on her face.

Tears formed in Daddy-O's eyes. He could not believe it.

"Suzy-Q. Suzy-Q. It's me. I'm your Daddy-O."

"Ain't got no Daddy-O no more. I'm a Queen. Do you hear? A Queen!" She sunk into unconsciousness, laughing and moaning as she did. "The King . . . oh where is my King?"

Daddy-O left the room. He closed the door. He couldn't help it now as the sobs rose and caught in his throat. What had happened to his Suzy-Q? He felt chilled and feverish all over at the same time and could hardly stand up because his whole body was trembling. Why had this happened? Why did the King have to die? Daddy-O was afraid.

Daddy-O could not understand.

He walked slowly back into his store. He switched on the record player and the voice of the King filled the room. "Oh my angel, come be with me in a rock & roll paradise . . . " Daddy-O stood there, as if he were in a trance. He didn't say a word. An unlighted cigarette dangled from his lip. The record played over and over.

As it grew slowly brighter in the east, the morning star hung high above in the purple sky. Daddy-O did not look up to behold the star, but he did see its shimmering light reflected on the hood of the gold Cadillac, and how it seemed to be breaking all over it into a thousand dazzling little pieces.

THE FATHER

I gave no reasons to my son the day I left his home, though I had them all the same.

So long ago. I remember so well.

On that particular day there had occurred only the usual episodes—episodes which portended a myriad of possible motives, possible actions, possible consequences. And as a result of the inexorable evolution of a situation of utter hopelessness, a situation which required my utmost and constant attention, I had grown more and more dissatisfied with my lot and resolved to drastically change things. While the dynamics of such a situation, its tacit assumptions, its specific structure, its inner logic, its unique patterns of expectation (so to speak), force one to wait until all alternatives are exhausted and each day becomes as unvarying and wearisome as the one preceding, suffice it to say, I could tolerate no more. I was forced to act. And I gave no reasons to my son the day I left his home. So long ago. I remember so well.

*

The sun has not yet risen. I sit up quickly in my bed at the sound of footsteps falling in the darkened hallway outside my door. They grow steadily louder as he approaches, then gradually diminish after he passes by and is headed towards the bathroom. I am now wide-awake.

"Pick up your feet!" I repeat his mother's former admonitions. "You heard me. Pick up your feet I say."

I can still see him as a boy. A shrug of the shoulders. Hands in his pockets. Stringy blonde hair hanging in his eyes. He would always listen to her of course. But with an unconcerned nod of his head in my direction, he affects an air of total nonchalance while continuing to slouch away from my door.

Through my window on this final morning I perceive faint streaks of light piercing the waning nighttime sky. First signs of the sun.

The water is running for his bath. I hear him urinate. He has difficulty when he urinates because he is unable to relax and let things flow naturally. Instead he goes in short, quick spurts all the while grunting and groaning which calls even more attention to the entire procedure.

And when he gargles it sounds like someone being strangled. My God! It's as if he's in the same room with me. All I want is some sleep. All I ask is for just a little more time to doze off and dream of former days. I lie back for a moment, beset by the despair of an old man.

(And even now, as I am remembering this, my forehead grows feverish. My limbs ache. I am soaked with perspiration.)

It's no use. The sound of him splashing in the tub. The thought of the bathroom floor covered with water. The way he continuously turns the faucets on and off in order to maintain a stable water temperature. HOT/COLD. I know him so well. But never do I let him suspect how much his morning toilet disturbs my sleep, upsets my tranquility, and spoils my entire day. Every day.

I must cover my head with my pillow to shut out the moaning and shuddering noise of the pipes.

I know that soon he will open my door, approach my bed,

and place his smooth, cold hands upon my shoulders. I must pretend to still be asleep.

He shakes me a second time.

"Father. Father you must wake up."

I open my eyes wearily. Oh for just a few more minutes of peace. Why must I always be forced to get up at first light of dawn?

All during breakfast he stares at a newspaper and chews the special high-fiber, high-vitamin cereal which he has dutifully prepared for the two of us. For my benefit he has turned on a radio program with morning stock market summaries and forecasts. Although it has been years, I still keep up.

But this morning I tremble with fear, with outrage, with disgust. My trembling causes ripples to swirl through my cup of coffee. When I raise it to my mouth it overflows and spills down the front of my shirt. No reaction from him. He won't help me at all. As if I do not exist, he leans back in his chair— so unconcerned, so oblivious to everything—and incessantly rattles the pages of that damned newspaper of his. Silently I curse him. Not another day of this. I swear I cannot bear it. Action is called for. Plans materialize. I must free myself once and for all from his home, his compulsive routines, this intolerable existence.

He speaks.

"Father, would you like to get outside today? The weather is so fine. Perhaps Mrs. Green can stop by for you this morning. She's been telephoning my office everyday, offering to take you for a drive. Wouldn't that be nice? Where would you like to go?"

Panic!

Not Mrs. Green! That loathsome old dowager. Constantly yakking unceasingly about things I don't understand or care about in the least. I simply will be unable to cope with her today. My stomach begins to ache. I am having chest pains. I am not a well man. Mrs. Green! Oh that does it!

"Father you must get out for awhile. It's no good for you to spend the whole day at your desk, sorting your papers until I come home."

Can this insensitive idiot be my son? Does he really believe that I sit alone in my room shuffling meaningless papers all day, anxiously awaiting his return? Soon he shall find out differently. Soon he shall have the answers to all of the questions he is too obtuse to think to ask.

But why insist that Mrs. Green come by at all? He seems so determined as he folds his paper, looks at me so sternly, and speaks in a low, firm voice. How can he presume that she and I have the slightest thing in common? If my son could only comprehend the resentment I have for this woman. If I could only convince him that Mrs. Green is a highly unsuitable companion for a man in my position . . . But for the moment I must surrender. I give my grudging assent in order to prevent him from wasting any more of my time. Yes. What I need is time. For myself. To think. To prepare.

Later he comes into my room after he has dressed for work. It's all settled. She will arrive at 10:30 in her car to take me for a drive. We will have lunch in a restaurant of her choosing and then cruise around for another couple of hours in the afternoon. By 3:30, if all goes well, she will have brought me home. Enough time. Just enough.

"Can I help you with your papers Father?"

NO. NO. NO! I want him to leave me alone and be gone.

When he finally does leave, right at 9:00, I can begin to get ready. I quickly review my lists. The secret phone numbers. Extra clothing. Plenty of cash. I must be ready to go without arousing the slightest suspicion on her part. She must be caught completely unaware.

(Perhaps I really believed, or even unconsciously desired that I would fail—that I would break down under the strain of a day with her, lose my will at a most embarrassing moment, find myself in a highly compromising position, and remain a prisoner forever. I knew that sonny-boy wouldn't dare to alert the authorities when he came home from work and discovered my escape. I figured he might have even deduced my destination, though perhaps I was overestimating his powers of observation. Still, there had been clues I tell you. But I was determined to act, to not miss my main chance, to actually remove myself to another location in time and space. Damn the consequences.)

Very busy. I hastily arrange the papers atop my desk in the remaining minutes into two separate piles. Business on the left, personal on the right. Later in the afternoon I will put them in the proper drawers. The tickets in my pocket. An address written on a scrap of paper. So much to do. So many actions to contemplate.

Suddenly a car horn honks. The doorbell chimes. Mrs. Green has arrived. Oh no. Just like that old crone to show up early. As if she has been alerted to my plans, she is now standing at the door, intruding her meddlesome presence into my preparations for freedom.

But there are limits, genuine limits to our liberties. And yes, these limits define not only the boundaries of our few, miserable liberties, but are the bases for all meaningful future actions. In fact, in my case, real freedom would be unthinkable without them. Take it from an old man who has learned to roll with the punches. I know what I'm talking about.

I suppress my first impulse to beat a hasty retreat. To do so will surely mean immediate apprehension. I know. Mrs. Green would be wise. Would be at my back door. Waiting so patiently. Anticipating so keenly. And even if I did get past her while trying to make a break for it, she would then be hot on my heels, dogging my every step, swooping down upon me like some hideous bird of prey. Such is the radar of her nosiness, coupled with an uncanny clairvoyance. I know.

The doorbell chimes again.

Strategy must be employed.

"Mrs. Green. How splendid."

"Mrs. Green. Come right in."

"Mrs. Green. Can I get you a chair? A cup of tea?"

"Mrs. Green—my son tells me that you have been ever so anxious to renew my acquaintance."

"Mrs. Green. You're quite right. Let us leave at once. Why hang around the house. Let's make the time fly. And yes your car is so very impressive with its tinted glass, leather seats, chrome wheels, and that enormous engine under the hood. Wasn't aware they still made them like that. Custom made you say? Oh my goodness I am very impressed."

Off we speed into the tangle of late morning rush hour traffic. Horn sounding, tires squalling, radio blaring, cigarette dangling—Mrs. Green puts on a masterful display of driving. I suppose the air of total self-assurance and dare-devil adroitness is a distinctive trait of the big city driver such as she, with her effortless weavings in and out of slow-moving traffic lanes, such smooth clutch and stick synchronization with every shift, and the sudden accelerations to out-race the other cars for a changing traffic signal which if we do not make we simply barrel through at full speed. The radio is tuned to a phone-in talk show. The topic of the program concerns do-it-yourself absolution from original sin and features a noted European psychoanalyst with a heavy accent and a supercilious attitude. Mrs. Green, dear dear Mrs. Green, can hardly stand it. Every five minutes she stops at a public phone, calls the radio station, and fights back her disappointment upon finding a busy signal waiting for her at the other end. No wonder the poor woman is always complaining that no one will ever listen to her.

But I will.

And so the morning passes. It seems to take forever. We criss-cross town via east-west expressways and north-south tollways with an occasional tree-lined parkway thrown in to break the asphalt and neon monotony. The city streams past our moving windows. No passive witness she—Mrs. Green constantly fiddles with the knobs and buttons of the radio. My earlier pleasantries are long forgotten. I have exhausted all of my resources, and here she is just getting started.

So to me she talks and talks and talks. Because she has

been unable to broadcast her voice into half a million homes, cars, schools, and offices, she finds it necessary to take advantage of "our time together." And during the all-too-few and all-too-brief respites from her conversation, I am now subject to wistful looks my way and deep swelling sighs that issue from the depths of her soul.

As the lunch hour approaches, the random patches of slowed cars become more and more frequent until it seems as if the whole world is nosing around, inch by inch, in search of something to eat. Including me and Mrs. Green. Suddenly she spots an opening. She whips into a drive-in hamburger stand, eases into a narrow stall, puts down the window, and cuts the ignition. The car's enormous engine needs a rest. Lunch is ordered by talking into a two-way radio speaker concealed within the smile-painted face of a jug-eared clown's head which hangs from a post just outside her door. When the bulging eyes of the clown-face light up, a siren sounds, bells ring, and smoke puffs from his misshapen ears. Our order is ready. It is brought to us by an androgynous midget who suddenly appears, balancing little white paper bags of food on an orange tray which he?/she? then shoves through the window on the driver's side. I'm still not certain at what point the money for our purchases was negotiated. Perhaps Mrs. Green had made prior arrangements. Or could it be that my son is somewhere about, pulling invisible strings?

I sit quietly with our hot cheeseburgers on my lap, their juices dripping through the thin paper wrapper and staining my trousers. My companion's voice is finally lost in the din of a tinny Muzak piped into the car by means of that two-way radio which no doubt possesses the capability to monitor every word we say.

But.

(But it was all an alembic for my schemes.) (I realize that now.)

I stare at Mrs. Green's sagging face, her white fright-wig shock of hair, those rouged cheeks which are nothing more than a futile attempt to disguise her Old World, sickbed pallor. I love her. Yes! I love her fat lips so yellow with mustard and encircled by a little milk shake mustache which she can never quite dissolve with her short, darting tongue.

Love perhaps?

Inspiration so often arrives like a bolt from out of the blue. Satori and the voice of the thunder right there in the front seat of her car. I struggle to maintain my composure. Oh the beautiful disposition of the mind—to dispense with all difficulties and resolve all contradictions. I am certain that freedom will soon be mine.

(I prefer not to divulge all the details. Besides, my son will have already arrived at his own conclusions.)

I silently chew my cheeseburger. Two coffees with cream and sugar in equal measure. The world is getting fed all around us.

We later arrive at a high bluff overlooking a deserted beach and a somber body of gray water. Lunch had been quickly finished . . . 1:00 deadline . . . we're back on the street . . . Mrs. Green took a fancy . . . I was ready . . . My only request is that she not play the radio. Capitulation. We sit quietly for a long while watching some small boats bob up and down on the impatient tides.

"Mrs. Green, there is something I must tell you—"

But she smiles me back into silence. She no longer sighs or fidgets. Instead, she is now lost in a trance of post-prandial bovine tranquility. No matter. Things will soon be settled. We each have a smoke. I watch and wait for my chances.

A pair of white seagulls fly by. Describing a long, ascending arc above the gray horizon, their wide wings are made invisible by the sun which emerges at that instant from behind an enormous bank of clouds. Vast blue regions of sky and water suddenly spread out above us and below.

Oh yes Mrs. Green. Here we go. That's my girl. Close those big eyes and let me sing my song for you.

"You see Mrs. Green, my son and I have been together for

such a long, long while. We don't often agree on very much. We . . . " Etc.

So long ago. I remember so well.

*

And so it has come to this . . . while I wait for the end I must contemplate the physical properties of this, my private New World: the dirty, paint-peeling walls shot through by a network of cracks and fissures running from floor to ceiling; the faded carpet, worn-out in several places and bearing the marks and scars of Mrs. Green's high-heel shoes and discarded cigarettes; the black dust which outlines the grooves of my fingertips after I run them across the night table beside the bed and hold my hands up to the light. And as I lie on my bed I stare at the ceiling and wonder how many others have studied these same flowing patterns of water stain on moldy plaster, eased into unconsciousness, breathed their last, and surrendered their souls.

And do I think of my son?

Mrs. Green left for good today after a very noisy morning toilet. We so often quarrel over money when she comes home in the evening. Or is it because she can never have dinner ready soon enough to please me? But these things are only the result of the underlying problem. Last night things went too far. I struck her. I admit it. She locked herself in the bathroom and cried for hours then later stormed out of the apartment and did not return until after midnight. When I asked where she'd been she said she had met up with an old boy friend who was very rich and still interested in her, but I knew that she had only been out drinking or bowling or just driving around in her car. Perhaps someday, I taunted her, this rich boy friend will marry you and take you to Florida where you can spend the day sunning yourself and eating oranges off the trees.

No reply. Hurtful silence.

And now she is gone. Car keys and all. Nothing remains but the smell of the cabbage that she kept boiling in an iron pot on the stove for twenty-four hours a day. The heavy, sour odor has infiltrated the greasy walls to such an extent that everything in the room—the shoddy furniture, my clothing, my own body even, has the stench of decaying vegetables about it.

And do I think of my son?

For hours I love to sit alone, wrapped in a blanket, propped up beside the broken window, and gaze upon the endless procession of life below me in the street. Day and night they pass. The businessmen and brokers; bankers and lawyers; workers, mongers, peddlers, and cops. Hustlers and four-flushers; bullies and thieves; losers, dealers, hookers, and pimps. Good-time gals cling to the arms of strutting hoodlums. Squadrons of bums sleep it off in the gutter while a pariah priest watches over his flock. The plaintive notes of the street musician's song reaches my ears, his saxophone glittering in the streetlight's shine. And oh the lovers still embracing on all night street corners. They're all out there. The entire human race. Dressed to the nines. So down and out.

Ah world. Ah this life.

And do I think of my son?

Bah! What do I care how he reacts? A puzzled stare around my room, a frantic search throughout the house, the doleful tone of his voice as he cries out "Oh Father—my Father." But Father isn't there. How I relish the thought of all his pointless shouts and curses being directed at Mrs. Green. Undoubtedly he blames her for letting me slip away. The fool. No doubt he'd really like to get his hands on the old gal and work her over. He wouldn't stop until he had her weeping and begging for mercy. Of course there is nothing—nothing!—that she could have done to change things. Unfortunate woman. A victim of her own curiosity. But I know how he is about these things. He can be most unreasonable.

But that is another lifetime. I must not allow myself to settle back into old patterns of expectation.

And do I think of my son?

Observe now, if you would, the old steam radiator that sits in the corner—popping, whistling, and sputtering throughout the day. And in the evening, as the twilight dies in every part of my room, that radiator stops trying to produce even the slightest amount of heat. I sit by the broken window and the chilly night air invades my lungs. They have become so congested that I can hear my chest rattle with every breath. A bargain with the devil is being negotiated inside my body.

And do I think of my son?

The early morning hours pass, so slowly, so inexorably. The stifled sighs and muffled screams, the moanings and groanings of the night world leak through my walls from the neighboring apartments, mingling now with distant memories conjured up by the spell of sleeplessness.

A dim strip of light from the corridor seeps under the door to my room. I lie back on my bed. I close my eyes.

And do I think of my son?

A sudden hiss of steam. A flood of sunlight through the window. The honk, rush, and roar of morning traffic. The sound of footsteps in the hallway, nearing my door. Someone enters without knocking, speaks, "Father—I must insist. You have to get outside today."

I remember so well. So long ago. Everything.

*

Did I mention this couple across the way? They live on the 7th story of an inelegant apartment building and residence hotel. They never close their curtains or lower their shades. Every afternoon he sits with his back against the railing on the narrow balcony outside their one-room flat and plays the guitar just for her. I can never hear him, but judging from the way she looks at him she seems to be extremely interested in his every move.

LIA

A taxi racing through cold, dark, empty NYC streets. Grand Central looms Cathedral-like at the end of the Avenue. Moments later, a figure emerges from the cab and hurries through the 42nd street entrance and down the corridor into the vaulted expanse of the great concourse. A dismal early morning scene of sleeping bums, staggering drunks, muggers on the prowl. A shopping bag lady leans against a shuttered ticket window. A pair of bored cops sip coffee, smoke cigarettes, and spin their nightsticks. The giant Kodak ad depicts snow-covered northern woods with a lonesome log cabin throwing golden slivers of light through tiny windows into the gloom of darkness surrounding. And standing there at the foot of the escalator, waiting, as per instructions—Lt. M.

They say Lt. M. is beautiful. Long raven hair; hazel eyes; high, fine cheekbones; wide mouth; delicately sloping nose; elegant, even aristocratic manner. Don't know about her figure. Never seen her without an overcoat on. She has it on now in fact, and wears a long black scarf tied around the outside of her turned-up collar. She's also holding a large attaché case. Again, as per instructions.

"Got the tickets Lt.?"

"Got them Capt."

Aboard the 6:05 to New Haven just as the doors close and the train lurches out of the station.

"Sorry to keep you waiting Lt. A lousy time of day to start out."

"I didn't wait that long. And I wouldn't have missed this assignment for anything. I even had time to get us some coffee and bagels. Here you are Capt . . . . " She opens the attaché case and takes out a white paper bag with dark, coffee-stain rings on the bottom.

We drink our coffee and eat our bagels as the train emerges from beneath the Park Avenue tunnel and crawls past the wall of East Harlem housing projects. The sun has not risen but is shooting up spikes of color over the horizon on our right. The long winter has been unrelenting. Weeks of accumulated snow and garbage remain piled along the curbs and in the gutters of the city streets like mounds of lava after a volcanic eruption. The bitter wind whips through the crumbling facades of abandoned uptown tenements and even penetrates the car in which we are riding when the doors momentarily open and close at the 125th Street station where no one is getting on or off. We cross the bridge over the Harlem River and proceed through the red-brick warehouse gloom of the Bronx dawn. A sleepy-eyed conductor punches our tickets. The poor stiff looks exhausted—like he's been riding this same train back and forth between New York and New Haven all night long without once setting foot in either place.

Coffee finished, half-eaten bagels tossed on the floor and pushed under the seats with the rest of our trash, Lt. M. lights her first cigarette of the day. It won't be her last. I mooch one from her and we get down to work. It's a No Smoking car, but it doesn't matter. There's no one else around and the conductor is "wise"; he's been making these New Haven runs for quite some time so he's probably one of ours.

"Okay Lt. fill me in. What've we got this time?"

"I thought you'd never ask Capt.," she says, smiling almost.

I think they're right. She is beautiful. But after a moment she's all business again as she opens the attaché case and produces the files.

"A poet. Fellow by the name of Riddley, first name Jason."

"Jason Riddley . . . Jason Riddley . . . . Name's familiar."

"Ought to be. He's published all over the place. *New Yorker,* *Atlantic Monthly,* not to mention all the major university literary magazines. Gives lots of readings too. Churches, college campuses, bars, art galleries. The usual."

"Ever come into the city?"

"Apparently so. Here read this." From the attaché case she takes out a well-thumbed copy of a collection of poems by Riddley entitled *Lunar Lights.* I flip through it quickly and come to a page marked with a paper clip. The poem in question is something called "Snowscape/Nightscape in Central Park."

"What's this all about Lt.?"

"Just read Capt. You'll get the picture."

It's a short, free verse lyric in which the "I" of the poem— the poet—Riddley himself evidently, has ventured into Central Park one evening while a "gossamer sky of falling snow softly enfolds the hills and meadows and trees like a bride's wedding gown . . . " The poet continues walking through the park— "unafraid in the frozen folds of the snowscape," while ahead of him he sees "a line of glittering city lights which seem far away—as if viewed through the wrong end of a telescope."

"He's got to be kidding," I say, clinching my teeth. "But still there's nothing we can really nail him on, nothing that would convince a jury."

"Read on Capt.," orders the Lt.

And she's right. When the poet is almost out of the park he catches a glimpse out of the corner of his eye of something moving beneath a bench in the shadows. The something moving turns out to be a large brown rat.

I look at Lt. M. and communicate with her by means of a single, upraised eyebrow.

"I know. I know," she replies, understanding immediately.

The climax of the poem comes when the poet, in his state of heightened consciousness, induced partly by the "laser-beams of starlight which pierce the veil of falling snow . . . " is able to comprehend how even a rat in the shadows has its place in this world. The last lines of the poem go, "And I then offer a lonesome prayer for a solitary rat/Crawling beside me into the ineffable void."

I whistle through my teeth at that one. "No doubt about it Lt. this is right up our alley."

"I knew you'd say that Capt. That's why I volunteered for this case."

We exchange looks.

"You know something Lt., I'm beginning to think you can read me like a book." I laugh out loud and so does she. This is the first time we've worked together, but it won't be the last.

"The next thing I want to know Lt. is who his connection is. Who in New York I mean."

Lt. M. is frowning. Her troubled expression almost makes me think that her interest in this case is something beyond the merely professional.

"We're just not sure at this point Capt. Apparently the guy is a real expert at working both sides of the street. Uptown—Downtown. East Side—West Side. He's even been spotted in Brooklyn."

"Good Lord Lt.! If that's true then we've got to work fast." My throat suddenly feels as dry as the inside of a banker's glove. I start to understand why she's so interested in this case.

"We've infiltrated various groups and questioned several informants but still haven't really worked our way to the top," she adds.

"You mean to the bottom," I sneer.

But Lt. M. is dead serious and doesn't react to my joke. I tell her to relax. We have another hour to go on the train and a ways to drive after that. Lt. M. is good at what she does I can tell—damned good—but I've had more experience. The main thing is to be ready when the time comes. "Don't worry Lt. I've dealt with these types before—these poets. It'll be like shooting fish in a barrel."

But if anything she becomes even more intense. She sits and pores over the files again and again for the rest of the trip. By the time we are slowing down for New Haven and the sleepy-eyed conductor is walking through the car shouting "Last stop!" she's as restless as a cat. A cat on the trail of a rat.

As we walk out of the New Haven station we're met by the morning crowds surging in. We stand in the numbing cold and try our luck at hailing a cab. Finally one pulls up to the curb and we get in. When I tell the driver where we're headed—a little town up the turnpike called Guilford—like some kind of a wise guy he starts in with, "Guilford? Where's that? Never heard of it." I see him grinning in the rear-view mirror, real pleased with himself because he takes us for a couple of suckers. I slip him a C-note and tell him to buy himself a road map. "Now quit stalling Jack and let's get moving!" Miraculously, he remembers the way.

Thirty minutes later we're arrived in downtown Guilford. If you want to call it downtown. Mostly a bunch of churches facing the snow-covered town green on three sides while on the other side is a row of shops—a drugstore, a grocery store, an art gallery, and a bookstore that serves coffee where you can no doubt buy books by people like Jason Riddley.

"Quaint little burg," I remark to M.

"Yeah ain't it though," she sneers, no trace of an aristocratic manner showing through her professional facade.

We drive down a residential street where the houses are all old colonial types with most of them having dates like 1683 or 1735 posted on them. We go past the town cemetery and turn down a little country lane that recently had been plowed. Some of the houses out this way aren't so bad—are almost modern in fact. But others look even more run down than the ones in town.

"I'll give you ten to one that our Mr. Riddley lives in one of these old-fashioned jobs. What do you think Lt.?"

"I think I wouldn't touch that bet at a thousand to one Capt.," she replies, rapidly shifting her eyes from side to side and keeping her chin pressed down so that her head seems to be sinking into her turned up collar. Can't fool M. She doesn't miss a thing.

We stop in front of an ordinary-looking, two-story saltbox type house, glistening with a fresh coat of barn-red paint and smoke coming out of a chimney. It sits well back from the road and at the foot of a steep, snow-covered, wooded hill.

I slip the cabby another C-note and tell him to go back to town and find a tin can to kick around for a couple of hours and then come back out here and pick us up.

As we approach the house by means of a weathered wooden plank walkway I ask M. what our cover is going to be.

"*Paris Review.*"

"Again?"

"Yeah they fall for it every time. I'll bet he won't ask for any ID either. Imagine!—letting someone into your home without checking their ID. That's New England for you."

Before we can even knock, the door opens and we are greeted by a smiling, late middle-aged woman in a plain housedress who wears a heavy, woolen shawl draped over her shoulders. Mrs. Riddley.

"Do come in and warm yourselves by the fire. I've made coffee. Would you like something to eat? You must have had to leave the city so early." She offers to take our coats but we tell her we prefer to leave them on. She doesn't insist like some people do and ushers us immediately into the living room. The room is surprisingly warm for an old house like this. There's a fire roaring in the hearth and the walls are lined with books and various sorts of antique knickknacks. Except on one wall, where hanging all by itself is an oil painting in a varnished wooden frame. It's a portrait of an old man, a very old man, with a long skinny neck and a furrowed brow and a shock of white hair that cascades down his forehead. He is holding an open book on his lap but his stern gaze is directed straight at the viewer. The face is somehow familiar. And it's also one of those creepy pictures where the eyes seem to follow you around the room.

"Jason will be with you in a moment," says Mrs. Riddley between trips back and forth to the kitchen as she brings in a coffee set-up and several platters of pastries and cookies.

"He's been working all morning. He always gets up early, around five, and works until breakfast."

M. and I exchange looks as if to say, "Where've we heard that one before?"

"He's really been looking forward to seeing you, I know. He mentioned it several times during dinner last night. We had guests as we so often do—we just love company, I do hope you can stay for lunch—and when Jason told them that someone from the *Paris Review* was coming today and how excited he was—well, I tell you, I haven't seen Jason in such a mood since I don't know when."

"Mrs. Riddley, do you know who the person in the painting is?" I ask when she finally stops talking and comes up for air.

"Oh that was in the house when we bought it years ago. We found it in the basement and had it restored, we liked it so much. Jason thinks he must be the ancestor of someone who owned the house before or perhaps even lived here at one time. But we've never found out for sure and probably never will. It's still a mystery. Jason has written a poem about it you know."

"I'll just bet he has."

Lt. M. is busy setting up the cassette tape recorder, which she has taken out of the attaché case. On my lap I balance a cup of coffee and a legal pad on which I had jotted down some questions concerning poetry while on the train—just in case. I pretend to be making notes of what Mrs. Riddley is saying when we hear the sound of footsteps and the stairs creaking and then into the room walks Jason Riddley himself.

To tell the truth, he looks not at all as I had expected. I had thought he would be an older man, more like the fellow in the painting. These poets so often go in for those glowering expressions and penetrating stares. But this guy, even in his plaid shirt, blue cardigan sweater-vest, and wrinkled corduroy pants—a poet's get up if I ever saw one—has more the style and air of a Midwestern dentist, all smiles and glad-hands and overflowing with cornball jokes.

"Well I had no idea that the *Paris Review* sent out such attractive interviewers."

He winks at me then leers at M. the way a dentist does after his victim is strapped down, doped up, and unable to offer the least resistance. But the Lt. ignores him completely and continues fiddling with the knobs on the tape recorder.

"I see my wife has taken good care of you. But what's this? She didn't take your coats. Martha! Please take our guests' coats."

Mrs. Riddley starts to protest but I speak up and explain that we're just fine and prefer to go on wearing our coats.

At this point Mrs. Riddley leaves the room. "Give a holler if you need anything else. More coffee, more cookies, more anything."

Riddley remains standing with his hands behind his back, in front of the fireplace, staring at M. for a long while. But finally he takes a seat in an overstuffed reading chair.

"Will the microphone be able to pick up my voice from over here?" he asks. "Perhaps you'd like to move closer, dear. I can get you another chair."

"It's a very powerful microphone Mr. Riddley," I say. "It'll pick up everything, even the slightest noise."

"Oh well—yes of course—I mean—I only thought—that is—since it's warmer here by the fire, perhaps—"

"No one complained about being cold Mr. Riddley. How about you M.? Are you cold?"

"No I'm not cold. Not at all," she replies, still without looking up.

Riddley's Midwestern smile fades briefly but soon flashes again. "I suppose you'll be asking me all the usual questions regarding work habits, influences, the sources of my ideas.

Perhaps I should begin by telling you about my boyhood days on an Indiana farm. Every morning at four we would arise, my brothers and I, to help our father milk the cows. Often I would be sitting there squeezing a warm teat as the jets of white liquid resonated in the vastness of the cold metal bucket and I would be thinking—"

"Excuse me Mr. Riddley," interrupts M., an unlighted cigarette dangling from her lips. "Do you mind if I smoke?"

"Well, actually, I am getting over a cold and sometimes the smell irritates . . . "

His voice trails off and once again the smile fades when M. pulls out her stainless steel Zippo and lights up. She takes a deep drag, leans back, and exhales a long plume of smoke. "Damn! I really needed a cigarette," she declares.

I know right then and there that Lt. M. is going to be all right. Though I've worked in the field for over twenty years, with all kinds of partners, in all kinds of situations, I think I've found the one for me.

"Well if you're such an addict," Riddley says sarcastically, "then be my guest. But where was I? Did I tell you about my work habits? It's true I never use a computer except to prepare a final draft of something I'm sending to an editor or to a magazine. And I always work in the morning because I feel that's when I'm most in touch with my deeper self. I suppose it has something to do with my upbringing on the farm I mentioned a moment ago. And—excuse me young lady, are you having some sort of problem with the machine?"

M. is randomly punching buttons on the tape recorder— rewinding the tape, advancing it, and playing back what Riddley has just said: first at a fast speed so that his voice becomes all high and fluty like a TV cartoon character's, then slowing it down so that it drags and wheezes and he now sounds like some kind of asthmatic basso profundo.

"No problem at all Mr. Riddley. What makes you ask?" M. has a gleam of sheer inspiration in her eyes, as the ashes from the tip of her cigarette keep falling on the floor.

"Oh I should get you an ashtray. The Mrs. would die if she found ashes on the sofa."

"No need for that Mr. Riddley," M. shouts while springing to her feet. "I was just finishing my cigarette." And saying that she drops it on the polished plank floor and grinds it out with the heel of her boot. Even I am amazed at her behavior. What an agent! What a woman! What an—aristocrat.

Now Riddley is on his feet. "Young lady! Whatever is your problem? I've never met anyone as rude and inconsiderate as you. How on earth could the *Paris Review* have sent someone like you out to conduct an interview? I'm going to have to ask you to leave immediately if you don't stop behaving in this outrageous manner."

I decide that things are getting out of hand. Since Lt. M. and Riddley are both standing, I stand up as well. "I'll take it from here M. Have a seat. And you too Mr. Riddley—have a seat. From now on I'll talk and you'll just answer my questions."

"How dare you come into my home and speak to me this way. I don't have to put up with you or anyone else from your magazine for that matter."

"Look Riddley we're not from the *Paris Review*, in case you haven't figured that out, and I'm telling you once more to sit down."

Riddley moves a couple of steps toward me. "Not from the *Paris Review*? But I thought—"

"I don't care what you thought Riddley, but if you take one more step toward me or my partner you'll regret it."

"Well who are you then? Why are you here?"

M. and I exchange looks. The time has come. I open my coat and show him my badge.

"LITERARY INTELLIGENCE AGENCY—New York Metro Division—Dead Metaphor Squad. I'm Capt. T. and this is my partner Lt. M., Deconstructionist/Post-Modernist Special Investigator. We've got some questions to ask you Riddley and you better have the answers."

"Not the L.I.A.!" Riddley cries out, horror stricken. He backs up and plops down into the overstuffed reading chair as if all the muscles in his legs have turned into sawdust. But after a moment he recovers and a sneer crosses his face.

"You two got nothing on me."

"Is that right."

"Yeah that's right. I've heard about you people—always going around giving artists like me a hard time."

"Just want to ask you some questions Riddley."

"Treating us as if we were criminals or something worse. As if we ought to be ashamed of ourselves because we're creative. What'd you ever create copper? I call you copper because that's just what you are! A dirty, stinking, lousy copper. My only mistake was letting you into my home without asking for any ID. I've told Martha a million times to not let someone into our own house without first asking for ID. Especially someone from New York City."

"Look Riddley, you can save your breath for the jury."

"What do you mean jury? You got nothing on me. I'm clean."

"Oh yeah."

"Yeah. You heard me—clean."

"All right Riddley, let's say you're clean. Let's just suppose that for a minute." M. opens the attaché case and gets out the book. She hands it to me. Riddley says nothing. He grits his teeth and continues to glare at us. He looks like he's posing for his portrait.

"Let me read you something Riddley. A poem. You like poems, don't you Riddley?"

I open the book to the page marked with the paper clip. "Here's a real pretty poem Riddley from a book you might have heard of by the name of *Lunar Lights*." I hold it up so that he can see the cover. The blood drains from his face until it's the color of an overcooked turnip.

I begin to read and continue reading in a low monotone without emphasis on any particular passage. As I finish the final line, his fingers are digging deeply into the arms of his chair.

"Notice anything strange about that poem Riddley?"

"Not particularly."

"You were doing fine Riddley, just fine. The snow, the park, the stars, the trees, the city lights. We could've let you off with nothing more than a warning or even an unfavorable review in the *Times*. Nickel-and-dime stuff Riddley. But there at the end, the part about the rat Riddley, the rat! You went too far. That's where you gave yourself away and now it's going to cost you."

"But good God man, it's only a poem! Besides, it's the truth. I swear. It all happened exactly as I said. It was some years ago and I was crossing the park on my way to a concert in Lincoln Center. It really was snowing and I really did see the stars and the lights of the buildings exactly the way I wrote. I swear I saw the rat too."

"No one doubts that Riddley. You say you saw a rat in the park? No big deal. Must be hundreds of them, thousands of them in Central Park. Doing all sorts of things like walking in the snow and looking for food or a warm hole to sleep in. Other people probably see them all the time too."

"Then so what? What's the L.I.A. want with me?"

"Most people don't go home and write a poem about it Riddley. To most people a rat's a rat. Something ugly, something disgusting. It scares them Riddley. For most people a rat would ruin the whole scene."

"But that's the point! Can't you see? The poet is in a higher state of awareness. He's uplifted by the beauty around him. He is in touch with the macrocosm by means of all he sees and feels. And when the rat appears, the poet is able to see it not the way most people would, not in a conventional way, not simply as a rat, but as part of a totality in which even the apparently ugly and disgusting is subsumed by the harmony of the Whole." He is talking excitedly and running his hands through his hair. His voice rises as he jumps up and spreads his arms. "It's not just a rat! It's something else. It's something completely metaphysical. It's like a glimpse of the universal order, an intuition which reveals the beauty of every single part, every aspect, in a way that we can't even begin to approach or comprehend except through poetry."

The smiling midwestern dentist has long since turned into an impassioned 19th century-style Romantic. He's a regular Brian/Sheats/and Kelley all rolled up into one as he stands there gasping for breath, clenching and unclenching his fists, his eyes ablaze.

I walk across the room and stand looking, as if in deep thought, at the dying embers of the fire. There follows a long silence.

"You know you poets make me sick," I say finally. "You tell us now it's not a rat at all. It's the cosmos or some kind of mumbo-jumbo like that. Like it's a big joke on anybody else who'd walk through there and just see a rat."

"But it's true. It's true. As far as poetry is concerned," he replies. And then he puts his shoulders back and puffs out his chest. His voice rises. "Maybe you people at the L.I.A. haven't heard that poetry proclaims a higher truth."

I have him right where I want him.

M. knows exactly what to do. She reaches once more into the attaché case and produces Exhibit A. She flings it in his direction and he cries out—just like they all do.

Mrs. Riddley, hearing the commotion from the kitchen, comes running into the room. "Jason! Jason! What's going on in here? Does anybody need more coffee? Why are you standing on the chair? But what's that on the floor? Why—it's—a—a—it's a—!!" and she starts screaming too.

"Don't worry Mrs. Riddley," I say. "It's only a specimen. It's filled with nothing more than sawdust. We only used it to prove a point." M. goes over and picks Exhibit A up off the floor. She holds it by the tail and dangles it like a pendulum in front of Riddley who is still cringing with fear. Then she tosses it back into the attaché case.

Riddley is trembling all over. His nerves are shot. "What happens now?" he mumbles.

"What happens now Mr. Riddley is that we've got to take

you in. You'll be booked and fingerprinted and there'll be some people who'll want to ask you some more questions. It'll be something like a *Paris Review* interview. And if you cooperate there's no reason why you won't be back at your desk in about six or seven years."

"And it I don't cooperate?"

I just shrug. "Put the cuffs on him Lt."

"Will you be taking him back to New York?" Mrs. Riddley asks.

"No ma'am that won't be necessary. We'll take him to our office in New Haven. They'll take it from there. My partner and I are only up here today on special assignment. However, since *Lunar Lights* does bear a New York imprint, your husband will probably have to go there to stand trial. We're just investigators Mrs. Riddley. We'll have nothing more to do with the case after he's booked."

"Oh I see. I see. Perhaps during the trial I can come to New York to be with Jason in court. Besides, there are so many museums that I've been wanting to visit. Is Placido Domingo appearing at the Met this season? Where can I pick up a Knicks schedule? And do you know if I can get *Phantom of the Opera* or *Lion King* tickets at the box office on the same day as the performance?"

"I couldn't say ma'am."

"Good Lord Martha—you're such an idiot!" Riddley shakes his head in despair.

"Oh Jason don't be so testy. You're always so testy with me when your work isn't going well. But you'll need your coat won't you? And will you folks need a ride to New Haven? I have some shopping to do and I can get the car warmed up in a jiffy."

"Don't bother Mrs. Riddley." I check my watch. "We've got a cab on the way. But it you don't mind I could use another cup of coffee. I think we all could use a cup. And say, I never did get anything to eat and those pastries sure look tempting . . . "

Mrs. Riddley makes some more coffee and we all sit around like a bunch of aristocrats—eating, drinking, and smoking M.'s cigarettes until the cab arrives, right on time. I slip the cabby another C-note and tell him to take us back to L.I.A. headquarters in New Haven. He knows just where to go. When we arrive, M. waits in the cab while I take Riddley inside. "I won't be but a minute Lt."

Riddley hasn't uttered a word since we left his house. I deliver him to the desk and the officer-on-duty whistles in amazement when he sees who has been brought in. "Jason Riddley—wow. We've been after him for years. What'd you nail him on? These free verse birds are hard to catch."

It's been a long day and I'm not in the mood to stand there yakking with some rookie desk jockey right out of grad school. I fill out the papers as fast as I can and turn Riddley over to him. As he leads Riddley away, down a long hallway, already putting questions to him, it makes me wonder about the kind of people they're hiring at the L.I.A. these days when I hear things like, "Mr. Riddley would you please compare and contrast the ramifications of the proposition that by the frequent employment of nature-imagery you are attempting to mediate between the post-millennial sensibility and a type of reality that evokes a pre-verbal, pre-gender conscious recognition, thereby eliciting a non-cognitive, non-reifying response on the part of the implied reader, with reference to the Lacanian axiom that holds that the phenomenological site of any poetic assertion is impossible to establish in so far as the symbological, semiotic, and the hermeneutical codes are evidenced by the textual performance itself rather than originating with the latent residual awareness or perhaps unawareness of any particular reader . . . etc." I'm glad I don't have to stick around for the full interrogation. It won't be very pretty. Thirty minutes of that, after they tie him down and shine the lights in his eyes, and Riddley will melt like a bar of soap floating in the Hudson. I would too.

Back in the cab on the way to the train station M. is pensive.

"It's not that Riddley is such a bad poet," she says," I mean if you consider his body of work as a whole."

"You're right Lt. But you have to remember how it is with some of these guys when they get down to the city, they think it's anything goes."

Once we're on the train to New York however, her mood brightens. Both of our moods brighten.

"What's your assignment for this evening Lt.?" I ask.

"Oh nothing very exciting. The library stakeout on 42nd Street. Not much fun. How about you?"

"Poetry reading up at the 92nd Street Y. But I was thinking of calling the office and begging off."

"Begging off? I didn't think you ever begged off assignments Capt."

"I don't usually. And if you'd like, I could make a phone call and maybe get your assignment switched as well. Like to a little Italian restaurant in the Village I know about, with candles and a red-checked table cloth, and a bottle of *Chianti*, and . . . "

"Sounds pretty dangerous to me Capt. I'd probably need a partner. Know anybody who might volunteer?" We exchange looks and both laugh.

"You know something Lt.? I'm beginning to think you can read me just like a book."

THE FRIENDS OF KEN

Dealing with the telephone often can be problematic for me. Maybe it's because I am not a good listener. More than once my wife has accused me of that both in person and on the phone. What can I say? I plead guilty. Besides, it's the only way to get her to stop talking about the subject. I've never considered a ringing telephone to be an interruption or a nuisance so much as an indication from the outside world that there really is an outside world. And then there's the element of chance. Whenever the phone rings you never know who might be calling.

*

Several years ago when I was living in a different town, a town much smaller than where I live now, my telephone number was very similar to one for a local bank—a matter of the last two digits being reversed. It was not the bank's main number, which was probably something that ended in a string of zero's, but a secondary number that was actually a connection to an automated service that provided the time and temperature. Everyone in the town knew the number. It had been the same for as long as anyone could remember and it was dialed very frequently. The law of averages determined that there should be at least an occasional error. My own phone seldom rang. This was before I was married and I knew hardly anybody in that town. But when my phone did ring I would always hasten to answer it. Most of the time when I said hello there would be a pause and then a click and the line would go dead, the caller realizing right away that he or she had dialed incorrectly. But there was a certain woman who did not hang up, who whenever she called would invariably ask me what the time and the temperature were.

If I happened to know I simply told her and she would thank me and that was the end of it. More than once however, when I didn't know the time or temperature or wasn't sure or was busy doing something else and tried to explain this to her, she became flustered and sounded distraught. She couldn't understand how there could be such uncertainty on the part of the bank. I would then tell her to hold on while I checked the clock in another room or even went outside in order to provide her with a rough estimate of the temperature. I had no problem with this woman whoever she was. She sounded elderly, and she didn't call all that often.

There was another woman that would call late at night or in the early morning. An ill-tempered drunk apparently. I didn't offer to provide her with any service. She called me repeatedly one night and demanded to know why I didn't know the time or the temperature or at least why I refused to tell her. She asked who my supervisor was. She said she kept a lot of money in the bank and if I thought I could treat her like that she was going to drive down to the bank that very minute and use the ATM to take every last penny out. I told her to go ahead, that I could care less what she did with her money.

For a long while, a couple of years perhaps, I regularly had encounters with another late-night caller. It had nothing to do with the bank's phone number—it was just some teenager with time on his hands. He'd started out with the typical stupid prank calls all kids make. But he had a real imagination too. He once disguised his voice and said he was from a radio station and that if I was willing to discuss some things of a personal nature I would be elegible to win $10,000. Supposedly it a was a kind of marketing survey, and he then proceeded to pose a number of detailed questions concerning my preferences as a consumer of peanut butter, of laundry detergent, of car wax, of condoms. Sometimes he'd claim to be doing political polls. Or he'd identify himself as a Detective Connor from the local police department and wanted me to come down to the station to be interrogated. I always caught immediately on and would then put him on as well. I'd provide nonsense or bogus answers. I'd pretend to lose my temper and he really enjoyed that. We both did. I would scream obscenities into the phone and tell him that I was going to find his skinny little ass then wring his pimply neck. I called him a sorry son of a bitch and a geek and a little bastard and a loser and said I was going to have the calls traced and notify his parents. He would laugh loudly and hang up. But when he did not call for some time, I found myself wondering what had become of him. Finally, one evening around seven just as I was sitting down to eat, the phone rang and it was him. He explained why the calls had stopped. He had been away at college. He'd gotten a scholarship to Wesleyan University in Connecticut and things were going exceedingly well. He said that after he graduated he intended to move to Boston or New York and become a journalist. I congratulated him on his scholarship and future plans and wished him well.

"Who knows, maybe you'll find a good job with a newspaper and become famous." I told him he could call me any time—collect if he wanted to, from school even, but I never heard from him again.

∗

It wasn't my idea to get an answering machine. A friend of my wife's from work had bought a new one and given her her old one. She brought it home one night and I hooked it up. It worked fine for awhile but then the little tape wore out and the messages didn't get properly recorded and couldn't be played back, so I unplugged the thing and threw it away. My wife insisted she still needed something for her incoming calls. She contacted the phone company because they offered a service such that you didn't need any type of mechanical device in your home. The phone would ring a certain number of times and an automated voice came on and told the caller to leave a short message and a number and their call would be returned. It was reasonably priced, only a small extra charge buried in a column of figures on the monthly phone bill, so it worked out fine. We each had a separate sequence of numbers to punch in that enabled us to check our own messages. She never told me her code and I never her told her mine. Not that it mattered. Neither of us received any calls of great importance.

But one day last January when I did bother to check, there was a long message from somebody who identified himself only as "Gary", and said that he was "a friend of Ken's." I didn't know anyone named Gary, or at least anyone who would have been calling me. I didn't know anyone named Ken either. Gary apologized for not having been in touch for a while and said he hoped I had enjoyed the holidays. He said he didn't know if I had heard that Ken had died in December. He went on to say that though it was neither sudden nor unexpected, still when death actually happens, there's inevitably a sense of shock and of loss. There had been no funeral—at Ken's request— but plans were being made to hold a memorial service later on and he would keep me posted. Gary ended by saying, "If you want to get in touch with Mary, she'd really like to hear from anyone who knew Ken or was close to him."

Since this was obviously a wrong number I immediately erased the message.

Some eight or nine months went by and I gave it not another thought until there was another message from Gary, and as promised he provided further details concerning the memorial gathering for Ken. It was to be held at a church although not in the main sanctuary, rather in a meeting room that the congregation used for its own functions and sometimes rented out to groups for various events—poetry readings, dance performances, art exhibits, community gatherings. Gary said that he would be there and so would Mary. "We both hope you will be able to come." My recollection of the previous message was that Mary had been married to Ken or involved with him such that she had needed consoling, but it sounded like she was with Gary now. Or perhaps this Gary had been closer to Ken than I had thought. Maybe he was a brother or a companion instead of just a friend. It was all unclear. The time of the event also seemed a little strange—10:30 PM on Friday night of the following week.

The next day there was yet another message on my phone and this one was from Mary. In none of these messages had they asked for anyone by name or left a number for a return call. This suggested to me that several calls were being made in a short period of time with the same message in order to notify those whose numbers were on some kind of list, mine by mistake presumably. It further suggested that the callers, Gary and Mary, were not necessarily acquainted with those whose names were on this list. Mary said she was following up on the flyer that had been sent out concerning the gathering for Ken. Apparently not everyone had received it. She very much hoped I could make it. She also said to spread the word and feel free to bring a guest. "The most important thing is to remember Ken and to celebrate his life and to let as many people as possible know about him and all that he accomplished." I had thought that if I happened to answer the phone and was able to actually speak to Gary or Mary I would tell them they had been calling the wrong number. But after hearing Mary's latest message I changed my mind. Whoever it was they were attempting to reach by phone had surely received the flyer and could decide for themselves if they wanted to attend Ken's memorial. As a matter of fact, I was considering going myself since Mary had said that it basically open to anybody.

I mentioned to my wife that someone named Ken had died in December and that there would be a memorial for him late on Friday night. "He didn't want a funeral," I said.

She asked me if I was going to the memorial and I told her I thought I would.

"Do you think they're expecting me too?"

"I doubt it. I mean you never met Ken so I don't see the point."

We both agreed it wasn't necessary for her to go.

*

It was a dreary, rainy night as I made my way to the memorial gathering for this fellow Ken. I had to wait for a bus near my house for nearly half an hour but at least I didn't have to transfer to another one. I entered the church by means of a side door beneath a low portico where everyone had been directed to by a handwritten sign on the iron fence in front of the building. I found myself in a small foyer with three doors. One of them to the left was marked *Sanctuary* and had another handwritten sign on it that read "Keep Out." The door to the right was propped open and one could see directly into the church kitchen. The door in the middle was unmarked but led into the meeting room. Thumbtacked to this door was a large black and white photograph of a strikingly handsome man with silver hair and a deep tan. A third handwritten sign below the photograph said "We Remember Ken—The Man Who Touched So Many." I opened this door and walked through it.

The large room was quite crowded. A young woman sat at a table a few steps inside. "Are you here for Ken?" she asked and I thought she meant I was supposed to pay or buy a ticket of admission from her.

I stood there for a moment in my dripping overcoat trying to decide what to say. When I finally told her yes I was she smiled and nodded and gave me a look that indicated I was now free to continue into the room. No ticket was necessary. She was just some kind of a greeter. On one side of the room there were three tables set up. On the one in the middle there was a large punch bowl filled not with punch but with water where several small candles floated like little boats with flaming sails. Next to the punch bowl was a memorial book in which people were invited to inscribe their names and share their thoughts and recollections of Ken. On another table, stacks multi-colored booklets and pamphlets were identified by a small handwritten placard as being "Ken's Works", and also "For Sale. Individually Or In Lots." There was also a copy of the flyer that Mary had referred to when she had left the phone message about this evening's gathering. "Friends of Ken will be coming together to share their memories . . . . Wine and cheese reception . . . . " the flyer read and then it gave the address of the church and today's date and the 10:30 starting time.

On a third table was a set up of wines—both red and white, already opened—and bottles of water. On this table there was also an array of cheeses and different kinds of crackers as well as a large bowl of mixed nuts with raisins. There were plastic wineglasses and plastic knives set out along with some small paper plates and napkins. Nobody was assigned to pour the wine or slice the cheeses. It was strictly a self-service operation. People were helping themselves without any prompting.

I looked around for a place to hang my coat and spotted a moveable coat rack in a corner near the back of the room. It was already packed tight with wet overcoats and jackets. A large bucket served as an umbrella stand and it too was jammed full of umbrellas of various sizes and styles. I found the last unused hanger on the rack, but instead of forcing my coat into the middle of things I hung it on one end so that the rounded tip of the hanger just barely caught hold of the horizontal rod which held all the other garments.

Everyone stood in clusters around each of the tables and a

line had formed to write in the memorial book. On the table with the pamphlets and the flyer was a poster-sized enlargement of the black and white photograph that was thumbtacked to the door in the foyer. Ken was a man with rugged good looks that were emphasized by his glowing skin and wind-blown hair. He appeared to be staring pensively at something that lay in the distance behind the photographer or the viewer. There were several large white unidentifiable masses in the background behind him. They could have been clouds or mountains, the sides of buildings, or the interior walls of a photographer's studio. But something about the image of Ken himself suggested he was outdoors and bracing himself against the elements.

Around the walls of the room hung similar pictures—similar in that they were also black and white photographs of what might be clouds or snow-capped mountains or even examples of post-modern architecture—but without the presence of Ken or any other human being.

I poured myself some wine and took a few of the nuts and raisins. I cut off a small piece of Brie and spread it on a cracker. The opposite side of the room was lined with rows of chairs that faced a podium with a small mic-stand. A fellow in a dark suit and a bow tie, one of the few people in the room dressed in anything approaching formal attire, was scurrying about setting up a sound system. Apparently the evening's proceedings would be tape-recorded as well as amplified.

More people were arriving. Something of a bottleneck had formed just inside the door as each person who entered stopped at the table where the young woman was sitting. I still kept expecting to see someone take out a wallet or reach into a purse and give her some money. Once inside, nearly everyone went right for the wine and the cheese and the mixed nuts with raisins then moved towards one of the other two tables. Clusters of people would form and chat, and then the clusters would break up as new clusters were formed when a particular conversation had ended and a new one commenced. It was a diverse crowd of young and old and middle-aged. Only a very few appeared to be in a similar situation to my own, that is, to not be acquainted with anyone else in the room. I was still trying to determine who Mary might be and which one was Gary. I poured myself some more wine and then stood near the table with the floating candles and the memorial book, hoping to get a clue.

"So how well did you know Ken?" Although I should have known that this question was bound to come up I still wasn't really prepared for it. I had not heretofore even noticed the woman who now was speaking to me. She was rather non-descript. Short brown hair. Thick glasses. Little or no make-up except for some bright pink lipstick that was slightly smeared on one side at the corner of her mouth. She seemed to have materialized out of thin air.

"Not all that well, I suppose. But Ken was a man with a lot of friends—that's pretty obvious." I hoped my interlocutor would at once decide I was a most boring and unimportant person and go find somebody else to talk to. I certainly didn't want to reveal my reasons for being here.

"When was the last time you saw him?"

"Oh—I don't really remember, to tell you the truth."

"Was it before he got sick?"

"Before?"

"So it was probably after."

"After? I suppose so but not too long after. But I never expected him to uh—to leave so soon. I didn't realize he was so sick."

"Well two years is not all that soon. Three actually, if you count the time when he wasn't talking to anybody."

"Yes, yes you're right about that. That's for sure. When was the last time you saw him?"

"I don't know for certain. Maybe that last spring. He was sick then. But not that sick. I mean I guess he was pretty sick but he wasn't really dying. I wanted to take some pictures but he wouldn't let me."

"Some pictures? Of what?"

"Of Ken of course."

"So you're a photographer?" As soon as I said it I regretted it. I didn't want this conversation to gather any kind of momentum.

"Oh I just like to take pictures. I'm not a professional."

"Interesting." I nodded.

"Ken let me take his picture only that one time. But that was before he got sick."

"Only once? Hmm."

"You would think somebody as vain as Ken would love to have his picture taken."

"Why did he let you take it that one time?"

"Do you mean why did he let me take it only one time or why did he let me take it that particular time?"

"I suppose I'd like to know the answer either way." Actually I didn't.

"Well so would I. He never told me. Maybe he didn't like me."

"Oh I'm sure that's not true."

"He was always afraid of being exploited."

"By his friends?"

"By anyone who knew him. But yes, by his friends, especially by his so-called friends."

She seemed to be quite perturbed about the matter, as if there had been some sort of recent incident.

"So no pictures after Ken got sick."

"Oh he let me take some pictures of the house and of his garden. I got some good shots of Al too."

Of Al? Who was Al? I could only nod.

"And then he showed me his leg."

"Ah." Whose leg did she mean? Al's leg? Ken's?

"I didn't ask to see his leg or anything. I would never have been so indiscreet. I tried to respect his privacy."

"And how was it? His leg?"

"It was awful. I've never seen anything like that before—so swollen and black and blue, as if it had been injured somehow. It looked all mangled. No wonder he lost it."

Now I could only slowly shake my head. We were back on firmer ground, perhaps. Somebody had lost his leg. A leg was missing. Did anybody find a leg? I felt like this conversation would never end.

"Oh Tim—how are you? So good to see you again."

At this point an older fellow with an ample stomach and red blotchy skin joined us. His white hair was thin and wispy. Nothing at all like Ken's thick mane. He was wearing a sagging pair of jeans and a denim jacket that was saturated from the rain.

"Can I get you something to drink? Tim McCarthy this is— oh I'm sorry I've forgotten your name. Do introduce yourself to each other while I get something. Would you like some wine Tim?"

"Would I like some wine? Yes, yes, ah yes. I really do want wine but I'll have to settle for water instead. I'd like some whiskey too but I'll have just the water. Just the goddamned water. The goddamned doctor's orders."

Tim assumed a wistful demeanor as if he were now recalling his long-ago whiskey-drinking days.

"What a night for this." He finally spoke. "Such a dirty night as the Irish would say. And starting so late. Why is it starting so late? I'll have to find somebody to give me a ride home. My daughter brought me here but she isn't staying. I wouldn't do this for anybody else but Ken. He was one of a kind that Ken."

I nodded in agreement with everything Tim was saying. The foul weather. The lateness of the hour. The uniqueness of Ken.

"How long did you know him?" I inquired after another lengthy silence.

"Ken?"

I couldn't imagine whom else he thought I might be referring to.

"Ken and I go back all the way. Sixty years at least, maybe longer. A couple of old salts we were."

"Sailors?"

"The sea was in our blood."

"You were in the navy?"

"I sure was—served in the Pacific during the war. Leyte Gulf. Battle of Midway."

"Ken was with you? You were onboard ship together? You fought together?"

"Nah."

"No?"

"Ken never served. He was a pacifist or so he claimed. He worked in a military hospital. He pushed gurneys. He changed bedpans."

"But I thought you both had the sea in your blood."

"That's because we both grew up in Gloucester, Massachusetts. Ken's father was a fisherman by profession. He used to go out on the boats with him."

"And did he follow him into the business?"

"Nah."

"I wonder why not?"

"It was because his father drowned during a storm when Ken was eleven. He was lost at sea. His body was never recovered. His mother said the one thing she wouldn't allow was for her son to become a fisherman. She worked hard so he could go to college and not be like his brothers and sisters. They all worked but he was the youngest so he didn't have to work. He had time to study. That's how he got to go to college. He would never have amounted to anything if he'd kept on fishing."

"Well maybe he would have." I kept thinking that even if I didn't know Ken I perhaps knew who he was. That he was someone famous.

"Well I wouldn't have known Ken. Because that's how we met in the first place. At the colony I mean. I had just left my second wife."

I was losing the threads of the narrative. "But you knew Ken before that, you said, in Gloucester when you were boys. The sea was in your blood. In his blood. In both of your bloods.

I mean you each had your own blood—" I really had no idea what I was saying.

"Ah but we had lost touch. I had moved away with my family. They were merchants. My father had a hardware store. And then we moved down to New York. My mother had come from there. Long Island. It was a long way from Gloucester and I never went back. I didn't come from a fishing family. There was no reason to go back."

"And that was how long ago?"

"Sixty years—maybe more."

"And this colony—"

"Here you are Tim." The woman had returned with a glass of wine and one filled with water.

"Oh on a night such as this to be drinking water. At my age." Tim seemed to be growing more despondent by the moment. The conversation came to a complete halt while he took a long slow drink.

What kind of colony was he talking about? Was it the name of a restaurant? An artist colony perhaps? A nudist colony? I tried to get things going again.

"This colony—where you say you met Ken—"

"I told you, we knew each other in Gloucester. We were boys."

"Then where you perhaps became reacquainted with Ken."

"That's right."

"Where was this colony?"

"It was in New Hampshire or Vermont, I don't remember. It moved from year to year. It's not around anymore."

"What kind of people were at the colony?"

"All kinds of people. You'd be surprised."

"And what happened at this colony. What did you do there?"

"Well every night at dinner for instance we would gather in a large room that was like a lodge. Afterwards, we would entertain one anther. Ken was always the life of the party—any party—and not only at the colony. What a talker he was. The stories he would tell. Everybody loved Ken. Especially the women. That's not news to anybody."

"I see." The sound of a piano came from another part of the room. I looked over to a corner beyond the podium and saw a young man in his mid-20's playing in an exuberant manner. The piano's existence was something else I had not noticed until then. It sounded as if the young man was improvising various chord sequences and notes, just making things up as he went along rather than playing any particular compositions.

"I don't see McMahon here yet. He's still supposed to come isn't he?" Tim's eyes darted all around. The woman with the pink lipstick was now distracted and talking to an older woman wearing a shawl over her shoulders and large hoop earrings.

I said I wasn't sure but I thought he would come.

"It's such a dirty night that he might not make it."

Tim and the woman in the shawl were staring at one another without speaking. I didn't know if they were already acquainted. It could be they were total strangers, but neither would I have been surprised to be told that they had once been married. I wasn't sure if I should say something or just move quietly away.

"Hello Rita, hello Tim." A past middle-aged woman in a flower-print blouse and with a flower behind her ear now joined our group. She had thick dark hair with a wide streak of silver in it. She was holding her drink in one hand and a cigarette in the other. Apparently in a church was the one place you were allowed to smoke these days. She was speaking to Tim and the woman in the shawl as if she knew both of them quite well although I still couldn't tell if they knew each other. "And you're Louise aren't you?" she said to the woman with the pink lipstick I had been speaking to at first. "I'm so glad all of you could come."

Could this be Mary?

"Yes I'm Louise and you must be Vivian."

Vivian? Now who is Vivian? What about Mary?

"That's right."

I stood there and said nothing. I glanced around the room.

I was distracted by the piano music. I didn't realize this Vivian was speaking to me and didn't hear what she said even though she was looking at me fixedly, as if expecting me to respond to a question. It felt like a bit of cracker or a small piece of peanut was caught in my throat. I took a sip of wine. I coughed. I could only shrug my shoulders in order to indicate I was momentarily indisposed and unable to answer.

"Well aren't you being rather curt," she said somewhat icily.

I felt embarrassed, falsely accused. How could she have formed such an immediate opinion? Perhaps she was just being witty or ironic. Perhaps the others hadn't heard.

Before I could respond—and I still wasn't really sure what she meant or how I ought to proceed—the woman in the shawl, Rita, speaking in a slightly raised, slightly fluttery voice said, "Oh so this is the famous Curtis we've heard so much about."

"I don't know—I mean—I can be—that is—what exactly have you heard?" My throat was clearing slightly. I took another sip of wine.

"Only what Ken used to say," answered Vivian.

"And what did he say?"

"That he admired your work. He thought you had a lot of talent—that you were brilliant in fact—but you could never finish things. That you often dashed from one project to another."

"Too many irons in the fire. Too many pots cooking on the stove." Tim was studying his glass of water and he spoke as if he had found these phrases floating around in there like ice cubes. Each of the women stared at me intently. The piano music was growing louder. I wondered if the pianist wasn't actually Curtis. He played short riffs and condensed pieces that sounded as if they had been taken from longer works but without any sense of completion or closure. One thing was just melding with another thing.

"Of course Ken was one to talk. If there was anyone who had a hard time finishing things it was Ken." It now sounded as if Louise, the woman with the bright lipstick, was coming to my defense.

"But he didn't really move from thing to another, although it would have been better if he had," Vivian interjected. "He had a very focused mind even if he did keep a cluttered desk with his files and papers always scattered everywhere. And of course there was what he always described as his *grand projet.*"

"Oh Ken and his great work. Mostly a series of pilot projects." Louise gestured in the direction of the table where the booklets and pamphlets were stacked. "Was anybody familiar with it in its entirety? Did he ever show it to someone? I mean he let people see parts of it but I don't think anyone had any sense of what it was going to be in its completed state." Louise had at least been able to take those pictures of Ken's house and garden so one would assume she must have known whereof she spoke. And of course she had seen the leg.

"You see for Ken it was a kind of immortality. Like a never-ending song. Like *Finnegan's Wake*—where the first line of the work is the same as the last. But there was always more to be done. Always more worlds to conquer." These words had burst from Tim all at once in a startling fit of eloquence, and then he resumed glumly staring at his glass of water.

"Well perhaps Ken saw things in Curtis that he was able to recognize because he likewise saw them in himself. Maybe that's all he meant." It sounded like Rita was also somewhat sympathetic. I was uncomfortable at being the center of this conversation. I would have liked to steer it in another direction, to say something a propos Ken and the *grand projet,* if I only had some clue as to what it actually was. I noticed the ash from Vivian's cigarette was just about to fall. Looking around for an ashtray and seeing none, I offered her my plastic wineglass containing only the dregs of some white wine.

"Oh aren't you nice?" Apparently Vivian wasn't aware or didn't care that nowadays one was customarily obliged to go stand outside and smoke. But it really was a dirty night, as Tim had described it. I was glad she had changed her opinion of me. As she spoke, she glanced past me towards the door at a man in a dripping overcoat and sporting a wide-brimmed hat. With the right upright bend on either side and perhaps a leather cord around its high crown it would have passed for a cowboy hat. Whatever it was, it was one impressive hat.

McMahon was here at last, Rita declared, and now the program could get underway.

But Tim objected vehemently. "That's not McMahon! McMahon is stockier and has a dark beard. Some people mistake him for a Negro or a Mexican. Besides, McMahon would never wear a hat like that."

If indeed McMahon was short and heavy and dark featured then this fellow was definitely not their man. A helmet of blonde hair was revealed as soon as he took off his hat. He was in fact very tall with bushy blonde eyebrows and fierce blue eyes like that of a Viking warrior or a Nazi SS Officer. He removed his overcoat in a most dramatic fashion and looked around as if he expected someone to come out of the crowd and take it from him. And that's exactly what happened. My own coat was still barely hanging on the portable rack in the corner. It was not a particularly tall piece of furniture and the bottoms of the longer coats jammed onto it were touching the floor. The fellow in the bow tie who had been setting up the mic-stand minutes before took the Viking's coat and hat and gestured toward the tables with the wine and the *hors d'oeuvres*. The newest arrival nodded without smiling and his gaze took in the rest of the room. His eyes rested momentarily on my little group before his attention was captured by the pianist who had now worked himself up into a positive fury.

I wanted to ask if someone knew who this strange pianist was. For all I knew it could have been Gary or Al or someone else who was close to Ken. It certainly wasn't McMahon. The SS Officer looked resplendent in a dark blue, expensively tailored suit and a white turtleneck. He was easily the best-dressed person in the room.

And Vivian recognized him. "Oh my it's Günter. I can't believe he came. I haven't seen him in years. He and Ken used to be inseparable until they had their famous falling out. I don't think I ever heard Ken utter one kind word or flattering remark about him in the last twenty years."

And then a flicker of recognition appeared on Günter's face when he happened to take a second radar sweep across the room with his eyes and spied our group once more. At least he was Günter and not the famous Curtis, whose role I was still playing. Of course I could not be sure that Curtis wouldn't also be arriving late. As Günter approached our group I wondered to whom he would speak first. I was taken aback, and so were the others, when he came up and stood in front of me. Ignoring the women as well as Tim, he put his left hand on my right shoulder and offered his other hand. Staring at me intently he said, "So my friend, we meet again."

I felt as if I inhabited some sort of x-ray force field. The eyebeams directed at me must surely have been burning through my clothing and skin and tissue to expose the collection of bones that constituted my actual skeleton. I met Günter's gaze, but for some reason blinked my eyes and held them shut for several seconds. I'm certain none of them had the slightest idea what this gesture was supposed to mean. I certainly didn't. When I opened them again Günter had shifted his attention. He was now staring at the nearly empty wineglass I still held in my hand that contained the butt of Vivian's cigarette. His bushy blonde eyebrows quivered slightly.

"One can smoke in here?" Günter didn't wait for an answer. He produced a silver filigree cigarette case and removed a short stubby filtered cigarette that was no doubt of non-American origin. He didn't offer one to anyone else before putting the case away and then lighting his cigarette with a slender lighter that produced a prodigious flame. He had an air about him suggesting that he not only expected to be catered to, but that his every gesture and remark carried great import. He took a drag on his cigarette and exhaled an enormous cloud

of smoke and then uttered a long sigh. Was it because he and
Ken had never reconciled that he was sighing or because he
had had to come here in the first place? I wasn't sure if I was
up to it, but it now seemed incumbent upon me to find out
which, if not for my own sake, then for everyone else's.

"Would you care for something to drink?" was the best I
could come up with under the circumstances however.

"Of course. I'll have the same as whatever you are drinking
my friend."

"Yes, I do need to freshen my drink up a bit." That was
supposed to be an amusing riposte but no one was smiling. I
sort of slunk away from the group and tried not to think about
what they might be saying about me. Why Günter claimed he
recognized me I had no idea. He obviously had forgotten the
name of the person he took me to be. I saw that his coat had
been carefully hung while mine had been removed from its
hanger and was draped precariously over the top of the coat
rack. I made my way through the crowd that was gathered
near the wine and cheese table and past the line that was waiting
to write in the memorial book next to the floating candles in
the punch bowl. I tried once more to have a look at the booklets
and pamphlets that were displayed on the third table along
with the flyer announcing the evening's gathering. They
resembled high school literary magazines but the titles made
it impossible to discern exactly what the contents might be or
even what field of endeavor they dealt with or were an
expression of. *The Oldest Lie . . . Seven Cities Below the Dam . . . The
Cry of the Hawk . . . Who Is To Say? . . . The First Sunday of the Last
Month . . . Follow the Drums . . . The Thunderbolt Brigade . . .* They
could have been brief works of fiction or poetry or some type
of criticism or conjectures on historical topics. They might just
as easily have been religious or philosophical or some other
type of speculative tracts. I picked up a copy of *The Earnest
Man Who Refused to Choose* and was about to put it in my pocket
when Louise, my original interlocutor, once again approached
me.

"I had no idea you knew Günter."

"Well, I—"

"Did Ken know?"

"Did Ken know what?"

"That you were a friend of Günter's too. That you knew him."

"Well I wouldn't exactly say we were friends."

"An acquaintance—whatever. Did Ken know that?"

"I don't think so."

"Because if he did I can't imagine how he would have tolerated your presence to the extent he apparently did. I simply can't fathom such a thing."

"He didn't really tolerate me. He did criticize me after all. He said I didn't finish things."

"Oh he criticized everyone. You should have heard what he said about me."

"Like what."

"Do you really want to know?"

Actually I could have cared less. "Tell me, I'm very curious now."

"It was when I was taking the pictures of his house and the ones of Al."

"What happened?"

"I thought a picture of Al sitting on his lap would be appealing . . . "

Appealing to whom? "And?"

"But you would think that I had suggested that the two of them assume some kind of pornographic pose."

"Perhaps it might be slightly provocative, but surely not pornographic."

"But Ken was livid. He said I was always trying to exploit Al. That I would no doubt be trying to make a buck off her by putting any picture I took of her on the cover of a calendar."

"Of her?" Did Al = Alexandra? Or Alexis? Or Alex? Still, a picture—any picture—of a woman sitting on a man's lap might be considered suggestive, even if one of them was missing a leg.

"Ken was sick by then. There was no way to reason with him to try and change his mind. And perhaps he was right. But one thing's for sure, Al was right there to the end with him."

I wondered now about Mary. If this Al was there with Ken to the end—bad leg and all—whoever's leg it might have been, then where was she? And what about Gary?

"Did Mary call you afterwards?" I was hoping to break up what had become a hopeless logjam in my mind. Who was who at this gathering and why were they here? That is, while I had learned several people's name, I still had no idea what they did or how they knew Ken. It was still unclear to me who Ken was or what he did or how he was able to touch the lives of so many.

"Mary? Why would she call me? She's the last person I would expect to call."

"Maybe she called one of the others—Rita or Tim or even Günter."

"Maybe. But she hasn't spoken to me in years. Everyone knows that. Even before Ken got sick she had crossed me off her list."

These were certainly murky depths. I didn't want to get into the nature of Louise's relationship with Mary. Or anybody's relationship with anyone for that matter. But it was too late for that I suppose.

"Of course it's so ironic that his Al is with Mary now."

"Al? With Mary?" I was genuinely surprised. And perplexed. I also detected something about the way Louise said the name 'Al'. She pronounced it more like 'Owl', rhyming with 'howl' instead of with 'Hal'. It was a very slight alteration and I wasn't certain I had just heard her say it that way. Or had she been perhaps saying it that way all along and I had simply not noticed? I would have to pay more attention and also try to think along two tracks. His 'owl' was with Mary?

"He wouldn't have her around after she bit him."

"She bit him? Where?" On the leg perhaps? Before he lost it?

"On his arm. And she scratched him on the face too. I

asked him again if I could take a picture of only him but he wouldn't hear of that either."

But not on the leg. "He refused?"

"He didn't want anyone to see him bleeding or wounded. He had a thing about scars."

"And he was sick too."

"Exactly."

"Where did this happen? What were the circumstances?"

"In bed. Evidently he had rubbed her the wrong way or she became so over-stimulated that she attacked him. It wasn't the first time this had happened but she had never actually drawn blood before. Something had to be done."

"I should say so. But what can Mary do with her?"

"Oh she was Mary's before she was Ken's."

"She was Mary's—?" What?

"Exactly. She was just left behind sort of. It was sad. Ken had taken care of her for such a long time. He loved her and she loved him but she could be so—vicious. There's no other way to describe it."

I had already disposed of the wineglass with the doused cigarette and now poured two more glasses of wine, one for myself and one for Günter. Louise was pouring water for herself and for Tim apparently. Neither of us had a free hand for getting any mixed nuts with raisins or slicing off a piece of cheese. I went to find Günter to give him his wine. He was holding forth in fine fashion to both Rita and to Vivian. Tim stood to one side, still burdened by the knowledge that he was without a ride home on such a dirty night. Another couple, and they definitely were a couple, had joined them. They were each dressed entirely in black—black leather pants, black turtlenecks, and identical black baseball caps. A couple of New Age types wearing unusual necklaces. Hers was of multi-colored polished stones of different sizes and shapes and his looked to be fashioned from the teeth of some kind of animal. Perhaps this was Gary and Mary at last. I wondered when they had come in, I certainly hadn't noticed them before, or if they had perhaps been here all along. That was unlikely though. Surely I would have seen them, their appearance was so striking. I strode up to Günter and handed him his wine, which he took without acknowledging me or pausing for even a moment while discoursing on whatever the topic was. The pictures on the wall once again caught my eye. I wondered if they hung there permanently or if they had been put up just for the occasion. The pianist was beating out what now seemed to be random notes and chords struck several seconds apart. It was hard to tell if he was improvising or if this was actually the way some composer had intended the piece to be played.

I wandered away from my group to look more closely at the photographs. None of them contained a single human figure. While they still appeared to be black and white abstract studies of cloud formations, snow-capped mountains, or post-modern architecture, upon closer examination one could conclude they might also be extreme close-ups of foaming waves pounding a rocky shore or something being examined through a microscope. In one of them there were what might possibly have been streaks of lightning illumining a vast treeless plain. Or the Northern Lights? It could just as well have been some type of bacteria or virus. Another one of them caught my attention because it was somehow different from the others. It featured the outline and the shape of what I thought was a tree growing in deep shadows or in a chasm. After studying it intently for some minutes I slowly became aware that there was something in the tree perched on a branch. Perceptible only by its even darker but distinctive contours, I began to discern the silhouette of a type of bird. An owl!

Something about the room made me feel uneasy. My head was aching. There was a roaring sound in my ears. I hadn't had that much to drink so that couldn't be it. Perhaps it was the floating candles in the large punch bowl or the loose ends of the various conversations I had participated in. The music, if it could be called music, wasn't helping things either. Perhaps it was the spirit of Ken himself. At any rate, as I made my way across the room more and more people were starting to arrive. The place was getting packed. Once again I passed through the foyer with the three doors and then stood outside under the portico that protects one from the rain but not the chilling wind and stared at the churchyard. A dirty night indeed. I remained there for several minutes. On the other side of the iron fence that enclosed the churchyard I saw ghostlike figures moving beneath the street lamps in the rain and I decided I wanted to be among them. I'd had enough of this gathering. How I wished I had removed my coat from the rack before coming out when I had had the chance. I decided that was exactly what I was now going to do. When I turned to go back inside however, I noticed for the first time that I was not alone under the portico. A woman in one corner wearing a dark overcoat and smoking a cigarette was engrossed in an animated conversation on a cell phone. Perhaps she had been there when I had come out or perhaps not. Something about her made me suspicious. Why had I not heard her talking before this, before I had seen her? And there was something else too— something in her manner and tone of voice that made it seem as if she wasn't really talking to someone on the cell phone at all but was merely using it as a prop.

But no matter. All I was concerned with was getting my coat and being on my way. Whatever she was doing out here was of no interest to me. Suddenly the door to the foyer was thrown open and storming onto the portico was a visibly furious Günter in his overcoat, the belt-ends flying, with his hat pushed down on his head, followed by Vivian. They both came up and positioned themselves on either side of me and stood there glaring at one another. It was as if they had sought me out to referee their dispute, whatever it was about.

He spoke first.

"It is always the same with Kenneth and these people who call themselves his friends. Those people are not his friends. They are merely acolytes. He always surrounds himself with them so that they can tell him what he wants to hear." Günter put another cigarette between his lips and again produced his fancy lighter. He once more uttered a long sigh and then spewed smoke from his mouth and nose directly into my face. I noticed that he had not put his arms into the sleeves of his coat and was wearing it draped over his shoulders.

"But Günter—Bruce is counting on you. You can't just leave." Vivian had a pleading tone but an exasperated note now crept into her voice. "You've known Ken longer than anyone. It's not important what the others say or think or why they are here."

They continued to look past me, still glaring intently at one another. But after a few moments Günter took a step backwards and then acted surprised to see me standing there.

"Ah Curtis, I am sorry I forgot your name inside." Günter apparently wished to change the subject of whatever it was that he and Vivian were disputing. "Where was it we last saw each other? Was it in Paris?"

"No, I don't think it was."

"You're right it was after Paris, but before California I seem to recall. It was certainly a long time ago, no?"

"Oh yes—a long, long time ago. And far away too. Far from here."

"Yes—just like in a fairy tale." While Günter spoke fluently there was a trace of something in his speech that suggested that English was not his first language.

"And you Curtis—are you one of Kenneth's many acolytes? Are you also one who desires to bask in the reflected glory of another?"

"Not at all. I suppose I came tonight as much for Mary's sake as for Ken's."

"And did you receive the famous flyer?"

"Actually I didn't. There was a mix-up. And so she called me."

"Mary called you? You certainly must be among the chosen few."

"She didn't call you?"

"She hasn't spoken to me in years. Mary call me? Hah! Oh Curtis you make me laugh. But then, you've always had that knack."

With his coat draped over his shoulders and by the way he held his cigarette in a sort of backhanded, V is for Victory fashion, Günter possessed the air of a European film producer. For all I knew, he really was a European film producer.

"Maybe Gary called you then?"

"Who is this Gary that everyone keeps mentioning?" he asked dismissively.

"Gary is perfectly nice," said Vivian. "He was a great help to both of them while Ken was having his troubles. He's a very competent young man."

Ken's troubles? Financial troubles? Or did she mean when he was sick?

"Kenneth's troubles? What troubles are these? Is this Gary a nurse or something?"

"You know exactly what I mean Günter. Don't pretend that you don't."

"One man's troubles are another's opportunities. I am sure that Kenneth would have understood that."

"On Günter, you can be so outrageous sometimes. You and Ken were too much alike. That's what the problem was. Please, let's go back inside. It's cold out here."

"You're entirely correct no doubt my dear in that particular assessment. But I am not going back inside because I am now ready to depart."

"But Kelly and Pat are here! Think about how this will affect them?"

Kelly and Pat? Who are they?

"Kelly and Pat? Who are they? I don't know anyone named Kelly or Pat."

"You do too. You were just talking to them. They're Ken's grown children. How could you have forgotten their names?"

The pair dressed in black with the necklaces.

"I am not good with names I admit. Didn't I forget Curtis's name here? And he is my friend. But those two inside are now dressing in black and calling themselves Kelly and Pat? They used to have such exotic names, from near-Eastern mythology. One was Marduk and the other Erishkigal. I can't remember which was which. Kenneth named them himself. He researched it at great length in the library.

"They changed their names when they went away to boarding school, that's all."

"So once again Kenneth's grandiose ideas did not stand the test of time."

"It's not a matter of time Günter."

"Perhaps time was the wrong word. He displayed a certain lack of vision. No that is not right either. Kenneth was a man of vision. Even I must concede that."

"Of course you must. And now you must come inside. Bruce will be wanting to begin."

"If Bruce wants to begin then let Bruce begin. He can begin and end at the same time. And then everyone can go home."

"Oh Günter—honestly."

"Wasn't McMahon supposed to be here tonight?" I interjected.

"McMahon here? McMahon won't dare show his monkey's face if he knows that I, Günter, am going to be present. Not since the colony have we so much as set eyes on each other."

"Would this be the same colony where Tim and Ken also were?"

Günter stared at me with raised bushy blonde eyebrows. "Of course it was the same colony. There was only the one colony. And now you say that McMahon is here? I must see this for myself." With that he turned around and he and Vivian went back inside.

Once again I decided that what I was going to do was just go find my coat and depart. It really was chilly out here on the portico. I heard her voice once more. The woman was still conversing on her cell phone, or pretending to be.

"Excuse me," I said, interrupting her. "Excuse me, but do

you have a light?"

Her first reaction was one of annoyance and then she hunched her shoulders and dipped her head and pressed the phone to her ear as if to concentrate all the harder and to ignore me. But I would not be ignored.

"Excuse me Miss—Miss—I really need a light. Can you please help me?"

Giving a deep sigh à la Günter she removed the phone from her ear and turned it off. She put it into the pocket of her jacket and then quickly removed her hand. She was holding something. It was a cigarette lighter, an inexpensive Bic butane, and she manipulated the gas jet and flicked it on in one rapid movement so that it seemed that she had been carrying a perpetual flame in her pocket. I fumbled around and patted the outside of my own pockets and made a dumb show of pretending to search for a cigarette.

"I suppose you'll be needing a cigarette too."

"Oh no thanks. I just remembered. I don't smoke."

She stood there with her arm still extended. She increased the butane supply to the flame for a few seconds so that it rose and illuminated the immediate area around her hand. And then she released her thumb and cut the flame. She put the lighter back into her pocket. I waited to see if she would bring out the telephone again. She didn't. But something in her manner suggested that she was expecting it to ring at any moment.

"So how long have you known Ken?" "So how long have you known Ken?"

We both spoke simultaneously.

We each waited for the other to proceed.

Finally. I spoke again.

"Oh not as long as some of the others here tonight. And yourself?"

"The same."

"Ken was certainly a man with many friends."

"That's for sure."

"They say that McMahon is supposed to be here."

"McMahon?"

"From the colony."

"The colony?"

"Ken and McMahon and Tim—they were at the colony. Probably Vivian and Rita too. And Günter of course."

"So many."

"Yes, yes. That's why it was called a colony I suppose."

"Well you do need a lot of people in order to have a colony."

A long awkward silence ensued. I would have reached for a cigarette if I had one and if I smoked. I almost asked to see her lighter again.

"So many came."

"Tonight?"

"Yes."

"Yes."

"And it's such a dirty night and all—"

"Excuse me?"

"The night. It's dirty."

"Dirty?"

"The night."

"The night?"

"Dirty."

"I'm not sure I—"

"The weather. It's dirty."

"The weather?"

"Foul. Dirty."

"Ah."

"The rain."

"The rain is dirty?"

"It doesn't make a lot of sense I suppose. It's Irish."

"The rain is Irish?"

"No, the expression."

"Ah."

We both stared across the churchyard towards the sidewalks and the streets where people beneath their umbrellas were still hurrying along. The cars and busses moved slowly and splashed through the intersections where the water was standing. The wind was whipping and the beads of rain visible in the streetlights' shine were moving in furious and divers directions.

"Did you ever see Ken's leg?" I now inquired.

"His leg? I mean if I saw Ken I suppose I would have seen his leg. Both of them as a matter of fact. He used them to walk I believe."

"No just the one leg."

"He walked on one leg?"

"No, I mean the one that was—you know—"

"That was what?"

"Lost."

"Well he couldn't have then?"

"Couldn't have what?"

"Shown me his leg if it was lost."

"I mean when he was sick. Before he lost his leg. It wasn't because of Al or anything."

"Al made Ken sick?"

"Well I don't know if there was a direct cause. But she did attack him."

"She did?"

"Yes, she bit him and scratched him too."

"Ah. On the leg you mean."

"No it wasn't on the leg exactly."

"Not on the leg? Then where exactly?"

"On the face. And the arm."

"Well there you are."

"What—?"

"That's certainly not his leg—his face and his arm. But what happened to his leg?"

"I suppose it's something of a mystery."

"Indeed."

Somehow this conversation wasn't going anywhere. This woman knew less about Ken than I did and yet she had succeeded in making me exquisitely uncomfortable. I would have liked then to go inside to get my coat were it not for the fact that I'd have to get past her in order to do so. She had nothing to say but still seemed to be coaxing all sorts of information out of me unbidden. It felt as if I were being cleverly interrogated. Now I really did want her cell phone to ring so that she would have to occupy herself with answering it. I don't know why but I spoke again.

"That's what makes it so ironic."

"What's ironic?"

"The fact that Al is with Mary."

"Al is with Mary? Where?"

"Here."

"Here?"

"Tonight."

"They're both here? Tonight?"

"Possibly. Maybe."

"Are they inside?"

"Possibly. Maybe."

"You didn't see them?"

"Well there are so many people in there."

She nodded knowingly. I nodded too.

"Did Mary call you?" I asked.

"Mary? Call me? About Al?"

"No I mean about Ken."

"About his leg?"

"No—about his death."

"Ah—his death."

"Actually it was Gary who called me first."

"Gary?"

"Mary called me later about the flyer."

"The flyer?"

"She wanted to know if I ever saw the flyer. I told her no. Apparently there was some mix-up."

"And did you."

"No I never did. Until tonight."

"You saw the flyer tonight?"

"Oh yes."

"There's a flyer here? Where?"

"Inside?"

"Where inside."

"On the table beside those booklets and pamphlets that Ken supposedly wrote. Some of his pilot projects."

"How on the table—this flyer?"

"Just sitting there."

"The flyer is sitting on the table."

"Yes. I suppose it's for the benefit of those who didn't see the first flyer."

"There's more than one?"

"I should think there were several of them in fact. Ken had a lot of friends."

"But there is a flyer inside sitting on a table. At this very moment."

"Oh yes. Right there for everyone to see."

"But not the original flyer."

"It's hard to say that there was ever an original one."

"And what happened to the others then?"

"Probably some of Ken's friends brought theirs with them."

"They brought their flyers with them? They had their own?"

"Possibly."

"Maybe this Ken doesn't have as many friends as it might appear."

"Why do you say that?"

She was acting suspiciously and growing suspicious at the same time. I now had some real questions for her. She no doubt had some more for me.

"Do you mind if I smoke?" she asked.

"Why not? This is a church after all."

"Are you sure you won't have one?"

"Oh quite sure." Actually I could have used a cigarette but I didn't want her to go about the business of lighting first mine

and then hers, or hers and then mine, and then having to look
at her with gimlet eye through a cloud of smoke. Of course
there was nothing to prevent her from looking at me that way
whether I smoked or not. But by taking one of her cigarettes it
would have put me in her debt in some way and therefore at a
disadvantage. I would have owed her something.

"So tell me more about Ken's leg."

"There's not much to tell. Louise saw it. It was all black and
blue. Except it might not have been Ken's leg."

"His face then? His arm? You said—"

"Oh it was a leg all right. No doubt about that. But—"

"But what?"

"It could have been Al's leg."

"I thought Al was the one who bit Ken."

"And scratched him too. But not on the leg apparently."

"So perhaps Ken did something to Al? Something to Al's
leg?"

"I don't know."

"Well who would know?"

"Louise would know. She saw it. She wanted to take a
picture of it but Ken wouldn't let her."

"Of his own leg."

"Or possibly it was Al's leg. Just because Ken let her take
pictures of the garden and the house didn't mean he would
let her take pictures of the leg."

"Unless it was Al's leg." She burst out with this like a TV
detective having some sort of revelation. "Who else would have
seen the leg? Would Mary perhaps have seen it?"

"Why do you say that?"

"Because you said Al was with her now. And that it was
suspicious."

"I didn't say suspicious. I said it was ironic."

"You implied it was suspicious."

"I did no such thing. I only repeated what Louise said—
that Al was with Mary before she was with Ken and is back with
her again."

"And that they were both inside. Does Al walk with a limp?"

"I just said possibly."

"Possibly walks with a limp? You can't be sure?"

"No just possibly inside. Of course it's possible that Al doesn't walk anyway."

"Al is crippled as a result of this leg injury?"

"Not as a result of anything."

"Then how does Al get around?"

"The usual way I suppose."

"By flying perhaps?"

"Well some of the time I guess."

"Al is a flyer perhaps?"

"Possibly."

"So maybe Al is inside there sitting on the table."

"Who?"

"Al."

I thought she was now saying owl too, like Louise. For all I knew that's the way it sounded when I said it. It was hard to discern what exactly she knew or why she was asking all of these questions. Either she knew nothing or she knew everything. There was no way to tell.

"Do you mind if I ask you some more questions?"

"Weren't you going to have a cigarette?"

"No thanks. I'm trying to quit."

"I'd better go inside now. I think things are starting."

"Maybe I'll come inside too and take a peek at that flyer. I'm curious about this pilot project."

"You won't learn much from the flyer."

"Maybe I will and maybe I won't."

"Suit yourself."

We both entered the foyer. I stopped for a moment and bent over to tie my shoe. She stopped as well and looked around in a confused manner. I had the distinct impression she did not know which of the three doors to go through next. When I made a move she fell into step behind me and followed me into the room. I walked past the young woman still seated behind the table but my new acquaintance stopped short and said something about having left something outside and that she'd be right back. What could she possibly have left outside in the rain I wondered? Not her telephone. Not her cigarettes. I figured that was the last I'd see of her.

The fellow providing the music was engaged in what sounded like a final all-out assault on that piano. He was pounding it with his fists and then smashing his elbow down upon the keys in the manner of a professional wrestler. And then he had his head tilted back and was staring at the ceiling and his long blonde hair dangled almost down to his waist. He appeared to be in a kind of trance. Little pools of spittle glistened at the sides of his mouth. The fellow was literally foaming at the mouth.

I looked toward the coat rack and didn't see my coat at first. But there it was, lying in a heap on the dusty floor. No doubt when Günter had yanked his coat off the hanger mine had fallen. Of course no one bothered to pick it up, least of all Günter. I would have to do it myself. I bent down to retrieve it and brushed it off with my bare hand and started to put it on.

"You're not leaving are you?"

Rita was speaking to me, accompanied by the pair in the black turtlenecks.

"Oh no, I was just getting something out of my coat." I didn't want to have to explain my reasons for leaving early to anyone, anymore than I wanted to explain why I was here in the first place. I took the opportunity to slip my coat onto the hanger that was now available since Günter was still wandering around the room wearing his draped over his shoulders. The three of them stared at me as if questioning what it was that I had needed to get from my coat. A telephone? A cigarette? What could it be?

"You remember Kelly and Pat don't you Curtis?" Ken's grown children who had changed their names. The two of them stood there with their chins pressed to their chests still eyeing me warily. I had no clue which was which. They seemed

very confused. Apparently they weren't sure if they were
supposed to know me or not. I didn't know if it was this
particular situation that was disorienting them or if they went
around in this condition on a permanent basis. At last the
female half of the sibling tandem spoke.

"Curtis, Curtis—so this is Curtis. Yet I am not able to put
the face together with the name." The two of them stepped
back in a sort of choreographed lockstep and regarded me as
if from a great distance. For my part I didn't know exactly what
to say either. I couldn't claim not to have seen them since they
were children because their ages were unfathomable. For all I
knew they could have been older than me.

"Your father was a man with many friends." I used my stock
line. It was all I had.

"Persons of all sorts were drawn to him." The male sibling
now spoke.

"For better or for worse—in many cases for the worse." The
sister added somewhat archly. Impossible to know if she was
referring to the present case. After all she had stated she
couldn't put my name together with my face.

They moved even closer together until it looked like they
were joined from shoulder to hip. And then there was still
more choreography as they lapsed into a weird alternating-
voice singsong riff.

"Our father only had to put out the word—"

"And his minions would come running."

"We never saw our father after we were sent to boarding
school—"

"And he returned to the colony."

The colony again.

"Mary was always the one who was there for us—"

"She changed our names. And she was there for him."

"But in the end what could Mary do."

"Mary was only Mary."

So this Mary wasn't their mother after all. She was just a
slow-witted stepmother.

"What could anybody do?"

"Our father refused to have his picture taken. He didn't want to see us."

"Isn't that rather strange Curtis?"

Not altogether, I was thinking. Frankly, in my opinion, if Ken was sick and had an injured leg, the fact that he didn't want his picture taken with these two seemed perfectly reasonable. If nothing else it was inconsequential.

They might have carried on in this fashion indefinitely had not Tim then appeared in our midst carrying his signature glass of water.

"Word is that McMahon came early and left early," he announced.

The female sibling now directed her long hard gaze at him. The brother followed suit. I was glad to no longer be the object of their attention.

"But I thought that this fellow was McMahon," she said, indicating Tim.

"Oh no, he's not McMahon," Rita exclaimed.

"Not McMahon? Were we mistaken? Were we duped?" the brother chimed in.

"No this is Tim—from Gloucester. He knew your father from there and from the colony as well." I was just trying to be helpful.

"Tim, Tim, the hardware merchant's son—ah yes, yes, yes."

"He knew our father when he was young."

"Of this Tim we've heard many a tale."

At this point I couldn't tell which one was speaking. The pitch and timber of their voices was very similar even though they were brother and sister—male and female. But I wasn't listening anymore either. Their whole act was becoming rather tiresome. For all I knew their father had given them exotic names and put them in a freak show in addition to boarding school and that's why they were so resentful.

"Oh there he is! We were afraid you had left already. Curtis—?" It was Vivian's voice coming from behind me. I turned around. I welcomed any opportunity to get away from Kelly and Pat.

"Oh Curtis, do you know Bruce? Bruce this is Curtis. Curtis this is Bruce."

"I think we may have met somewhere before. The face is familiar." This according to Bruce, the fellow with the bow tie who had been setting up the podium and microphone and the tape recorder previously. He offered a limp handshake. Of course we'd never laid eyes on each other before tonight.

"Yes—yes—possibly some time or another with Ken."

"Ken was a man with a lot of friends." He had stolen my line.

"Oh Curtis I know this is a huge favor to ask," Vivian was saying, "but Günter absolutely refuses to speak and no one has seen McMahon or heard from him either . . . "

"I understand that he was here earlier but left already."

"McMahon was here?"

"McMahon was here."

"Who said this?"

"Tim just told me."

"Oh Tim—pooh. He doesn't know anything." I noticed that Vivian was no longer wearing the flowers behind her ears.

"Well you heard what Günter said about McMahon. Maybe he came and then left when Günter arrived."

"Oh don't pay attention to Günter either. He and Tim and McMahon were all at the colony. You can't believe a word of theirs about anything. That's why it's important for you to be the one to say something. Everyone else has such an ax to grind."

"For me?"

"Yes."

"To say—what?"

"Something."

"Something?"

"Yes something, anything."

"About?"

"About Ken."

"About Ken?

"About Ken."

"What about Ken?

"Something."

"What?"

"Whatever."

"Whatever?"

"Whatever."

Vivian and I had fallen into this hopeless echolalia. It was almost as ridiculous as the Kelly and Pat routine. Not that it was inappropriate to the situation however.

"But—"

"Oh Curtis, I know Bruce can count on you."

"On me?"

"Yes, you."

"But—"

"The program will be simple," Bruce said. "First I'll welcome everybody and then introduce you and you can talk as long as you want. And then we'll open up the mic and if someone else wants to speak after you they'll have the opportunity."

"But."

"Oh Curtis you are a darling. Curtis saves the day in my book. And Ken was ever so right about you too."

"Ken was right about me? What did he say?"

"That you were a clutch hitter. That if he ever needed something in a pinch, you were the person he would turn to."

"Ken said that? About me?"

"Perhaps not that exactly. His remarks might have been of a more general nature. But I should think that this certainly counts as saving the day."

I looked longingly in the direction of the coat rack. How I wished I had taken my coat with me the first time I left the room. I even wished I had left it behind when I was standing on the portico and had just disappeared into the dirty night.

And once again here was Louise speaking to me.

"I was wondering where you had gone."

"Oh just to get some air."

"I thought maybe you didn't care for the company."

"What do you mean?"

"Ken's friends that is."

"He certainly had a lot of them."

"Oh I don't think everybody that came tonight would consider themselves a friend of Ken's. Not a close friend anyway."

"Not Günter, that's for sure."

"Oh Ken and Günter—they were like brothers."

"Brothers?"

"Like twin brothers almost."

"Not according to Günter."

"They had their moments and then they grew apart. That's not unusual. Günter came tonight, that's the main thing."

"But Günter says he won't speak, that he has nothing to say about Ken."

"He's probably still angry at Mary."

I looked around the room. There were at least twenty women present who could have been Mary. I kept hoping that Louise would give some indication which one of them it might be. Although come to think of it, I wasn't sure I really wanted to meet her, or Gary for that matter.

"Wasn't that all in the past?"

"Nothing is ever in the past for any of them. And then there was the whole situation with the owl. She always thought that the owl belonged to her anyway."

Owl! I heard her distinctly. Not Al. Owl. A nickname? But she had said—"the owl".

"You mean because Ken was bitten by [him? her? it?] the owl?"

"Even before that. She claimed that the owl was hers all along and never was his. Ken just butted in and took possession."

"But where does Günter enter into this."

"Günter enters into everything. He pretends to be aloof

and bored by things but it's only an act. Gary says that Günter would call every day asking about Madame Owl, as he called her."

"Günter claims he doesn't know Gary."

"Oh he knows him, perhaps not by name, or not by the name of Gary, but he knows him all the same."

Once again it felt as if the murky waters were rising. The dirty night had fallen all around me. I needed another glass of wine at the very least. My head was still aching. The roaring noise still filled my ears. And then there was that hideous fellow on the piano. He was now for all intents and purposes in the process of dismembering the instrument. All around the room the buzz of conversation continued without anyone paying him the slightest interest or showing the least concern over the fate of the poor piano.

And then Bruce in his bow tie was at the microphone. He stood there clearing his throat for a moment and then bent down to announce that we were going to get started. People made one last stop by the wine table and then drifted towards the folding chairs that faced the podium. Louise poured Tim some more water. I eyed her carefully to see if maybe she was adding something to it. I thought one last time about grabbing my jacket and making a break for it but there she was again— that woman in the dark overcoat, hovering in the doorway, neither coming in nor going out. She had her cell phone in her hand. Who could she be talking to now? Günter with his coat still draped over his shoulders and wearing his hat sat glumly in the back row. He had his hands on his knees and was rocking back and forth like a bored child. Vivian, ignoring him, was right beside him with a smile and poised countenance directed towards the front. The piano player finally stopped, mercifully, but the damage done to the instrument was no doubt permanent. The buzz of conversations and scraping of chairs grew fainter and fainter until there was complete silence. And then Bruce was making a few preliminary remarks regarding Ken to which I was mostly oblivious. "Ken was certainly a man with many friends . . . " was the only thing I heard him say. Again he had stolen my line. He introduced me in some sort of vague fashion, as if to say while he wasn't really that well acquainted with me, everyone else no doubt knew about my relationship with Ken.

I walked to the podium. I felt the eyes of every person in the room upon my back as I approached it. I turned and stood in front of the microphone and looked out at the gathering now assembled in the rows of folding chairs. I let my eyes roam around the room on either side and in every corner. I noticed that my coat had once again fallen on the floor.

"I want to thank everyone for coming tonight on such short notice. Many of you may have seen the flyer but I'm afraid that some of you did not. Mary was trying to contact everyone who may have known Ken or come into contact with him and it had been left to her and to Gary the task of searching through the contents of Ken's cluttered desk and examining the papers that were scattered across the top, not to mention delving into his files. We all owe a debt of gratitude to Gary and Mary for their heroic efforts." I expected at this point that everyone would turn towards Gary and Mary, wherever they were, whoever they were, and the two of them would smile and nod and graciously acknowledge this recognition. But the faces in the room remained placid and fixed in their attention upon me as the speaker. I didn't want to ask Gary and/or Mary to stand up and take a bow since I still wasn't sure they were even here. I had no choice but to resume.

"We all know that Ken certainly possessed a unique capacity to re-invent himself. He was truly a man of whom it could be said, he was all things to all people. Everyone who was even slightly acquainted with him will attest to that. But Ken's genius, if I may be so bold, was a many-faceted one as well. We—and by we, I mean all of us—we only knew the part of him that he would show to us. One might assert that if we were to put all of our stories together we would then come close to approximating the whole man. I disagree. I maintain that actually it's not really

necessary to try and put all the parts together because I believe
that Ken's multi-layered genius is revealed just as fully in these
various fragments. And it is our task, and will remain our task
after we leave here tonight, to more seriously contemplate the
constituent parts of him that we knew or that he let us know
and then perhaps we will have enough evidence to understand
Ken, to take his measure, or at least say something insightful
about him." Surprisingly, this was all going over better than I
expected. "Certainly one could discuss Ken's *grand projet* all
day and conclude on that basis that he was a definitely a genius.
But one man's *grand projet* is another's man's pilot project. By
this I mean that one aspect of being a genius, and we all agree
that Ken was a genius, is simply possessing the ability to deal
with the issue at hand—unhesitatingly, enthusiastically,
courageously. Ken was able to do this repeatedly. It was
astounding the way he went about it. And yet the evidence is
clear. It's right in front of us. That he was able to do this with
respect to all of his several interests, which in the end
constituted his life's work as much as the various fruits of his
labors, is *grand projet* enough for any man to accomplish in his
lifetime in my book. Perhaps others will differ. But we are not
likely to find them assembled among us tonight.

  "Ken came a long way from Gloucester, Massachusetts, the
son of a father lost at sea. One of us here has traveled much of
that journey with him. Not step by step of course, but with the
awareness that in one's beginnings there necessarily follows
one's endings. Others of you probably never had any idea he
hailed from such a place, assuming he had been fully-formed
from some unique essence particular to our neck of the woods.
Certainly Ken was one of us. The fact that he chose to live
where he did cannot be overlooked. But it is likewise important
to consider where a man comes from, the point of origin of his
life's journey, in order to understand the nature and the
ultimate purpose of that journey. Gloucester is a seafaring town,
a fishing town, and the spirit of adventure, of danger even,
coupled with a diligence to duty never left Ken no matter

where he went. Even during his time in the famous colony, where Ken certainly was one of its most lively members, ever the ready wit and raconteur by all accounts, but even then, Ken was about his business and full of high purpose. Even in the matter of naming his children, Ken delved deeply into the subject. You can bet the librarians had to drag out their heaviest books and really be on their toes when Ken was around." Fortunately Kelly and Pat, or Marduk and Erishkigal, had departed the scene, though perhaps they were lurking in the church kitchen or even the sanctuary, still waiting for McMahon and rehearsing their act.

"Ken's final days were filled with pain. No doubt he suffered terribly even if he didn't care to reveal the full extent of his suffering. But his physical tribulations were ameliorated by the comfort of knowing he was a man of many friends and the satisfaction of having completed his life's work. Perhaps not entirely completed—because there is always additional work to be done, another mountain to climb, one more pilot project to get off the ground—but certainly fulfilled. And once he had climbed that mountain and gazed upon the valleys that lay below him and surveyed the vistas that lay in the distance, he could say to himself: 'Mission accomplished. Good job Ken.'

"Like the eagle that soars, like the pilots in the earliest days of aviation, Ken did not know fear. To venture to those places where no one has ever ventured before was all the greater inducement. Others might look around themselves as they prepared for the quest, a 360 degree contemplation of one's own navel perhaps, but Ken had the inspiration to look up and look down, to stare at his feet and to ponder the sky. Ken's genius was a vertical genius by this reckoning. And if he was a man with many friends, who himself could sometimes be a difficult friend, there's no getting around it, if he was a man who constantly had the urge to re-invent himself, he also constantly had the need to seek out new friendships as well. One of the questions, if not *the* question, that must be asked, is how many lives can one man live over the course of his own life. Certainly the number is plastic, is indefinite. Ken is proof of that.

"Yes Ken suffered in the end. Those who cared for him, or who knew him even slightly, could not take his place, anymore than we can take each other's places when our time shall come. Even his beloved Al, or should I say Madame Owl, could not be with him in the end for reasons it would neither be appropriate or helpful to belabor. And if he didn't wish to be photographed either alone or with his owl—Al, except that one time, then we can say nothing, can conclude nothing, and must move on. Judgment is not ours . . . "

I had no idea what I was saying or what I might say next. After a pause—

"There are so many others who will be standing here later tonight, others who are much better qualified than I to speak of Ken and will provide their own stories of their encounters with him. But if it is I who must first perform the necessary, preliminary responsibility of being the means by which Ken is remembered, then I too will have fulfilled my task. I too will have discharged my obligations to this man whose life we are gathered here tonight to celebrate and to recall. And if Ken is here even in spirit then he can certainly render his own judgment. Not some kind of ultimate judgment by the dead upon the living—that's not where I intend to go. But he would certainly offer a criticism. Ken never hesitated to offer his criticism. Ken was a man with many opinions. I see many of you smiling and nodding in agreement." Actually no one was doing anything of the sort. The silver streak in Vivian's hair had not so much as quivered the entire time I had spoken. Everyone in the audience with the exception of fidgety Günter had a sedated quality about them, as if they had all partaken of the same waters from the same source as Tim. Maybe they all needed rides home on such a dirty night. Or perhaps it really was because of what I was saying they were sitting there so placidly. I had no choice but to continue speaking, wondering when or if I was going to provoke some kind of reaction.

"When I learned that Ken had died I realized at once that the world I had lived in for all these many decades was not going to be the same one without his presence on the planet. I'm sure all of you had similar such reactions. Even with ample time to prepare one's self mentally and emotionally, and especially so for those who were closest to him, it was still a shock to receive the news. I know I'll never forget where I was and what I was doing when I first heard that Ken had gone beyond the mountain. But now that I have had time to reflect on it, I can only be grateful that there was someone like Ken—and that would be Ken himself of course—and that he was my contemporary. Thanks to Ken, and his example, I've learned more about myself and so many other things than I ever would have thought possible. And though I was never fortunate enough to be physically present at the colony like some of you, I think it can be rightly said that everyone here tonight who has ventured forth on this dirty night, is in essence a member of the colony. What a gathering that must have been. But what a gathering we are here tonight as well. We are all truly among friends."

I then had a sudden inspiration. "I want everyone at this time to turn to the person seated on either side of you or in front of you or behind you and greet them and acknowledge your connection to them by means of the man we knew as Ken. Even if it is someone you don't know at all, even if it is someone who accompanied you here tonight, please make this gesture not for the sake of Ken but for your own sake."

There was an awkward bit of movement. People regarded each other warily, but in the end nearly everyone offered some sort of half-hearted handshake or air kiss or pat on the back. Except for Günter of course. As a result of my entreaty he was now slouching there in his chair with his coat pulled up over his head so that he looked like he was inside of a tent. Vivian was still doing her best to ignore him. The woman with the cell phone was no longer by the door. Perhaps she had used this moment to make her exit. But no I was wrong. There she was. She was sitting beside the piano player on his bench on the side of the room, still wearing her dark overcoat. Surely she hadn't come with him!

And then there was the low rumble of thunder from outside. No doubt the dirty night was going to turn filthy.

Some in the audience eyed the coat rack and then stole glances at the door with what can only be described as hopeful expressions upon their faces. Those expressions became positively joyful when I uttered my next words—"In conclusion, we must always be mindful of the teachings of the prophet, who I would remind you comes by his gift not by the means of his ability to foretell the future, but rather by his profound knowledge of the present. Perhaps it's merely a case of cause and effect, of one conclusion after another following from a particular set of premises. It's the vision thing all over again. But to stand astride the mountaintop requires the enormous effort of climbing the mountain in the first place, don't ever forget that. And as for glimpsing the tops of the other mountains, no particular gift of sight is required. You just have to be there, in the right place at the right time, because while standing on the shoulders of giants every dog has his day. And Ken, our good friend Ken, or in some cases our father ('hallowed be thy name', I almost added)—we say we sure won't forget you Ken. And all of you that are here also can leave this room tonight with the certain knowledge that you won't be forgotten either."

All at once Bruce was standing right beside me and inclining his face toward the microphone. "Thank you Curtis for your most appropriate words. We are now going to open the mic. Anyone with something else to say, and I know there are many of you, please feel invited to come forward at this time and to share your own thoughts and memories." I noticed a contented expression on Vivian's face. Günter was still hidden in the tent of his overcoat. Louise was bringing more water to Tim who was sitting next to Rita. Neither one of them appeared to have any idea where they were or why.

I wasted no time. I hurried to the back of the room where my coat still lay in a heap on the floor. I didn't bother to put it on. I just picked it up and held it in front of me and hurried for the door in order to escape as quickly as I could. The smiling young woman who had greeted everyone upon entering had finally quit her post. Outside on the portico once again was the woman with the cell phone. How did she accomplish this? Had I only imagined she was in there sitting next to the piano player?

"Are you leaving now? So soon?"

"I'm not feeling well. I got up from my deathbed to be here."

"I wonder what happened to McMahon?"

"McMahon was here. He came earlier."

"And he left?"

"So I was told."

"I never did see that flyer you mentioned."

I put on my coat. I had nothing more to say. I was ready to go.

"Well good night to you."

"And good night to you. Perhaps we will meet again."

"I wonder where?"

"I have no idea." And I truly didn't.

I ran through the churchyard in the pouring rain. The thunder had stopped but the rain had intensified. I didn't care. I felt feverish. I wanted to feel the cold rain beating upon my face. I walked for several blocks and then caught a bus that took me someplace near my house. Thankfully there was no one else on the bus except for the driver. After I got home I sat in the kitchen listening to the radio. My wife had long since fallen asleep. There was a ballgame on but I wasn't really paying attention to the score or even who was playing. Finally I turned it off and went to bed.

The next morning my wife asked how the evening had been. I told her it was all right. "Ken certainly had a lot of friends." I didn't go into any details. She said she was sorry she hadn't gone, but that she hadn't known Ken all that well. I said she might have considered going, if only for my benefit.

She replied that it wasn't like one of my parents had died or even a brother or sister.

Since it was Saturday morning she had to go out and run some errands. The rain had let up somewhat. While she was gone the phone rang but I made no attempt to answer it. I once again sat in the kitchen listening to the radio, this time to some classical music. I waited a minute for the phone to stop ringing and then dialed the number and then the code for the automated answering service.

"Hello this is Gary calling all friends of Ken. Since Mary and I were able to meet and talk to only a few of the many people at the memorial last night, we're inviting you to her house for brunch tomorrow. Nothing fancy of course—that's not our style. In case you're wondering, McMahon definitely will be there, and of course Owl."

Owl? Not the Owl? Not Madame Owl?

"If you're coming then please call back and RSVP. If no one's in just leave a message on the machine. We'd love to see you."

I made myself some coffee and sat at the kitchen table for a long while. I then took my coffee into the living room and sat on the sofa. The curtains were closed and the room was dark. I put the coffee down on the coffee table and got up and opened the curtains. The skies were still gray and swollen and again it looked like rain. I thought of my wife out doing errands and wondered if she had taken an umbrella with her. Of course if her hands were full then she wouldn't have been able to use the umbrella anyway. No doubt she was prepared for this possibility and had worn the yellow rain slicker that she'd ordered from a catalog last year. I sat down and watched as the clouds thickened further and as the rain began to fall. I waited for the telephone to ring once more as well. Maybe I should look into this business of buying a cell phone. One for me and one for her. You see them more and more now. I'm really not one for gadgets but perhaps this one is a good idea.